...his mouth covering hers roughly. His hand covered her breast and she arched into it. Her pulse plummeted to join the ache between her thighs.

He smiled down at her, and a rush of heat swirled almost painfully through her, making her thighs shake. His body pressed into her, hard and demanding.

Beau repressed the wanton need to let him have his way. He liked to win, but so did she.

"You are the most maddening woman alive. Do you know that?"

Beau nodded, trying not to smile. She was winning.

"The simple truth is that if I let you do as you're asking, I'm not entirely sure where it will end. But the most likely scenario is with me taking your maidenhead in this blasted coach."

"Think of it a challenge. Or a bet. Men love a good bet, don't they? I bet you, Gareth Sandison, that no matter what I do, you *can* resist me."

"Did you ever stop to think I might want to lose that bet?"

Ripe for Scandal

ISOBEL CARR

FOREVER

NEW YORK   BOSTON

Forever
Hachette Book Group
237 Park Avenue
New York, NY 10017
www.HachetteBookGroup.com

Forever is an imprint of Grand Central Publishing.
The Forever name and logo are trademarks of Hachette Book Group, Inc.

The publisher is not responsible for websites (or their content) that are not owned by the publisher.

Printed in the United States of America

First Edition: September 2011

10 9 8 7 6 5 4 3 2 1

ATTENTION CORPORATIONS AND ORGANIZATIONS:
Most HACHETTE BOOK GROUP books are available at quantity discounts with bulk purchase for educational, business, or sales promotional use. For information, please call or write:

Special Markets Department, Hachette Book Group
237 Park Avenue, New York, NY 10017
Telephone: 1-800-222-6747 Fax: 1-800-477-5925

For Tracy Grant

ACKNOWLEDGMENTS

I owe a special debt of gratitude to the fabulous Tracy Grant, who helped me work out the intricacies of the plot. Without her help, I'm pretty sure at least one character would still be waiting somewhere offstage, forgotten. I want to thank my friend Jess for the fabulous art for my Web site, and Poppy Reiffin for the Web site itself. Since I'm going to try and keep this short, as always, I'd like to thank my friends, my family, and my dog for the patience and support. My RWA chapters (San Francisco and Beau Monde) are vital to my process and my sanity. Special thanks to Monica McCarty, Jami Alden, Bella Andre, and Carolyn Jewel for listening to me whine and helping me celebrate. Major thanks to my History Hoydens pals for always being there. Last, my kickass team of "Alexes": my agent, Alexandra Machinist, and my editor, Alex Logan. These two make me rise to the occasion and become the writer I want to be.

Ripe for Scandal

~ PROLOGUE ~

There are three private gentlemen's clubs on St. James's Street in London, each with its own rules and regulations governing membership. They are filled each day with peers who can't be bothered to attend to their duties in the House of Lords, let alone what they owe to their estates and family. Their ranks are frequently swelled by the addition of their firstborn sons, who gamble away their youth and fortunes while waiting for their fathers to die. What's less commonly known is that there is also one secret society, whose membership spans all three: *The League of Second Sons.*

Their charter reads:

We are MPs and Diplomats, Sailors and Curates, Barristers and Explorers, Adventurers and Soldiers. Our Fathers and Brothers may rule the World, but We run it. For this Service to God, Country and Family, We will have Our Due.

Formed this day, 17 May 1755. All Members to Swear to Aid their Fellows in their Endeavors, Accompany them on their Quests, and Promote their Causes where they be Just.

Addendum, 14 April 1756. Any rotter who outlives his elder brother to become heir apparent to a duke is hereby expelled.

Addendum, 15 Sept 1768. All younger brothers to be admitted without prejudice in favor of the second.

❧ CHAPTER 1 ❧

London, October 1784

He had the saddest eyebrows in the world.

They were straight and well defined, but they dipped from the center downward to their end, leaving him with a melancholy expression that didn't entirely dissipate even when he smiled. Every time Lady Boudicea Vaughn saw him, she found herself wanting to cup his cheeks, smooth those brows with her thumbs, and kiss away whatever it was that haunted him.

Not that he'd ever noticed...

Gareth Sandison, second son of the Earl of Roxwell, still thought of her as his friend Leonidas's scrubby little sister. He treated her more as a boy than a woman, when he bothered to acknowledge her existence at all. Mostly he seemed to do his best to avoid her.

As the Season progressed, Lady Boudicea had found herself missing his taunts. Missing his scathing wit and withering set-downs. Fighting with Sandison was far more invigorating than flirting with her London suitors. He might not like her, but he saw her. Truly saw her and sparred with her as an equal, or he had until she'd grown up and made her curtsey to the king.

Their roles had changed seemingly overnight. Instead of being her brother's friend, he was a rake to be avoided. Instead of being simply Beau, his friend's baby sister, she was Lady Boudicea, marriageable daughter of a duke. It was maddening.

The dance reunited her with her partner, Mr. Nowlin, and she dragged her attention away from Sandison. Nowlin smiled at her, brown eyes teasing her for missing her step. Beau smiled back. He might be an Irishman with a penchant for too much scent, but he was certainly handsome enough, and the lilt in his voice was charming. Half the ladies in London were enamored with their newest addition with his pretty coats, gleaming buckles, and fulsome compliments.

Sandison's pale head caught her attention again, and she jerked her eyes away from him. He was standing against the wall, flirting none too slyly with the very married Lady Cook. Her husband was, no doubt, in the card room oblivious to the set of horns sprouting from his head.

The lady and Sandison were rumored to be lovers, but gossip made such allegations about people on a regular basis. According to the scandalmongers, Beau herself always seemed to be on the cusp of contracting some grand alliance or on the verge of covering her family in mortification.

The scandals she'd nearly caused—or that had nearly

been inflicted upon her by various overeager suitors—
didn't bear thinking about. Better by far that the *ton*'s
gossips distract themselves with rumors of unsuitable
engagements and heartless flirtations. The truth would
ruin her.

A trickle of hot wax fell in a drizzle onto her chest
and splattered across the silk of her gown. Her skin stung
and she bit back an oath, missing the next series of steps.
She sucked in a sharp breath and pulled the wax from her
breast, flicking it to the floor with disgust. This was the
second time tonight. Beau glanced up at the offending
candles and stepped carefully back into the dance. Getting it out of her hair was going to be pure hell.

Beau glanced over her partner's shoulder, meeting
Sandison's gaze for the briefest of moments. A smile hov-
ered about his lips. Whether it was for her or Lady Cook
she couldn't say, but given the way his companion was
thrusting her ample bosom at him, it was likely the latter.

Light glittered off Sandison's hair. He'd been silver-
haired as long as she'd known him, as were all the men in
his family by the time they finished their teens. He never
bothered to wear a wig, just his own pale locks, clean and
immaculately dressed.

His family was reputed to be the illegitimate descen-
dants of the disreputable second Earl of Rochester himself. A rumor that lent him a certain air of titillation, a
deliciously illicit cachet. It drew women like moths to a
flame...or maybe it was just his eyebrows.

She couldn't be the only woman undone by them.
Could she?

· · ·

She was watching him again.

Gareth could feel her gaze upon him as distinctly as if she'd reached out and run her hand down his arm. Lady Boudicea Vaughn: possessor of two gigantic brothers, a father who was legend with the small sword, and a mother who was herself distractingly entrancing even as fifty became a distant memory.

Lady Cook reclaimed his attention, her lovely face pulled into a pout. She wasn't used to being ignored, nor was she likely to be forgiving about such a breech. Especially over Beau. They were of an age, and she'd married one of the many suitors that Lady Boudicea had declined.

Gareth traced one finger along the exposed skin between the sleeve of Lady Cook's gown and the top of her kidskin glove. The tiny tassels dangling from the edge of her ruffle swayed. She shivered and stretched her neck out like a languid vixen. He circled his finger over the pulse point at her elbow, and she let out a small, indiscreet moan.

If their host's garden wasn't so well lit and filled to overflowing with guests, he'd have steered the oh-so-willing Lady Cook outside and satisfied them both. As it was, he'd have to wait and see if her husband accompanied her home.

Lady Boudicea disapproved of his dallying with married ladies. Hell, she disapproved of *him*. She always had. She'd been scathingly disapproving as a girl, more haughtily so since she'd left off playing with dolls and taken her place among the *ton* in London. Even muddied from head to toe and only twelve years old, she'd already had the ability to make him feel like an impudent fool. A decade later, he still couldn't say that he'd ever come out on top when they'd clashed.

And clash they did. It seemed inevitable at this point. Unavoidable. Was it wrong of him to enjoy it? To look forward to their little skirmishes? Probably so, but it was too delicious an entertainment to give up. Or it had been. He'd made a concerted effort to avoid such interactions of late.

He schooled his expression, concentrating on Lady Cook's breasts, the creamy flesh overflowing her bodice, begging for admiration. Anything to keep from glancing across the room, from meeting Beau's frosty gaze, from crossing the room to see if he could tease a smile out of her, make her rap him with her fan, provoke her into some small indiscretion...

Lady Cook inhaled, holding her breath for a moment, breasts rising until the edge of her areolas peeked out of the fabric. Full, soft, ripe. But somehow not as tempting tonight as they'd been previously. Tonight her smile was brittle, and the powder obscuring her skin was too heavy, making her corpse-like rather than luminous. The small taffeta beauty mark she'd placed beside her mouth was half-obscured in a frown line.

Beau's laugh caught his attention like a whip. He clenched his jaw and forced himself not to follow it back to its source. She was haunting him this season. Her brother Leonidas had asked him to keep an eye on her while he was absent from town. It hadn't seemed much of a burden at the time, but now that March was giving way to April and the Season was well and truly underway, a mild irritant had become outright torture.

Why was she was still unmarried? Were his fellow Englishmen blind, deaf, and utterly stupid?

She'd been out for several years, and while rumor had

her engaged a dozen times over, nothing had ever come of any of it. It was maddening. *She* was maddening.

She was the daughter of a duke, with a dowry that was likely to be immense, and she was far from being an antidote. Her one fault—aside from that temper—was her height. At nearly six foot, few men outside her own family were tall enough not to appear ridiculous beside her.

Look at the poor fop she was dancing with now. Gareth blew his breath out in a disgusted huff. Even in his evening pumps, the man was barely her match. If not for the poof of his wig he might even have appeared shorter than she. But still, somewhere there must be a man who was suitable? They didn't call the *ton* the top ten thousand for nothing. Even if you discounted those who were too short, too old, too young, and female, that had to leave a score or more who would suit? Didn't it?

Life would be so much simpler if she were married and happily domesticated somewhere far away like York or Dublin or Edinburgh. She was Scottish, after all. That should have expanded the pool of suitors. And everyone knew Scots tended to be great tall fellows. Surely there was a Highland laird or two in need of a wife.

Yes, life would be simpler if only she were somewhere else. Somewhere where she couldn't spend her evenings glaring at him and making him wish that he were something other than a penniless younger son.

That fact was like a flea biting deep below the layers of his clothing, niggling and occasionally sharply painful. He had more than enough for a life of elegant leisure for one, but it wouldn't stretch to supporting a wife. Certainly not one of Beau's quality and station.

They had a term for men like him who married girls like her: fortune hunter. Her father would shoot him before he'd give permission for such a match. Her brother Leo wouldn't bother with the gun. He'd use his bare hands.

No, men of his sort didn't marry, unless they took orders or found themselves a wealthy widow. There was no reason to do so, and every reason not to. And they certainly didn't marry girls with Lady Boudicea's pedigree and prospects. Not since Hardwick's Marriage Act went through anyway. Damn the old blighter.

Gareth forced a smile as Lady Cook pressed herself against his arm suggestively. She leaned in, close enough that he could almost feel her lips on his skin.

"I feel faint." Lady Cook opened her fan with a flick of her wrist, the sound causing heads to swivel toward them.

"Of course you do, my lady. Perhaps some air?"

Lady Cook smiled in response. Gareth propelled her through the thick of the crowd, circumventing the dancers. Her fingers slid possessively over his biceps.

A lady with the heart and soul of a whore from the gutter. She was everything a man such as he needed in life. Beau passed them in the whirl of the dance, so close her skirts struck his leg, silk and wool clinging to each other. Gareth ground his teeth and swallowed hard, ignoring the way his pulse leapt.

He'd known since the first time that he'd seen Beau with her hair up that he was done for. She'd come down the stairs in her father's house in a spangled silk gown, hair dressed and powdered, eyes glittering with excitement, and his lungs had seized.

Gone was the muddy child. Replaced, as if by fairy

magic, with a startling young woman whose vivid green eyes had a secret dancing behind them. A devilish, teasing secret.

If he'd thought for a moment that he had any chance at all, he'd have made himself miserable over her. As it was, he simply avoided her when possible and picked fights with her when avoidance wasn't an option.

Tonight, Lady Cook was going to be all that he needed to keep Beau at bay. They cordially loathed one another. Had done since their very first encounter. Beau would never seek him out so long as Lady Cook was on his arm. Lady Cook glanced unhappily around the garden. It was brightly lit with colored lanterns, and revelers had spilled forth from the house to choke its narrow walkways.

"My husband will be here all night playing cards and drinking too much port. Escort me home, Sandison. It will take hours simply to extricate my carriage from the mess outside...I'll need something to keep me amused."

Gareth nodded, tucking her hand securely into the crook of his arm. Lady Cook's idea of entertainment would no doubt prove entirely unimaginative, but it was better than spending half the night watching the unattainable Lady Boudicea Vaughn dance with other men, one of whom might someday actually get to call her wife.

His chest felt empty, soulless, as he hurried Lady Cook toward the door. This was his lot: unchaste wives and widows with an itch to scratch.

There'd been a time when he thought his life perfect.

~⚜ CHAPTER 2 ⚜~

Rush off to Firle Hill? Now?" Gareth's friend Roland Devere stared at him across the table. Sunlight streamed in through the window, casting half of Devere's face into shadow. Gareth squinted and slid his seat so that he wasn't staring directly into the light.

The taproom at The Red Lion was nearly empty. Most of his fellow League members had taken themselves off to a mill and the rest must still have been abed, exhausted from their exertions the night before.

Gareth blew out his breath in a disgruntled sigh and nodded. "Got a letter from Souttar this morning demanding my presence in no uncertain terms."

"How much trouble could your brother possibly have got himself into? He's only been married three months. Perhaps he needs advice of a very delicate nature?" Devere grinned wickedly.

"More likely he's bored, mired in the country, and simply wants Sandison at his beck and call," Lord Peter Wallace said with a shake of his head. "Someone to order about, someone to go shooting with, someone to play cards and chess with. You know what Souttar's like."

"Likes to have a fag. Always did," Devere said with a hint of disgust. "Never happier than when ordering someone about. I remember that much clearly. You'd think his new wife would fulfill that role admirably."

Gareth wrinkled his nose. The summation was perfectly accurate when viewed from the outside. He'd always been his brother's favorite subject, but it had also always been the two of them against their father. They might treat each other dreadfully, but when it came to dealing with the earl, he could always count on Souttar to have his back. He'd been close to refusing when he'd first read Souttar's summons, but truth be told, there was a hint of desperation in the wording, and a week or so away from town and Lady Boudicea would be a welcome relief.

He'd very nearly called out her name while fucking Lady Cook in her plush carriage. Whatever his brother wanted—and it was sure to be petty; it always was—it would still be better than causing a scandal of epic proportions because his mind was endlessly bent on a single subject. He'd come so very close to disaster with Lady Cook…

Gareth shuddered as the implication of his near slip worked its way down his spine: death, dismemberment, scandal, ruin. One simple word, one mistake, and he could have destroyed both their lives. Lady Cook wouldn't have taken the mistake lightly, and she wouldn't have spared either him or her former rival. The gossip would have lit up London like the Great Fire of 1666.

Not a soul would have believed either of them innocent. He was a rake, known for dallying with other men's wives. The leap to seducing virgins wasn't all that far... and when the girl in question was the outrageous Lady Boudicea Vaughn? Well, very few would want to believe her innocent. Seduction and ruin were her just deserts. Her entire family was considered either mad or depraved, and her brother marrying a courtesan had only added to that image.

Gareth shook off the sensation of doom. Better to put up with his family's decidedly feudal ideas for a few days or weeks. He'd be happy to see his mother, at least. His father's idea of her rights and prerogatives was nearly as ancient and restrictive as what he thought the dues of an elder son. Everyone was there to serve the earl first and the heir second. No one else really mattered.

Gareth could only be thankful he had no sisters. Their lot would have undoubtedly been worse than his, mere pawns for his father's machinations. At least he, as a man, could escape the greater part of his father's control now that he was grown.

The small independence that his maternal grandfather had left him had helped immensely. His father hadn't even bothered to threaten to stop his allowance for the past year or so. The earl took no pleasure in making empty threats, but Gareth knew with a cold certainty that his father would eventually attempt some new method of bringing him to heel. The earl simply couldn't help himself.

Devere waved his cup high, and the landlord's daughter appeared scant seconds later with a pot of steaming coffee. He heaped lump after lump of sugar into his cup until Gareth nearly gagged at the thought of drinking it.

"How long do you think you'll be gone?" Devere asked. "You'll be back for our cricket match, won't you?"

"Cricket's a sacred trust, especially when it's us versus the chuffs from Eton. Even my father wouldn't seek to prevent my returning for that." Gareth grinned and topped off his own cup.

"Bloody Etonians." Devere blew on his coffee, steam curling up and obscuring his eyes for a moment. "It's Harrow forever, and we'll show them this year as we have for the past ten."

"Now, now," a deep voice scolded from the door, and Anthony Thane crossed to join them. "League first; school second."

Gareth watched as the largest of his friends settled onto a chair that appeared far too small to hold him. Thane was certainly tall enough to be in the running for Beau's hand, but like himself, Thane was hobbled by his status as a second son. That and his position as an MP.

If Thane ever did marry, it would be to someone who could be a brilliant political hostess, not to a girl who preferred hunts to the balls that followed them and hobnobbing with dusty squires to playing games of political intrigue with the king's courtiers.

"League first, now and always," Devere agreed. "But all such bets are off when it comes to cricket. You shall be on one side, and we shall be on the other."

Thane chuckled, showing an expanse of teeth that seemed almost predatory. "Enemies on the field; friends off it. You should be aware that we have a new man. A bowler of unusual skill. Crawley's youngest brother. He's

seventeen and preparing to take orders. But for now"—
his smile grew—"he's all ours."

Devere grinned in return. "I wish you luck with
your Crawleys, but I doubt one green boy will make the
difference."

Thane nodded sagely, but a confident smile lurked in
the corner of his mouth. "We shall see. Our luck has to
turn eventually."

Gareth sipped his coffee, letting the bitter liquid linger
on his tongue, and settled in to watch his friends bicker. It
was likely to be the last amusing conversation in his life
for several weeks, knowing Souttar.

Beau stepped out of the circulating library on Pall Mall
and was nearly bowled over by a mob of running boys.
Curses flew between them as they dodged around her in
a swirling mass. The ball they were kicking bounced off
the window of a passing carriage, earning them a rebuke
from the driver, who pulled to, the axles groaning in protest at the sudden change in speed.

"My lady?" Beau's footman eyed the roving pack of
boys with distrust.

"I'm fine, Boaz. Just apprentices on the loose."

"Yes, my lady." As he spoke, his eyes widened, and he
dropped the carefully wrapped stack of books that he was
carrying and lunged for her.

Hands grabbed her from behind, dragging her into the
stopped coach. Boaz was shouting furiously; she could hear
him even after the door shut behind her. He hit the side of
the coach hard enough to rock it, but the coach rolled into
motion all the same, leaving him and his tirade behind.

Beau flailed, hands fisted, feet lashing out. Her foot connected with some part of her abductor. He yelped, and then she was being crushed into the seat, the man's weight bearing down on her. Further struggle became impossible. Futile.

Musk flooded her nostrils, the man's cologne so strong that it choked her. Nowlin. Her eyes watered, and she held her breath, trying to clear her head. This close, inside the small coach, the scent was overwhelming.

"Get. Off. Me." Beau lay still, heart beating madly, as though it might claw its way out of her chest. The seat creaked and sagged as Nowlin finally clambered off her.

"Oh, my darling, tell me I've not hurt you."

Beau clenched her jaw until her teeth ached. His Irish lilt didn't make his preposterous blandishments one jot less ridiculous. Her pulse dropped so suddenly she felt dizzy. She blinked, eyes adjusting to the dark interior of the coach. He sat poised near the door, a patently false smile lifting the corner of his lips.

"Mr. Nowlin. What do you think you're doing?"

"Isn't it obvious? We're eloping, my sweet love."

Beau's throat tightened. She'd been abducted before. Her fortune almost guaranteed such rough-and-ready attempts to acquire it, and she seemed cursed to inspire acts of deluded romance. But neither of the men who'd attempted to gain her hand and dowry had been a mere acquaintance as this one was. "Mr. Nowlin." She laced her voice with steel, doing her best impression of her father. "Stop this coach and put me down at once."

"Can't do that." His smile grew, cocking up on one side. "Can't, my sweet love. We must make haste."

"Do stop calling me that. You sound like a moonling." She struggled with her hat, which seemed to have been irrevocably crushed and was now drooping over her eyes.

A hearty laugh answered her, and she felt the first flush of real concern. She freed the ribbon that held her hat and stared down at the broken circle of straw.

Her father and brothers would catch them long before they reached Scotland—of that she had no doubt— but she'd been warned not to get herself into any more scrapes. A wave of panic radiated through her limbs.

Her brother had suggested that perhaps they should have left her to Granby. But this was entirely different. Granby had admittedly been one of her flirts. One of her favorites. A man who might, in his wildest imaginations, have convinced himself that she would welcome his advances, even if her father wouldn't. Nowlin was very nearly a stranger. She'd only ever danced with him the once, for heaven's sake.

Leo couldn't be so cruel. He wouldn't. She forced herself to breathe and watched Nowlin for any hint that he might be creeping toward her. If he touched her, she couldn't possibly be held responsible for what she might do.

Her stomach threatened to turn itself inside out as he turned to look at her, but her glare kept him pinned firmly in place. He didn't look like a man inflamed by love—or even lust—and there was something grim about his eyes. Something serious that belied his smile.

Beau swallowed and hunched into the corner, refusing to give in. Panic and terror wouldn't serve her at all. At some point, they'd have to stop. They'd have to change horses, and he'd have to let her out of the coach. It was six days or more to Scotland. She simply had to be ready to seize whatever opportunity for escape presented itself. She'd done it before, and she could do it again.

When they stopped for the first change, Nowlin sat with his foot propped up on the opposite seat and his leg pressed hard against the door, barring the only exit. At the sound of a knock, he dropped the window. A cool breeze, promising rain, washed over her. Beau found herself inhaling deeply, as though there'd been not enough air inside the coach.

Nowlin took a parcel wrapped in brown paper from his servant and shut the window up with a loud bang the moment that the coachman's hand disappeared. Beau sagged back into the squabs. Tension drained out of her. This stop offered her nothing, no chance of escape, no opportunity to bolt.

Once the coach was back in motion, Nowlin unwrapped the paper and offered her a small loaf of brown bread and a chunk of grayish cheese. Beau took the bread and gnawed on it in silence, shuddering at the thought of even touching the cheese. The stench alone was enough to set her stomach roiling.

Her abductor shrugged one elegantly clad shoulder. "There's scant time for hot meals taken in taprooms, so you'd best learn to make do. No? Have it your way." He ate her portion in two healthy bites and washed it all down with the contents of his flask.

Beau methodically chewed the leathery crust of the bread. She was certainly hungry, but not hungry enough to eat that cheese. Not yet, anyway. A few more missed meals and she might be regretting her choice.

A few miles on Nowlin tapped the roof and the carriage rolled to a halt. He flicked his gaze over her and climbed out. The scrape and a *thunk* told her that he'd latched the door shut from the outside. Beau eyed the small window in the door. If she took off the pads that held out her petticoats, she *might* be able to squeeze through...but her bright, floral jacket would be all too visible if she was forced to run. She might as well be waving a flag.

Beau peeled off her gloves and took her purse from her pocket. She hurriedly counted the coins. Nearly a pound. Plenty of pocket money for an afternoon's shopping, but not nearly enough to get her home even if she could somehow manage to slip away from Nowlin.

Beau cursed under her breath and shoved the purse back into her pocket. Even with her brothers both out of town and her father likely ensconced at his club, the wheels of her rescue must already be in motion. Boaz would have seen to it.

Leo might have threatened to leave her to her fate in a fit of anger, but surely he wouldn't actually do so. Beau worried the seam of her glove with her teeth. No, even if Leo wouldn't come for her, her father would.

Of that she was sure.

Shadows lengthened as they rolled swiftly northward. Shivering, Beau rummaged through the small storage spaces under the seats: empty wine bottles, a single woman's shoe, a scanty wool blanket, slightly moth-eaten, and smelling oddly of dog and mold. What was more telling was what was missing. There was no gun. Either there never had been one, or Nowlin knew better than to leave her alone with one. Aside from the bottles, there was nothing to arm herself with, not even a traveling set with a dull knife.

Still shivering, she curled up under the blanket, the sturdiest of the bottles clutched in her hand.

❧ CHAPTER 3 ❧

A heavy mist cloaked the day in misery. Nowlin had spent the night on the box with his servant as they rolled through the darkness, but Beau hadn't slept a wink. She'd been too busy waiting for him to creep inside and join her. Her nerves were raw from waiting, anticipating, and planning. But this morning it was cold and gray and wet, and he was back inside with her. She touched the bottle under her skirts where she'd hidden it and waited.

"You'll be lucky if my brothers don't rip you limb from limb."

"Promises, promises, my sweet." He sounded utterly dismissive, but then he hadn't met either of her brothers. He had no idea what he was in for.

"It's not as though this is the first time I've been abducted, you know."

"An old hand at it, are we?"

Beau bit the inside of her cheek and studied him for a moment. He was so cocksure, so confident that he would get away with abducting her and that her family would simply acquiesce to such a marriage, and that she would, it was baffling.

"Yes. First, it was Mr. Martin. My brothers say that perhaps they should have made me marry him. Only by the time they caught up with us, he wasn't willing anymore."

Nowlin grinned at her. Deep dimples appeared on either side of his mouth. It seemed impossible that a man with dimples like those could be so treacherous, that a man so handsome should need to be.

"Scared him off, did you?"

Beau shook her head and batted her eyes. "Stabbed him. With a fork. The tines went all the way into the bone and stuck there. So much howling. So much blood. My brothers caught up with us because we were waiting for the surgeon."

"I guess you'll be eating your meals with a spoon on this trip."

Beau sighed. He wasn't listening. Having only a spoon wasn't going to stop her. "And then there was Mr. Granby." She shook her head sadly. "He lives abroad now. Only one eye left. Father felt that was punishment enough."

The Irishman frowned, his dimples deserting him momentarily. Beau smiled wider and continued. "It's quite amazing what happens when you press your thumb into a man's eye socket with all your might."

"Well, well. You are a cold bitch, aren't you?"

Beau smiled and tilted her head, looking at him out of her lashes. "I am my mother's daughter. The best outcome here—for you, that is—is that one of the men in my family catches up with us. Left to my own devices, I'm liable to do permanent damage."

"It would cause quite a fuss if you did. Exactly the kind of thing that a woman in your position should be trying to avoid." His words were confident, but the tone was less so.

"And you think blinding a man didn't have that very distinct possibility? But not one whisper of either affair has ever reached the scandalmongers, has it?"

The worried frown returned, marring his handsome face. He rapped on the roof, and the carriage slid to a stop. Beau leaned forward to press her point. "They might—*might*—only have sent you packing back to Ireland. But you had to go and abduct me in public."

Without a word, he jumped down and slammed the door shut behind him, the scraping sound of the lock enraging her further. "They'll have to kill you. You know that?" she yelled after him, giving the door a good kick for emphasis.

Beau crossed her arms and hugged herself. Nowlin might not be ready to let her go yet, but if he failed to see reason, she'd see him cowering and bloody just like the others.

She was ruined already, and they both knew it. What he didn't know was that her father would let her choose ruin and a quiet life abroad, and she wouldn't hesitate to embrace the option. Paris, Vienna, Florence—perhaps even St. Petersburg or Tangier.

Hours later, the coach suddenly shimmied beneath her, shaking Beau out of a hazy nap. It bounced horribly and then sagged backward as it came to a stop.

A chorus of cursing swirled about her. Beau smiled to herself. There was something wrong with one of the wheels. That would slow them down. And if they had to stop for a repair, Nowlin would have to let her out of the carriage. She straightened her clothing and finger combed her hair, slipping the pins back into place.

Eventually, the coach resumed its progress, but with a jolt and a scraping sound that spoke all too clearly of increasing damage. After a painfully slow hour, they entered a small village of little more than an inn, a few shops, and a smattering of houses along an otherwise desolate bit of road.

The minutes stretched. Beau began to fear that Nowlin intended to keep her locked in the coach while the wheel was seen to, but eventually the door opened and he appeared to lead her inside.

"Don't bother telling tales to these kind people," Nowlin announced loudly as he dragged her through the taproom. "I've told them all about your little escapade."

Beau glared at him. Martin had done that too—poisoned the well so no one would help her. Nowlin pushed her into a private parlor and kicked the door shut behind them.

"Wives who run off and abandon their husbands and bairns don't sit too well with the common folk."

"And I suppose you're the forgiving husband come to fetch me home?"

"And I always will. Don't believe anything different for a moment, my love. Have a seat and eat something." He gestured to the table where a cold piece of steak and kidney pie sat waiting beside a tankard with a frothy head that promised ale. There were no utensils on the table.

"I see you remembered about the fork."

Nowlin laughed, his misleading dimples peeping out. "No forks, no knives, no candlesticks. I suppose you could hit me with a chair, but if you do, you'll eat the rest of your meals standing at the mantle." He bowed and slipped out of the room.

Beau swallowed down her anger and sat. Her stomach had been growling since dawn. Starving herself wouldn't help her situation one jot. She pulled off her gloves, thrust them into her pocket, and sat.

When she finished, she pushed the empty plate away and paced the room. A small commode was the room's only other piece of furniture. Beau rifled through it. It held a chamber pot, a few glasses, and an assortment of half-used candles of dubious quality.

She hefted the chamber pot with one hand. It was heavy stoneware. Nothing like the porcelain ones she was used to, with their fanciful flowers or pretty patterns of Oriental splendor. It was... she searched for the proper word: serviceable.

Clubbing Nowlin with it might not get her anywhere, but it certainly couldn't hurt. If she could wound him, it might at least slow them down, or delay them further.

She took up a position a safe distance behind the door and waited. He'd had fair warning, which was more than any woman owed under such circumstances.

The door swung open a few minutes later, and Nowlin, in a fresh change of clothes and newly shaved, stepped through. His cologne preceded him like a dog before its cart, the scent flooding the room.

Fury burst through her. *He* got a change of clothing and a wash while she was still wearing the same gown that he'd abducted her in and hadn't been offered so much as a basin of water to wash her hands in.

She raised the heavy chamber pot as high as the tight sleeves of her jacket would allow and swung it hard, putting all her anger and frustration behind it. Nowlin ducked, twisting about to face her, taking only a glancing blow to the head.

With a growl, he caught her wrists and squeezed. The chamber pot slipped from her grasp and hit the floor with the unmistakable sound of pottery breaking.

Beau twisted her wrists, wrenching one free. Nowlin let go of the other and backhanded her across the face, sending her sprawling. Beau hit the wall, tasting blood, pulse hammering through her like a military drum calling the troops to war.

She slid all the way to the floor, keeping the wall at her back. Nowlin stared at her as her hand closed around one of the shards of the pot. The edge was rough, jagged. It would hurt when she slashed it across his pretty face.

"Put it down, my bonny lass, or I swear on St. Patrick's staff, I'll beat you silly."

Beau tightened her grip and got a boot to the stomach for her defiance. She gasped and retched, her vision flickering as pain roiled through her. He'd kicked her hard enough to break the wooden busk of her stays, and now it was gouging into her, making it impossible for her to draw a free breath.

Nowlin stepped heavily onto her wrist, boot smearing her with mud, and wrenched the pottery shard out of her hand. He jerked her up, fingers digging into the flesh of her arm.

"Would you really rather be dead? That's not the plan, and I'd be hard pressed to explain it, but you're begging for a beating the likes of which you've clearly never had. We're leaving now, and you're going to behave yourself on the way to the coach or I truly will make you regret it, lass. Do you understand?"

Beau met his gaze. He didn't even look angry, just grimly determined. The taste of blood in her mouth made her stomach lurch painfully against her broken busk. She turned her head and spat.

"I see that you do understand." His smile returned in full force. "Good."

The mist had thickened, not quite turning to rain but heavy enough to coat everything with a damp layer of droplets every bit as cold and slippery. Gareth turned up the collar of his greatcoat and gave Mountebank his head. The gelding picked up the pace, breaking into a trot, as eager as Gareth to reach a warm, dry inn.

A few miles on, clear signs of habitation began. He was nowhere near St. Neots and the Swan and Bell, but whatever village this was would undoubtedly have an inn of some kind. He'd settle for a spot in the taproom if he had to at this point.

As he entered the village proper, it wasn't hard to spot the inn. A mail coach was just departing and a somewhat battered private carriage was drawn up outside, its groom in the process of checking the harness on what looked to be a fresh team. Gareth reined in. Monty shook like a dog beneath him, flinging droplets of water in all directions.

"I know, boy. It's high time we both found ourselves a…" His ability to speak deserted him.

A woman's head of curls broke through the mist, her hair so dark it seemed to bleed right through the gray. Her head was uncharacteristically bowed, but her height was unmistakable. A man ushered her along, hands familiarly at her arm and waist. Not her father. Not either of her brothers. Certainly not one of the handful of men whom her family might accept as a suitor. Gareth knew them all.

Lady Boudicea Vaughn was eloping.

A red fog filled his head. His vision tunneled out. Monty gave an impatient crow hop, and Gareth forced himself to loosen the reins and relax in the saddle.

The man bundled her into the coach and leapt in after her. The door shut and it rolled into motion. Gareth watched it go. The coach's wheels sprayed mud in their wake. It disappeared into the heavy mist in moments.

Monty was cantering after them before Gareth even realized that he'd made a decision.

~ CHAPTER 4 ~

The crack of a gunshot resounded like a clap of thunder. Beau leapt for the door, only to be dragged back by her hair. The coach skidded to a stop, sliding in the mud with a sickening, sideways lurch. A few shouts, muffled by the rain and the walls of the coach, and then the door was wrenched open and the wide-eyed groom slid hurriedly out of the way.

"Out, everyone out." The command came from some distance away, muffled but loud enough to be heard nonetheless.

Nowlin swore under his breath, let go of her hair, and stepped out. He attempted to keep Beau inside, but she squeezed past him. This might be her best chance. Her only chance. Highwaymen were, after all, seeking money. And if there was one thing her family had in abundance, it was money.

Rain droplets spattered across her skin, large but infrequent. A man on a huge dappled horse held a gun pointed at them, the barrel nearly the same smoky blue as the mist that swirled around their feet.

His mouth and nose were hidden in his cravat and the turned-up collar of his coat, but she'd know that horse anywhere. Lord knew she'd ridden him often enough before her brother had sold him. She didn't need the corroboration of Sandison's silvery queue and narrowed blue eyes, but she was relieved to see them all the same.

Beau bit her lips and tried to keep from smiling. Nowlin wasn't going to get a chance to follow through with any of his threats. Not today. Not ever. He'd be lucky to continue drawing breath.

"Your purse, sir."

Nowlin glared and tossed his wallet onto the ground at the horse's feet. Monty took a step back, clearly not happy about having things tossed at him in such a fashion.

Sandison's eyes met hers and narrowed, as though he were accessing the situation still. Beau lifted her chin and stared right back. What was he waiting for?

"If the lady would be so kind as to retrieve it for me."

Beau stepped toward him, but Nowlin blocked her with his arm, doing quite the impression of a man bravely guarding his own. "Get it yourself, bridle-cull."

"Ah-ah-ah. You were so hasty as to toss it to the ground. And I'm not fool enough to dismount. The lady seems the safest choice."

When Nowlin didn't remove his arm, Sandison trained the gun directly at him. "I suppose I could simply shoot you and then retrieve it myself. In fact, if you persist in this nonsense, I might take pleasure in doing just that."

Nowlin's arm sagged away from her, and Beau stepped around him, trying desperately not to appear too eager. Why didn't Sandison just shoot him? He had a clear shot. Was he choosing this moment in life to become squeamish?

She picked her way through the mud and bent carefully to pick up the wallet, hissing as her stays dug deeper into her flesh. She thrust the wallet into her pocket as Monty pivoted, swinging his hindquarters about, putting himself between her, Nowlin, and the coach.

Nowlin's shout of protest was lost in the loud report of Sandison's pistol and the splintering of wood. Beau grabbed Sandison's arm, fingers gouging into the wet wool of his coat. He swung her up in a flurry of skirts, and Monty sprang away, long legs eating up ground at a thunderous pace.

Gareth wrapped one arm around Lady Boudicea and gave Mountebank his head. The gelding flew through the trees. Small branches snatched at Gareth's hair. One struck his cheek hard enough that he was sure to have a welt.

Beau clutched at his coat, and he tightened his grip. He'd been lucky to get hold of her at all. Retaining her would prove difficult if she fought him. He didn't ever want to explain that he'd had to hurt Leo's sister in any way, for any reason.

"Did you shoot him?" Her question rattled through him, bringing a twinge of conscience in its wake. Lord knew that he'd wanted to in the moment, but he understood what might prompt a man to go to such lengths.

If he hadn't been friends with her brother, he might have done the same himself. Now that she was shivering in his arms, the urge to keep her for himself was nearly irresistible. It burned beneath his skin, live and hot and wicked.

"No, I'll leave that to your brothers. Rescuing you from yourself is effort enough for me."

She moved impatiently in his arms. "Can we stop for a moment?"

Gareth grinned. Get him to stop, give her swain a chance to catch up, give her a chance to slip away and run back to him. Cunning, conniving, and unstoppable. That was Beau. "Not just yet, brat. I'd like a bit more distance between us and them before I do."

"Agreed, but my busk broke when he kicked me, and it hurts like the devil. Monty's jostling is killing me."

He straightened in the saddle, stiffening his seat, and Monty planted his hooves and skidded to a halt. "He what?"

Gareth swung his leg over Monty's neck and took them both down to the ground in a single motion. That didn't sound like one of her tricks, and the thought of it brought the red haze back to the edge of his vision.

"What do you mean he kicked you?"

Beau swayed unsteadily as she got her feet beneath her. Gareth gripped her shoulders and looked her over. Her hair was a tumbled riot, and there was what looked like a bruise waxing across one cheekbone. She looked exhausted. The hollows beneath her eyes were deep and shadowed, the skin almost papery.

"He didn't take it at all kindly when I hit him with a chamber pot." Her fingers popped the hooks that held her jacket closed. "Now help me, please."

Gareth sucked in a breath and did as directed. That

might have been the first *please* he'd ever had from her. He tugged off her jacket, stripping the damp silk from her with difficulty. She dragged her trailing hair over one shoulder, and he jerked loose the knot that held her stays laced tightly shut.

"Are you telling me I should have shot him?"

"Yes!"

The venom in that single word took him aback. "My apologies, bantling. Next time I'll try to do better."

He took a deep breath and whipped the cord free with sharp, deliberate movements, trying not to think about the fact that Lady Boudicea Vaughn was about to stand before him, one damp layer from naked. Trying not to compare the reality of it to the daydreams he so often used to while away the time.

Damnation. The reality was so much better...and infinitely worse. The cord swung free of the last hole and she ripped her stays away from her body, flinging them to the ground as though she despised them as much as she did her abductor.

Her head was bent forward, exposing the nape of her neck, the visible trail of her spine leading downward into her shift. He traced it with his finger, stopping only when he reached the tie that held her petticoats in place.

Gareth stared at her back, at the sheer linen clinging damply to her skin, at the ties to her petticoats, lying quiescent beneath his fingertips.

Heaven help him.

She shivered and stepped away, and he told himself firmly that it was just the rain. That shiver hadn't been for him, because of him.

She retrieved her jacket from where he'd laid it across the saddle and turned to face him, fabric clutched to her chest. "You said rescuing me from myself." Her brow furrowed. "You thought I was eloping?" Anger and annoyance flared in her voice, bringing it down an octave.

"It wouldn't be the first time."

She blinked, drawing a clearly affronted breath. "Leo wouldn't have told you that. Never."

"I was with him when your father came to fetch him. It was impossible not to put the facts together and come to the obvious conclusion."

She set her mouth in a mulish line and shoved her arms into the sleeves of her jacket. "Well, you put it together as badly then as you did just now. I have *never* eloped."

Abducted. The flash of rage returned. That any man should presume to touch her, to force her. "You're right. I should have shot the bastard."

He stooped to retrieve her stays, his brain clearly picturing the sway of her breasts, the rosy shadow of her nipples, the way that the damp fabric clung to every luscious curve.

It was so clear in his mind that he might as well have looked his fill. Instead, he rolled the stays tightly and bound them with their cord and then jammed them into his saddlebag. When he turned back, she was nearly done refastening her jacket, though it gapped and pulled across the swell of her unrestrained breasts.

Chivalry withered in his chest, burnt to a crisp by the flare of desire, of lust and covetousness. He really was no better than the men who'd taken her. Or if he was, it was only because her brother was his friend. That single fact was the only thing allowing him to cling to honor even now.

"I think you've missed a few hooks, but you'll do." He remounted and held out his hand. She took it, and using his foot as her stirrup, leveraged herself into his lap.

Gareth unbuttoned his greatcoat and pulled her inside it, warding off as much of the rain as he could. She sat stiffly in the circle of his arms, clearly still affronted.

Rescuer or fellow villain, which was he? Which did he want to be? He'd told himself all these years he was a good man, but with every passing second it felt more and more like a lie.

～ CHAPTER 5 ～

Padrig Nowlin watched the rump of the highwayman's gray mount disappear into the rain and the mist with horror and sickening disbelief. This couldn't be happening. They'd planned everything so carefully. *He'd* planned everything so carefully.

Whoever heard of a highwayman acting as this one had? And what kind of woman threw herself into the arms of an unknown criminal? She hadn't done it because she was scared of him either. Lady Boudicea had proved to be everything he'd been warned she was: fickle, fast with her favors, and too cunning by far. A lady in name only. Not that it mattered. Padrig would have served up the Virgin herself if it meant saving his sister.

Panic welled up, flooding his chest, freezing his limbs. This couldn't be happening. She'd stranded him in the middle of nowhere with no means of paying the coachman or returning to London. The queasy feeling deepened, threatening to bring his lunch back up.

All he'd been asked to do was deliver Lady Boudicea

Vaughn to Gretna. One simple thing. One simple damn thing and his debts would be cleared. He'd have the title to his family's estate back in his possession, and his little sister would never hear from Mr. George Granby again. The world would never learn that Maeve had spent the better part of three months as Mr. Granby's mistress in London in some ill-conceived plan of her own to clear Padrig's debts.

Padrig had just wanted Granby gone. Him and all the trouble he'd brought. And if someone had to pay the price, better it was a stranger than Maeve. A duke would have the means to sugarcoat his daughter's disgrace. Padrig didn't have any such luxury, and neither did his sister.

What the hell was he going to do now?

❧ CHAPTER 6 ❧

Beau eyed the façade of The Pig and Whistle with trepidation. The sign swung in the wind, threatening to come free of its mooring at any second. The half-timbered walls appeared to be slowly sagging out from under the thatched roof, spreading like a warm pudding freshly loosed from the mould.

"They won't ask questions, and that's all that matters." Sandison's breath caressed her ear. His jaw brushed hers, the abrasive touch racing through her, making her tighten and pulse.

It was indecent the way he made her feel. The gossips could label her wanton, and they'd be right. Oh, so very right… She'd been all too aware of him since she'd turned and found him watching her like she was a Boxing Day feast.

He'd been calling her brat and bantling, as though she were still a child, but he certainly wasn't looking at her as if she were one. Finally. She'd wanted him to look at her in exactly that manner for nearly as long as she could remember, since before she'd even really comprehended what it meant... and now that he had, she had no idea what to do next.

Or rather, she had a very good idea—she had a sister-in-law who had been a courtesan, after all—but the odds of her brother's friend doing anything as suicidal as seducing her were nil. Only he didn't know the truth. She was already ruined. Nothing he did from this point forward could hurt her.

But it could hurt him.

She breathed in the scent of him: sandalwood and amber. He swung her down from the saddle, and her eyes pricked with heat. She could see her path out, her chance to stay in England with her family, to avoid exile, to salvage something of the life that she'd planned and wanted. But it was only possible if she sacrificed Sandison. And it would leave her at his mercy after she'd done so.

He leapt from the saddle, the skirt of his greatcoat flying out, shedding water like a bird's wing. Together they led Monty into what passed for the Pig and Whistle's stable. Sandison roused the stable boy with his foot and handed over the gelding's reins.

"There'll be a shilling for you in the morning if he's seen to properly. Rub him down, give him fresh water, and feed him."

Sandison tossed his saddlebags over his shoulder and led her into the inn. Beau's knees nearly gave out as they mounted the steps. She was really going to do this. There was no other choice. Sandison propped her up and pushed her forward into the nearly empty taproom.

A greasy man in a leather apron rounded the bar.

"A room," Sandison said, a hand nestled at her waist as though it belonged there. Heat pulsed through the wet fabric, radiating into her skin. "And dinner. Whatever the ordinary is will be fine, so long as it's hot and it's served in our room."

"Of course, sir. Such a nasty night to be out. Would you be wanting ale or wine with supper?"

"Wine if it's drinkable. Ale if the wine's going to strip my innards raw and leave me crying for my mother."

The innkeeper nodded. "Martha will show you to your room. Martha!" A stumpy girl appeared, wiping her hands on her drab skirts. She motioned to them and headed up the stairs without looking back.

Beau clutched her sopping wet petticoats in both hands and followed the girl up the dank staircase. The room they were led to was as dark and cold as the stairs, but Martha lit the coal that lay waiting in the grate and the candle stubs that sat upon the mantle.

"I'll be back with your supper quick as I can," the girl said as she clomped out of the room.

Sandison shoved Beau toward the slowly growing fire. She flexed her hands over the coals, wishing for the crackling warmth of wood. There was something a bit dismal about coal. He hung up his greatcoat and tossed his hat onto the table. His silvery hair was rumpled, strands falling loose from his queue to frame his face.

He looked wild. Like some creature out of a fairy tale. Her very own Tam Lin. He'd certainly abducted her in a forest. He even had a white—or nearly white—steed.

Beau bit her lip and shut her eyes. It didn't seem fair that under normal circumstances the world would never have let her keep him, that her family wouldn't have either. And there was nothing fair about what she had planned for him.

It was ruin or marriage. When Sandison discovered that merely retrieving her from Nowlin wouldn't be enough to salvage her reputation, would he baulk? Could she afford to leave him the option? Wasn't her mother always saying that the key to managing a man was letting him think everything was his idea?

Gareth took a seat by the wholly inadequate fire in the taproom and nursed his ale, trying—entirely unsuccessfully—to keep his very active imagination away from what was taking place upstairs. The Pig and Whistle's ale was bitter, but the bite was welcome. It slowly pushed the cold out of the pit of his stomach.

Upstairs, Lady Boudicea was no doubt even now sitting by the fire wearing nothing but his nightshirt. The erotic thrill of it was almost more than he could bear, more than he could face. Temptation incarnate.

If he were wise, he'd send fat Martha up for his greatcoat and spend the night here in the taproom, but there was no lock on the door, and an inn full of hedge birds on a wet night was too dangerous a place to leave Beau alone.

He dropped his head into his hands and massaged his scalp. If he'd taken a carriage rather than riding, he'd have had a way to push on despite the foul weather. If it weren't pouring rain, they might have journeyed on as well. If. If. If. What was it his grandmother always said? If wishes were horses, beggars would ride.

Gareth pushed his hair back from his face and propped

his feet up nearer the fire. As the leather warmed, steam drifted up from his boots in thin trails. His toes began to ache as circulation returned.

They were at least two days from anywhere that she might be safe: London, her brother's country estate, even his family's seat, if he were fool enough to take her there and subject her to the machinations of his father. And that was two days in good weather. In the condition the roads were in at the moment, they'd be lucky to make any of those journeys in twice the time.

And what would he say when they arrived at whatever destination they chose? *Good morning. So happy to have been of service. Please allow me to restore your sister to your protection.*

Her brother would rip his head from his body.

A tiny voice in the back of his mind pointed out that this was all the more reason to simply keep her for himself. Why bother returning her when the punishment would likely be the same? Why bother returning her when it was the very last thing he wanted to do?

His brain ran in circles, the wicked voice prompting him to take what he'd always wanted getting louder by the minute, drowning out common sense and decency. He knew that voice. It was his father's. Any action could be justified if one were a Sandison of Ashburn. Even if one was only a spare Sandison.

Martha swept by carrying a tray. He rose and followed her up the stairs. They would eat and talk over Beau's predicament, and then he'd roll himself up in his coat and sleep across the doorway like her dogsbody.

He stepped past the inn's maid and opened the door.

Beau was seated by the fire, combing out her hair. The dull glow was thankfully not enough to turn his nightshirt sheer. The obvious points of her nipples through the fine linen were trial enough.

She pushed her hair aside, curls tumbling down to cover her breasts, droplets of water slowly falling from the tip of each curl to bloom darkly on the linen.

"You can call me up when you're done, or I can get the dishes back in the morning, sir." Martha bobbed a quick curtsey and hurried out of the room as the innkeeper bellowed her name from the bottom of the stairs.

Gareth eyed the food on the table. "Looks like some kind of meat pie, mashed parsnips, a very hard loaf of bread, a few small apples, and pitcher of ale."

Beau stared at him, silent and still, her hands clutching the ivory comb in her lap. Was she afraid of him? That would certainly be an unprecedented first, but then so was everything else about the day.

"Come eat. We'll muddle through this. I promise you."

She let her breath out with a slightly giddy laugh. "Of that I'm sure." She caught her lower lip between her teeth, released it, and sighed. When she stood, he realized that he'd been mistaken about the coals. They provided exactly the requisite amount of light to turn the nightshirt to gossamer.

Gareth sucked in a strangled breath, blood surging through him thickly, pounding in his ears. She was beautiful. Always had been. But the sight of her in his nightshirt infused his blood with a possessive undercurrent that boded ill for his carefully leashed self-control.

•   •   •

Beau swallowed hard, throat working. Panic bubbled up. She could do this. How hard could it be to get a rake such as Gareth Sandison to tumble into bed with her? He was always one small step away from a carnal slip, wasn't he? She met his gaze and held it, stepping toward him.

She'd make him happy. She'd keep him happy. Whatever it took.

She came to a stop close enough that she could feel the heat of his body through the fine linen of his nightshirt. The eyebrows that she loved so much flexed and rose, the only part of him that hinted at escape.

She put one hand on his chest, fingers splayed out over his heart, curled them in over the edge of his waistcoat, holding on tight. If she let go, she'd lose him. She could feel the tension in him, the way his body coiled for flight.

But instead of pulling away, his hands gripped her hips. His thumbs circled on her hip bones, pushing and pulling the fabric across her skin. Heat flooded through her. She felt warm for the first time in days.

"What are you playing at, brat?" He sounded dazed, not confused but disbelieving.

She opened her mouth to speak but found herself pushing forward, reaching up to kiss him instead. Her hands slid over his shoulders. His locked across the small of her back. Action was almost always the best choice, and if any situation in her life had ever called for boldness, this was it.

His mouth took hers, hot and savage, a forlorn hope of a kiss. She pulled him down to her, one hand locked in his hair. She'd been kissed before, but she'd never been devoured. Had certainly never wanted to respond in kind.

His grip on her tightened, and he dragged his mouth away from hers. "Your brothers will kill me."

She leaned in, cheek to cheek, lips touching his ear as she spoke. "I won't let them." She pressed closer. She could feel his—her mind went blank for a moment, and she forced herself to find the right word—his manhood... his...his *cock* swelling against her belly. A blush burned her cheeks even as a triumphant thrill worked its way down her spine. His protest was nothing but bluster.

"If you don't want me, you should have left me to Nowlin." Lord knew that should goad him into action. She kissed Sandison's jaw, dragged her teeth along it, bit his lower lip softly. "In for a penny, in for a pound. I'm ruined either way."

Sandison pulled his head back, twisting his face to one side, but his hands didn't leave her. "Not if I get you safely back to your family," he said, each word coming out as though it hurt.

"There's no safe return." Beau pressed her advantage. "Not this time. Nowlin snatched me from Pall Mall in the middle of the afternoon in full sight of half a dozen members of the *ton*."

His breath hissed out of him. Beau cupped his cheeks in her hands and held his gaze with her own. "You can put me on a coach to London in the morning or you can run with me to Scotland."

"So I can play the villain or the scoundrel?"

A smile forced its way out, stretching her mouth in a grin that she couldn't even hope to mitigate or hide. "You'd be a secret villain. No one need ever know you had anything to do with my escape from Nowlin."

"You'd know." His voice was tinged with anger. "I'd know." For the briefest moment, she thought she'd lost the gamble, and then his hands flattened over her hips, fingers dipping to touch the dimples that bookended her spine.

Beau pulled loose the knot of his cravat while he stood frozen, as still as one of the standing stones at Avebury. She let the scrap of linen slip through her fingers and fall to the floor.

"Scotland?" Beau held her breath, waiting for his reply.

"Scotland." The word ground past his teeth like an animal clawing its way out of the earth. His mouth took hers with frantic need, lips and teeth clashing, tongue dancing, teasing. Beau locked her arms around his neck and kissed him back.

He was hers.

~ CHAPTER 7 ~

S he was his.

Gareth fisted his hands in the fabric of his own nightshirt and dragged her to the bed. He might be damned as a villain and scoundrel both, but he just couldn't bring himself to care.

Beau caught her hands in his coat and shoved. He shrugged out of it, letting it lie where it fell. She clawed open the buttons of his waistcoat and yanked his shirttails out of his breeches. He broke off kissing her long enough to toss his waistcoat aside, push off his braces, and yank his shirt over his head.

She didn't give him time to divest himself of his boots, let alone his breeches. She pulled him down onto the bed, hands roaming over his back, nightshirt already riding up around her hips, long, pale legs begging to be touched. He slid a hand up along her thigh until it came to rest where her thigh met the buttock. Sweet, impossibly soft skin rising to meet flesh that was softer yet.

He buried his face in the crook of her neck. Dragged

his open mouth up to the sensitive spot beneath her ear, where he bit down lightly. She gasped and arched, fingers gripping his shoulder blades as though she might rip them from his body.

Her earlobe beckoned, and he obligingly took it between his teeth, hand sliding over the top of her thigh, knuckles grazing the exquisitely soft flesh where leg met groin. Damp curls. Slick folds. The sensitive peak at the top of the cleft that ruled a woman's pleasure.

Gareth swirled his finger, and Beau made a strangled sound in the back of her throat. He continued the caress, fingers sliding between her thighs, down to the entrance to her body. Her flesh was hot, damp with her own juices, but the delicate web of her hymen was unmistakable.

Icy reality hit him full force. For all her wit, experience, and bravado, Beau was still very much a virginal daughter of the aristocracy. Gareth took a deep breath, cursing silently as the scent of her flooded through him, making his cock pulse and ache. He forced himself to break off the intimate caress, to thrust both hands safely into the blanket beneath them.

Her arms locked about him, preventing him from rolling off her. "Don't stop now. You can't possibly stop now."

The pleading note in her voice nearly broke him. "I can't possibly continue, brat. The fact that I trespassed as far as I did is bad enough."

Beau struggled out from under him. She pushed her hair back from her face and stared at him with dawning horror. There it was: sanity reasserting itself.

"You don't want me. Oh, God." She sounded sick, heartbroken. Gareth's own somewhat-damaged heart skipped a beat.

"Not want you?" The words raced out of him of their own accord. "You've no idea how badly I want you, Boudicea."

Beau's head snapped up at the use of her full name. Her damp eyes met his, passion sparking deep within them. She reached for him. Gareth caught her wrist and held her off.

"I chose Scotland, and I meant it," he said, willing her to understand. "But if, for any reason, we somehow failed to reach it, were prevented from marrying, your falling pregnant would make everything a thousand times worse. If your family—if Leo, damn it all—were to catch up with us..."

"You'd want to be able to assure Leo that I was untouched."

"I know you have a plan, and I've agreed to it, sweetheart, but your family might have an alternative. If you're carrying my child, if there's even a chance of that, then you're trapped."

"And you're trapped with me."

She said it flatly, as if it were the worst option in the world rather than a fate he wished for with every fiber of his being. "I'm not trapped. As you said, I could put you on the mail coach back to London in the morning if I chose. But when your brother and I meet again, I have to be able to tell him honestly that you married me of your own free will, not because I'd left you with no choice. Do you understand, brat?"

Beau nodded, but her expression remained disgruntled. She caught her lower lip between her teeth, an unmistakable glint of mischief lighting up her eyes. "I can't fall pregnant if all you do is touch me, can I?"

The look of dumbfounded disbelief on Sandison's face was priceless. Beau held her breath and waited. His touch had been far too pleasurable. She wanted more. Needed more. And she wanted him to push himself close enough to the brink that there would be no turning back, even if in strict honesty, he could tell her family that she was still a virgin.

"You're going to be the death of me," Sandison said as he reached for her.

He rolled her beneath him, his mouth hotly covering the pulse point just below her ear. He yanked the nightshirt up and his hand slid back between her thighs, long fingers splaying her open, circling and teasing until her breath caught in her throat and her limbs tingled.

Sandison caught her earlobe between his lips, the hint of teeth causing her to shiver. "Do you ever touch yourself?"

Beau bit her lips to keep from grinning. "Anyone who says they don't is a liar."

His palm slid roughly over her, dragging across the aching, sensitive peak between her thighs. His fingers circled the opening to her body, the tip of one pressed for entrance, slipped into her, and delved carefully deeper.

"Do you ever touch yourself and think of me?"

Beau caught a strangled breath and didn't answer. His finger slid in until his knuckles lodged against her. He curled his finger within her, and she gasped.

"If you didn't, you will now," he said, sounding pleased and possessive. He kissed her, tongue delving into her mouth. Beau kissed him back, a whimper rising in her throat as her release threatened to crest.

"Shall I show you something you could never have done for yourself?" Gareth asked. "Something far better than hands and fingers?"

"Yes." Beau's thighs tried to clamp shut around his hand, and Sandison used his hips to keep them spread open. For a moment, she thought that he'd changed his mind about taking her maidenhead, but then he slid down, his hand abandoning her.

Beau gave a cry of protest, and Sandison chuckled. He yanked her to the edge of the bed, legs dangling over, one knee on either side of him.

He planted a hot, open-mouthed kiss on the inside of her thigh. Beau felt her legs begin to tremble. Another kiss, this one with teeth behind it, where her leg met her torso. Sandison's hands slid behind her knees, pushed her thighs wide and held them as his lips took over where his fingers had left off.

Beau bit the heel of her hand to keep from screaming. His tongue swirled across her, and then his mouth locked over the already inflamed flesh of her clitoris, and her entire body throbbed and shook as she climaxed.

Sandison lapped the length of her secret folds. He dragged the flat of his tongue from the opening of her body to the bundle of nerves where her pulse hammered with unslaked demand for more.

Beau took hold of his hair with one unsteady hand and dragged him up. He kissed her hard, almost roughly. She could taste herself on his lips, sweet and salty at the same time.

Gareth swiped his jaw over hers, the stubble of his beard an oddly intimate caress. "We can do that as often as you like," he whispered. "Even after we're married."

"If we can make it to Neville's Cross, we can hire a coach. Or we could if three pounds and twelve shillings wasn't all we had to our names."

Gareth counted the coins again and swore. It wasn't nearly enough for a coach, changes of horse, rooms, food, and stabling for Monty.

"Don't forget," Beau said as she sipped her tea, "we've got whatever Nowlin had in his purse."

"You prigged it? Brilliant girl!"

Beau grinned back at him. "Clearly we're both meant to hang." She reached into her pocket and held up Nowlin's embroidered pocketbook.

"Well?" Anticipation clawed through his veins as she opened it.

"Nowlin was certainly prepared," Beau replied, pulling out a thick pile of bank notes. "I think we can afford to pay the piper here and stable poor Monty somewhere decent."

"And procure you a change of clothes."

"Another shift at least would certainly be welcome." Beau shrugged. "I know the poor make do with just the clothes on their backs, but looking like a shag rag hardly presents the image of a married couple who can afford to hire a coach."

Gareth swept up the pile of bank notes and quickly counted them. "We should have more than enough to reach Scotland and return to London, even with your sartorial needs. In Neville's Cross, we should be able to outfit you there swiftly and anonymously, as well as hire a coach."

"Shall we go then?" Beau finished off her tea and bit into the last bun, tearing off a chunk with her teeth. "Between my brothers and Mr. Nowlin, I'd like to reach Scotland as quickly as possible."

Gareth pushed a wave of guilt aside as he tossed the last of his things back into his saddlebags. Was there any way to explain things to her brother? Any chance of Leo understanding that, as bad as things looked, he really had done his best for her?

Beau finished off the sticky bun and licked her fingers. Desire flared. It was all Gareth could do not to drag her back to the sagging bed and repeat every delicious thing that he'd done the night before.

The true problem was that no matter how guilty he felt about betraying a friend's trust, he knew deep down that even if Beau hadn't stated flat out that marriage to him was the best of her options, he would still be dragging her to Scotland this morning.

Leo had every right to hate him.

❦ CHAPTER 8 ❧

Sandison ran one hand down Monty's neck and slapped the gelding on the shoulder. "I'll be back for you shortly, beast."

Beau bit her lips and clutched Gareth's greatcoat around her. Leaving Monty behind felt wrong somehow. Like a betrayal. Monty shook his head, making a familiar, blustery sound as he blew his breath out his nose.

"Come on, sweetheart." Gareth held out his hand, and Beau took it, clinging to it, suddenly afraid to let go. Last night didn't seem real, but this did. Something about leaving Monty behind brought it all into perspective and left her feeling suddenly unsure.

Sandison squeezed her hand and tugged her along, steering her through the streets, past puddles and steaming mounds of horse droppings. "The innkeeper said there was a pawn shop just a few blocks away. We should be able to find something for you there."

"A pawn shop?"

He grinned, showing a row of large, white teeth.

"What do you think most maids and valets do with the cast-off clothing of their employers? They sell it. And a pawn shop will give them far more for anything that's still serviceable than the rag-and-bone man."

Beau blinked and stepped over a small pile of refuse. She'd never really thought about where her clothing went when she was done with it. Some of it her maid reworked as clothing for herself, but not all of it. The idea of some stranger wearing her cast-off clothing seemed unnatural. As though she might someday meet a stranger with her own face.

They rounded the corner onto a small green, and Sandison pointed to a shop with a window full of silver. Inside, the shop was cleaner and more orderly than it appeared from the street. The man behind the counter looked up. The light from the candles that illuminated the shop bounced off his glasses.

"Selling or buying?"

"Buying," Sandison said. "My wife's trunk was stolen off the diligence, and we've got a good ways still to go before we reach home. The innkeeper at The Oak and Acorn said you'd be our best hope of finding something quickly."

The shopkeeper nodded. "I think we have a couple of gowns that might serve, and there's no shortage of shifts and the like." He stepped to the door behind the counter. "Mrs. Chandler! Bring those things Mrs. Stops's maid sold us last week. Yes, the two chintz gowns, Ma'am." He turned to face Beau. "Would you like to make a list of what else you might require, and I'll try to see what I can find for you while you examine the gowns?"

"Yes, thank you very much." Beau took the scrap of foolscap and the pencil he offered her and quickly wrote out a list of very basic items: one shift, two pairs of cotton stockings, a cap and hat, and a shawl.

Mr. Chandler took the list and glanced over it. His wife appeared with the promised gowns flowing over her arm, and he swept past her, disappearing into the bowels of the shop.

Mrs. Chandler looked Beau over with a careful eye. "Yes, indeed, ma'am. I think Mrs. Stops's gowns will suit you well enough. You might have to overlap the bodices when you pin them shut, but they'll be decent enough for all that. Do you have pins?"

Beau shook her head. "They were in my trunk. And the jacket I'm wearing has hook and eyes."

Mrs. Chandler made a tisking sound and rummaged in a drawer for a moment. She slid a paper packet of dress pins across the counter. "Not a spot of rust on these, though a couple of them are slightly bent."

"They just have to get me home," Beau said, warming to the tale that she and Sandison had concocted. "I'm sure they'll be fine."

The shopkeeper's wife nodded. "Such an outrage. Stealing a lady's baggage. I hope there was nothing valuable in it?"

It was all Beau could do not to laugh. She was so clearly hoping there was, and that it would end up here in her shop. "No," Beau said, shaking her head. "Just a few gowns and fripperies."

"Oh," Mrs. Chandler replied, clearly crestfallen. "Well then, not as terrible as it could have been."

"Not at all," Beau agreed. "And if your husband can supply me with the essentials on my list, the worst of it will be the loss of my trunk itself."

Mrs. Chandler nodded, an avaricious gleam sparking in her eye. "So inconvenient. Shall I find you a portmanteau to see you home?"

"Please," Sandison interjected. He stepped forward and put his hand on the small of her back. Beau felt her skin flush, heat rising from his hand to flood her chest and face.

The two hours she'd spent in his lap riding from the Pig and Whistle to Neville's Cross this morning had been pure torture. She couldn't stop thinking about what they'd done the night before...about what they hadn't done, and how very much she'd wanted to do more.

Wanton. There was no other word for it. Every time Sandison touched her, so much as looked at her, she could feel the desire for more welling up within her. The desire for Sandison. The fact that he had his own passions firmly under control ate at her.

It was somehow unfair, almost humiliating. The urge to drive him to the point of no return was irresistible.

Beau studied Sandison in the dim light of the shop. He was impossibly handsome. She'd have said beautiful except that it somehow implied a softness that Sandison utterly lacked. He was a collection of sharp angles and planes, lean in the way of a greyhound, strength and power tightly coiled over long lengths of bone.

He smiled at her, and her stomach clenched and then turned over. If she could just hold on to him until they reached Scotland, he was hers.

. . .

Gareth watched Beau shake one of the gowns and hold it up. The profusion of pink flowers blooming across the fabric was garish in the extreme, but it did look as though it might fit her.

The shopkeeper's wife folded everything carefully and stowed it inside a leather portmanteau with a shiny brass clasp. They'd had everything Beau had asked for except a hat, but they'd directed them to a milliner on the other side of the green.

With the half-filled bag in tow, Gareth escorted Beau across the damp green and handed over an exorbitant amount of money for a simple hat of chip straw with a jaunty confection of ribbons and feathers jutting forth from it.

His consternation at the expense melted away as she set it on her head and grinned up at him. "Come on, brat. We've miles to go before we sleep. And I'm sure you'll want to change before we set off."

Beau nodded, setting the feathers on her new hat dancing. "I'd burn every stitch I'm wearing if I didn't think I'd be ruing the decision long before we reached Scotland."

Padrig Nowlin patted his pockets as a riotous group of urchins burst past him. Then he suddenly remembered that he had nothing left for them to steal. His purse had been taken by Lady Boudicea and the highwayman. His watch, ring, and every bit of clothing that he wasn't currently wearing had all been pawned in order to fund his frantic search for the damned runaway heiress. He had to find her. Granby would accept nothing else.

For the thousandth time that day, Padrig found himself

wishing that he could abandon the entire project and simply return to Belfast. Wishing that he'd never met Granby, never played so deeply at the man's faro table, and that he'd stayed sober enough not to sign marker after marker, all for funds he didn't have.

But he had, and if he failed, Granby would call in those markers, take the house and the farm, and turn Padrig's mother and sisters out into the street. All except Maeve, whom he'd promised to take special care of.

Padrig swallowed his rising anger, stopping in his tracks as he spied a familiar figure across the park. Wonder of wonders. Lady Boudicea Vaughn, arm in arm with a man, laughing.

His mouth went dry and his heart surged in a series of uneven beats. He ducked into a doorway and watched the two of them wander down the street and disappear into the busy yard of The Spoon and Lion.

Everything was going to be all right. The luck of the Irish might not be reliable, but today it was damn timely.

Gareth watched until Beau disappeared up the stairs, straining forward to catch a final glimpse of her ragged, muddy hem. His. Every muddy, outrageous inch of her. His, if he could just reach Scotland.

By the time she reappeared in Mrs. Stops's pink floral gown, the coach was hitched, the postboy was in the saddle, and Gareth was pressing a vail into the hand of the stable boy responsible for caring for Monty until he could reclaim him. Beau dropped her bag onto the ground beside her and shook out her skirts. They were a tad too short, and the gown was clearly a bit too large, but all in all, she looked credible enough, like a country parson's wife, a bit down about the heels but happy with her lot.

"Clean," Beau said as he handed her into the coach. "Well, as clean as a basin of hot water and a change of clothing can make me."

Gareth tossed her bag onto the rear-facing seat and climbed in behind her, dragging the door shut as he did so. Before he'd fully settled in, the coach sprang into motion. Beau gave an exaggerated sigh and tossed her new hat across the coach. It landed on top of her bag.

"Scotland," she said, imbuing the word with almost mythic reverence.

"Scotland," Gareth echoed back.

She curled toward him, dropping her head onto his shoulder. "Thank you."

Her simple thanks cut into him, through him, made his heart shrivel just a little where it lurked inside his chest. He kissed the top of her head, choking back a dismissive reply. No thanks were due. Certainly not from her. He was getting everything he'd ever wanted, though the cost when all was said and done might be more than either of them had bargained for.

Gareth wrapped an arm around her, and she mumbled sleepily, nuzzling her face against his chest like a sleepy puppy. The steady beat of the horses' hooves changed as they left the confines of the town, and the postboy increased their speed.

They hit a bump, and the coach bounced awkwardly, shaking Beau loose from his embrace and rousing them both from idyllic stupor. She cursed under her breath and sat up.

"What did you say?"

Beau batted her eyes at him. "Just cursing this sorry, rutted excuse for a road."

"Like a jack tar."

She grinned, lashes skimming her checks in what he knew to be faux modesty. "I have been trailing after my brothers and all their friends for close to twenty-two years."

Gareth forced himself to smile back at her. She didn't seem to have the least understanding of what their marriage was going to mean to his friendship with her brother. Or maybe she did, and she—like him—was simply refusing to acknowledge it. The inevitable estrangement wasn't real until they voiced it.

Even if Leo understood that Gareth had acted in Beau's best interests, he was unlikely to accept that there'd been no other choice. It would still *feel* like a betrayal.

"No wool gathering," Beau said, sliding about on the seat so that she was facing him. "If we must be awake, and it seems that we must, then you'd best think of some way of keeping me entertained."

Sandison's jaw dropped, and he blinked at her, looking as stunned as he might have had she hit him upside the head with a bottle, just as she'd planned for Nowlin. Beau rolled her lip between her teeth and waited.

His eyes narrowed, and his nostrils flared as he straightened beside her. With no warning, he yanked her into his lap, his mouth covering hers roughly, heat seeking heat, tongue enticing her to play.

His hand covered her breast, and she arched into it. Her pulse plummeted to join the ache between her thighs, redoubled, spreading through her like a fever.

Sandison suddenly cursed and yanked his hand away. Beau shook her head and tried to reorder her thoughts. Why stop? Why stop now?

"Damn pins," he muttered, sucking on his finger, and then giving his hand a shake.

He smiled down at her, and the rush of heat flooding through her swirled almost painfully through her womb, making her thighs shake. His erection pressed into her, hard and demanding even through several layers of petticoats.

Beau rocked in his lap, grinding against him. She tugged at his coat. Sandison frowned. His hands gripped her hard, holding her still. "You're my playground, brat. Not the other way round. Not just yet anyway."

"And why is that?" Beau slid one hand down his side, fingers flittering over the button that held the fall of his breeches up. Sandison caught her wrist.

"I thought we covered that last night."

Beau leaned in to bite his earlobe, just as he had hers the night before. "Not to my satisfaction."

Sandison gave a weak laugh and kissed her again. "It was very much to your satisfaction as I remember it."

"But not to yours." Beau sat back enough to watch his reaction. His pupils widened, black pushing the blue to the edges. She couldn't tell if he was poised for flight or attack, but the silent tension spoke volumes.

"There's more than one kind of satisfaction." One of his hands began to work its way up her leg. "Bringing pleasure to your partner, giving rather than receiving, is a pleasure all its own."

His fingers skimmed over her thigh. Beau repressed

the wanton need to let him touch her. To let him have his way. He liked to win, but so did she.

"Show me how," Beau said, annoyance and frustration coloring her voice more than she would like. It made her sound weak.

"Not now, brat."

Beau pushed herself up, batting his hand away. "Why not? It's not fair that you get to touch me but I'm not allowed to touch you."

"Fair? St. Jude protect and defend us. You've got no idea what you're asking."

"I think I do."

Sandison shoved one hand through his hair, leaving his queue disordered and rumpled. His eyebrows dipped, pleading with her. Beau leaned forward to kiss one and then smoothed them both with her thumbs as she cupped his face.

"Show me."

"I'm a man, Beau, not a saint."

"And?"

"And? You are the most maddening woman alive. Do you know that?"

Beau nodded, trying not to smile. She was winning. She could see his defenses crumbling before her. The bleakness had left his eyes, replaced with dawning amusement.

"I hate to admit to being less than a gentleman, but the simple truth is that if I let you do as you're asking, I'm not entirely sure where it will end. But the most likely scenario is with me taking your maidenhead in this blasted coach."

"Think of it as a challenge. Or a bet. Men love a good

bet, don't they?" The smile that she'd been fighting won out. "I bet you, Gareth Sandison, the sum of one bawbee that no matter what I do, you can resist tupping me until after we reach Scotland."

Sandison's eyes widened. "Tupping? Where on earth did you learn that term?"

"Rude prints in the window of Ackerman's," Beau replied with perfect truth.

Sandison shook his head, the corners of his mouth giving way to a grin. "Did you ever stop to think I might want to lose that bet?"

"And let me lord that coin over you for the rest of your life? And I would, you know. I think not."

Gareth stared at Beau, fighting off the urge to roll her under him and lose the bet that instant. "You were born with the soul of a libertine."

Beau's smile turned into a full-fledged triumphant grin. Then she kissed him, lips and teeth and tongue all brought to bear, hands seemingly everywhere. She slid over until she was straddling him, and he gripped her hips and held her tight while he rocked against her.

She broke off the kiss. "I think that counts as touching me. Put your hands on the seat."

Gareth pressed himself against her one last time and did as she commanded. He's always known that she was a bit of a martinet. He'd just never known until this moment just how desirable that trait could be in a woman.

His fingers dug into the fabric of the seat. Beau, following his lead, settled her weight on him and rocked slowly. His cock swelled and her eyes widened.

"Well?" she said.

Gareth groaned. She was going to kill him. "Take off your gloves."

Beau caught the tips of each finger between her teeth and tugged. The glove slid off, and she spat it out. She did the same with the second one. By the time it landed beside its companion on the seat, Gareth thought that he might embarrass himself by coming then and there.

"Get on the floor."

She looked quizzically at him, one brow raised.

"I swear to God, Beau. If you're still straddling me when you open my breeches, I *will* fuck you. So get on the floor."

"You'd lose the bet," she reminded him, her tone egging him on to just that.

"And it would be worth it," Gareth said, letting go of the seat and shoving her off his lap. She landed in a disordered heap and glared up at him.

"That was uncalled for, Gareth."

"It was entirely called for, brat."

Beau's voluptuous mouth slid back into a smile, and she ran her hands up his thighs. She thumbed open the buttons that held the fall of his breeches and then loosed the waistband. A few more tugs and his shirt was pushed aside, freeing his cock.

She caught her breath sharply, thumbs pushing into the flesh of his upper thighs, the nails distinct even through the fabric of his breeches. She leaned in, close enough that he could feel her breath whisper across his engorged shaft.

"Spit in your hand," Gareth said. Beau looked slightly

disgusted but did as he directed. "Now wrap your hand around it."

Her palm was firm against his flesh. Her fingers drummed lightly, hesitantly, along the rigid length. Gareth grit his teeth and clung to sanity.

"Form a circle with your thumb and index finger. Pull up till you meet the head. Tighter." She did exactly as he said, and Gareth nearly came up off the seat. It felt as though every drop of blood in his body had drained to his groin. "Let your grip soften. Push back down. Again."

Gareth gripped the seat so hard that his fingers began to cramp. Beau passed her palm over the head of his cock, swiveled her entire hand around, and pushed down. Gareth shut his eyes and tried not to think about anything that didn't involve the immediate sensation of Beau's hand on his flesh.

How in the hell had she talked him into this?

He groaned, and her grip faltered. Gareth opened his eyes, met her gaze, and held it. He covered her hand with his own and led her through the motions, fingers entangled, impossible to tell which was touching him.

His breath rattled out of him as he came. He loosened his grip, but Beau gave his cock one last earth-shattering stroke. He caught her wrist, and she let go, falling back against the opposite seat. "You're still hard." Her gaze fastened onto his still swollen cock.

"Give the boy a moment to realize he's done for."

ᕦ CHAPTER 9 ᕦ

A dangerous swirl of horses and men flying in all directions greeted them at Neville's Cross. The busy yard had nearly a dozen coaches loading and off-loading passengers and baggage and swapping teams. Beau stepped out of the coach, only to flatten herself against it as the mail swept past, close enough that the wheel brushed her skirt.

"Damn it all," Beau said more loudly than she intended.

"I told you to stay in the coach." Gareth spun about and stepped over to brush ineffectively at the bits of mud—and worse—spattered across her petticoats like a foul sprigging.

"I need to use the privy."

Gareth glanced around the busy yard, eyes tracking the chaos. "Be quick about it and hurry back."

Beau clenched her teeth and wove her way through the throng that seemed to have filled the inn's courtyard to the bursting point. She stepped into the taproom to ask directions to the privy, and a harried-looking maid thrust a rough stoneware cup of tea into her hands.

Beau drank it without hesitation. Lord knew when Gareth would see fit to feed her next. He'd refused to stop to eat or sleep, paying extra for a new team to push on through the night. They'd changed teams again just before dawn, but all she'd got was a cup of ale and a stale muffin without so much as butter or jam.

She finished the tea, scalding her tongue in the process, and got directions to the inn's privies from a group of female passengers. Once the call of nature had been answered, Beau stepped out and hurried toward the back door of the busy inn. A harried woman with a child in tow passed her, scolding the child under her breath.

The door of the privy snapped shut behind them, and Beau was suddenly hauled off her feet. Her scream was cut off by a large, gloved hand covering her mouth. Beau wrenched her head to one side and bit down. The man cursed, wrapping his arm more securely about her waist.

Beau flailed, catching him a glancing blow with her elbow and a more solid one with her heel. His grip slackened, and she pulled loose. She threw a fleeting glance over her shoulder as she rushed inside. Nowlin. Not one of her brothers. Thank God.

Heart in her throat, Beau pushed through the crowd and into the busy yard. Sandison was impossible to miss, pale head shining above the rest. His brows drew sharply together as he spotted her. Beau fought the tears that she could feel building behind her eyes.

A groom ran past, leading a steaming bay, and she lost sight of Sandison for a moment. Beau forced herself to stand calmly. To wait. Sandison was right there. With a flick of its tail, the horse was gone, and Sandison was striding toward her.

He swept her across the yard, arm wrapped protectively about her. "I think one of your brothers has just arrived, so best hurry. No one's stepped out of the coach yet, but I swear that's Sampson on the box."

Beau's stomach turned over, and her hands went cold. "Mr. Nowlin as well. He tried to grab me."

"Here?" Sandison glanced hurriedly around. "Whatever happens, I promise you"—his voice dropped, the tone turning dark—"Mr. Nowlin will be dealt with." His grip tightened, the pressure welcome and reassuring. "Don't you dare vomit on my boots, brat. We'll brush through this. Thankfully the yard is still overrun. We should be able to slip away if we're quick about it."

Beau held her breath and ducked her head. Please let it not be Leo. Please let it not be Leo. The single thought burned through her like a prayer.

As Sandison thrust her into the coach, she heard her elder brother's voice, loud and brusque. "Get the team changed. I'm going inside to look for her."

Sandison stepped in, the door closed, and he knocked hard against the roof to signal the coachman to set off. "Glennalmond," he said. "I don't think he saw either of us."

"He wouldn't," Beau replied. "Glennalmond's looking for what he's found before: a trail of wreckage, woe, and blood, leading to a man who's rapidly coming to the realization that he's made a profound mistake."

· · ·

Lord Leonidas Vaughn stood rooted beside his horse, rage and betrayal crawling up this throat to choke him. Glennalmond had missed Beau entirely. Leo had very nearly done so himself. It hadn't been the woman in the ill-fitting gown who had caught his eye. It had been the tall, familiar figure of his closest friend.

Sandison. The man he'd left in charge of keeping an eye on Beau. A man he'd trusted without question. His sister's frightened face peered back over Sandison's shoulder as he shoved her into a somewhat battered coach. Leo swallowed hard. Nothing scared Beau. Whatever Sandison had done to make her look like that, Leo was going to make sure that he regretted it.

Leo caught the arm of an ostler and shoved the reins of his hack into the man's hands. "Saddle me a fresh horse. There's a crown in it for you if you're done by the time I get back."

With the man's "Yes, sir" ringing in his ears, Leo waded through the crowd and into the taproom. He found his brother, cup of ale in hand, surveying the room.

"No sign of her," Glennalmond said.

Leo let his breath out in a sigh and tried desperately to keep his temper in check. "That's because she just left."

Glennalmond swallowed wrong and spat ale onto the floor as he coughed. Leo thumped him on the back, plucked the glass from his hand, and finished the ale in one gulp.

"With Gareth Sandison," Leo added. Just saying the name brought a rush of renewed anger that flooded through him until even his fingertips throbbed with it.

"Sandison?" Glennalmond sounded as though he couldn't quite grasp what Leo had said. "But she and he—"

"Don't get on at all. I know. You should have seen her face. Stricken. Frightened. I've never seen Beau look like that. Not even when she stole grandfather's hunter and went on a cattle raid with Sean McDermid when she was ten."

Glennalmond's face turned beet red. "I'll kill him. Earl's son or not, I'll strangle him with my bare hands."

"Not if I beat you to it," Leo said.

~ CHAPTER 10 ~

Beau hugged herself, trying to rub away the prickle of gooseflesh that wouldn't abate. That had been close. Too close. On every front. If Nowlin had held on, she'd be Lord only knew where by now, and if Glennalmond had caught up to them already, Leo and her father couldn't be far behind.

"Can we go to ground somewhere?" she said, horrified by how pathetic and frightened she sounded. "Just disappear until they all give up looking?"

"I've been thinking the same thing," Sandison replied, his tone as grim as his expression. "You're not to leave my sight. Your Irish suitor will have to go through me if he's to lay so much as a finger on you ever again. As for your family, we could attempt to lose ourselves in Leeds. Put up in one of the smaller inns for a week or so. They couldn't possibly search them all."

"Or we could leave the main road," Beau said, twisting her petticoat in both hands. "We could turn off at Wakefield and go west. Or head east to Scarborough and follow the coastal road north." Anything. They could do anything and that would have to be better than following the prescribed path.

A look of disgust seemed to have settled permanently onto Sandison's brow. Beau's eyes burned, and she furiously blinked away the onset of tears. Was he starting to reconsider their plan? To regret it?

Beau bit her lip. "If you've changed your mind, you could leave me at the next posting inn. Glennalmond will find me, and no one need ever know..." She let the statement trail off.

His head snapped up, blue eyes piercing her. "Have you?"

Beau shook her head. No. She hadn't, but guilt rather than blood seemed to be pumping through her veins. She was selfishly ruining his friendship with her brother. Perhaps forever.

One side of Sandison's mouth curled into a smile. Beau's pulse steadied. She relaxed her hands, startled to find how tightly they'd been clenched. She knew that smile. It was the one he wore when teasing her, or torturing one of his friends with some prank.

Thank God.

"Then we'll turn at Wakefield and head west," he said, still smiling. "We can pick the road to Gretna back up at Manchester. Hopefully everyone else will continue north toward Newcastle Upon Tyne before cutting over."

Beau felt the tension drain out of her. Whatever happened, she trusted Sandison to keep her safe. Foolish as many would consider such conviction, it was true all the same. Though Leo would never forgive him, Sandison would do it for his sake as much as for hers.

"Abducting heiresses is a great deal of trouble," she said, poking Sandison in the shin with her toe.

"Being abducted by them seems every bit as much work to me," he replied with perfect seriousness, though this smile had grown into a full-fledged grin.

"I did *not* abduct you."

"Didn't you?" His dark brows rose in the center, mocking her.

Beau narrowed her eyes at him, knowing that he'd still see the smile pulling at the corners of her mouth. When you came right down to it, she had, hadn't she? And she'd do it again.

"I rescued you," he continued, "but here we are fleeing your brothers and running toward the border. One of us *must* have abducted the other. And since it most certainly wasn't I..."

"And it is my family after all which has the reputation for outrageousness?"

"It is, isn't it?" He sounded almost cheerful at the thought.

"As well you know, sir. Fine, I give in. *I* abducted *you*. What are you going to do about it?"

Sandison stretched out his legs and propped his booted feet up on the seat. "Sit quietly and pray for deliverance?"

Sandison leapt down from the coach, but before he could turn to assist Beau out, he was thrown back inside. Beau cracked her head against the far wall. Sandison's weight crushed her into the floor, her petticoats indecorously high about her knees.

Backlit by a rising moon, her brother Leo stood framed

in the small doorway. Beau froze, heart squeezed into a tiny, nonfunctional ball. Leo reached in, took hold of Sandison's coat, and hauled him out. Beau tumbled out after them, tripping on her skirts and landing in a crumpled pile.

She hadn't seen Leo this angry since the night he'd found her at a courtesan's masquerade at Vauxhall. "No, Leo!" She scrambled up and grabbed her brother's arm, clinging to it like a terrier with a rat when he tried to shake her off. "It isn't what you think."

Leo stared down at her, eyes blazing. Beau rapidly reassessed her opinion. She'd never seen him this angry. Never.

"Go inside, Beau."

Beau squeezed tighter onto his arm. "Leo, I swear to you—"

"Inside!" He peeled her fingers off his coat sleeve and shoved her toward the small inn. "Now, Beau!"

Beau took a step back and glared at him. He had to understand—had to be made to understand. Sandison was holding his jaw, waggling it back and forth, as though testing to see if it were still in one piece.

Leo glared back. "Glennalmond will be along in the carriage soon enough. Until then, wait inside. I've a parlor already hired for your use."

"Do as he says, Beau," Sandison said, the sound of his voice breaking the silent detente between Beau and her brother.

Without a word, Leo launched himself at his friend. Sandison blocked the first blow, but the second rocked his head back, and the third doubled him over. He wasn't going to fight back. Wasn't even going to try to defend himself.

Stupid man. Honor didn't demand that he allow Leo to beat him senseless. Or if it did, she wasn't about to stand by and watch.

Beau waded in and pulled her brother out by the skirts of his coat. Sandison pushed himself upright, wiping blood from his chin.

Leo spun toward her, yanked his coat from her grasp, and took one awful step toward her. Beau could feel her temper eating away at her self-control. She and he were very much alike when it came to that. Very much like their mother. But if she gave in and hit him, he might just be angry enough to hit her back.

"I said get inside." Leo's words were clipped, enunciated with awful precision. "If you choose to make me drag you there, so be it. But one way or another, you'll do as I say, Boudicea."

"Fine," she spat out, bracing herself.

When she didn't move, she could see the realization dawn on her brother's face that she meant *fine, drag me*, not *fine, I'll do as you say.* One side of her mouth quirked up. She couldn't help it. It was fine if he dragged her, but she'd be damned if she gave up and let Leo order her about. And she wouldn't stand by and let him punish his friend for something that she'd done.

Leo closed the gap between them and caught her by the wrist. Two steps, her heels leaving furrows in the damp earth of the yard, and they came to a halt as Sandison placed himself between them and the inn.

Tousled, bloody, his coat ripped and muddy—he still looked like a hero. Her hero.

"Let go of her," Sandison said in a tone that seemed

designed to provoke her brother into retaliation, just as her smile had been. Leo's grip tightened. Beau bumped against him, jostling him, forcing him to look at her and not at his friend.

Leo glared down at her. Beau searched his face. No tenderness. No forgiveness. She put her free hand on his chest. She had to make him understand. "Please, Leo. Just listen to me for a moment. One moment—" The clatter of hooves and the jingle of harness cut her off.

Beau stood frozen in place as her family's second best coach rolled into the yard, Sampson on the box, her footman Boaz beside him. Glennalmond leapt out before it came to a full stop. Leo shook his head, his expression hardening, and tossed her to their elder brother. Glennalmond caught her and held her tight, one massive arm locked about her waist.

"Take her to Dyrham," Leo said, not even looking at her. "If you drive all night, you should get there by morning. I'll follow when I'm done here."

Gareth checked his teeth with his tongue and spat. The coppery tang of blood remained. At least his nose didn't appear to be broken. Not yet, anyway.

The Vaughn family's servants stared down from the box of the coach, expressions as grim and unrelenting as their masters'. Beau's personal footman was fingering the blunderbuss in his hands as though he'd love to be given permission to use it.

Glennalmond was gesticulating widely with his one free hand, pointing repeatedly at Gareth. Leo was arguing back, his voice low enough that Gareth couldn't quite make out the words. He didn't need to. They were clearly arguing over which one of them got to kill him. Did being the eldest trump being the best friend of the villain?

Gareth choked down an utterly inappropriate laugh. This was one argument that Leo wasn't going to lose, and that was for the best. He'd be tempted to defend himself against Glennalmond, and he deserved what was coming.

If Beau had been his sister, he'd have wanted to kill him too. Leo turned, said something to Beau inside the coach, and then Glennalmond climbed in and slammed the door shut behind him. Leo nodded at the coachman and the carriage slowly turned about, circling him, the armed footman glaring at him under his powdered wig the entire time.

The scene was unfolding with all the absurdity of a staged farce. The thwarted lovers. The avenging brothers. The ever-present witnessing chorus of servants. The entire benighted cast was present and playing their roles to the hilt. Except perhaps for Beau, who clearly had no intention of being the quaking *ingénue*. If his world weren't caving in around his ears, it would have been damn funny.

Leo stood, still as a monolith, and watched until his siblings disappeared around a bend in the road. Once they were gone, he turned slowly back to face Gareth.

The silence stretched. Excuses swarmed Gareth's head. He opened his mouth and then shut it with an audible snap of teeth. What was there to say? No excuse was good enough. Even the truth wouldn't wipe the look of betrayal from Leo's face. And the whole truth—a true confession of his motives—would make things far, far worse.

"If you were anyone else," Leo said, "I'd kill you where you stand, Beau's reputation be damned."

Gareth nodded, not quite sure where that left them. Leo's expression was bleak. There would be no forgiveness, whatever the outcome.

"I've no doubt you can explain how it's all Beau's fault," Leo said with a hint of bitterness. "I'm sure this escapade happened by her express design—when did anything not?—but no matter what you have to say, it will merely be an *excuse*. She's my sister, Sandison. My baby sister. And I left her in your care."

"And I failed you both, but I swear to you, I didn't abduct her."

Leo shut his eyes for a moment, shaking his head. "When the girl is willing, or God forbid, actually complicit, it's usually called an elopement. I'll grant you that much. No, don't say another word. You can save your explanations for my parents. I don't think I can stomach to hear them."

Sandison swallowed down the urge to defend himself, to defend Beau. "Are your parents in London?"

"I imagine they'll be joining Beau at Dyrham as soon as Glennalmond's note reaches them. I'd advise you to do the same. Two days, Sandison. In two days, you'd best be at Dyrham, or I'll hunt you down and shoot you on sight."

⮞ CHAPTER 11 ⮜

W hat do you mean *'her brothers have taken her home'*?"

Padrig Nowlin flinched as Granby shot to his feet and his chair toppled back onto the floor with a reverberating crack.

"Just that, sir. She was snatched away from me at gunpoint, and before I could get her back, her brothers arrived."

Granby paced across the room, one hand fiddling with the patch that covered his left eye. Lady Boudicea had done that to him. With her bare hands. Padrig forced himself to ignore the shiver that went down his spine. If she was capable of such an action, what might her brothers do?

"I came as quickly as I could, sir," Padrig said, fully aware that nothing he could have said or done was going to mollify his employer.

"Snatch a girl and bring her to me. How hard is that?" Granby glared out of his one eye, his mouth quirked into a dismissive moue of disgust. "Lock her in the carriage and

don't let her out until you reach Scotland. Nothing could
have been simpler."

Padrig choked down the obvious retort. If it was so
simple, how had she got away from Granby when he'd
tried it? "I know, sir."

"But your *knowing* didn't get the job done," Granby
said, deep frown lines marring both cheeks. "And you
very much wanted to get the job done, Nowlin. Maeve has
already discovered a taste for the life of a harlot."

Padrig's hands curled into fists.

"Well," Granby continued, smoothing his coat, "she
likes the clothes and the money and the frills and furbelows that accompany her newfound place in the world. In
a few weeks, who knows, she may have passed out of my
keeping entirely."

"Breaking our bargain," Padrig growled.

"And whose fault would that be? Not mine. I promised to return the little slut when you brought me what I
wanted. If that's become impossible, I'll do with her as I
like. And so will my friends. There's always Bridget and
little Sorcha to take her place when she moves on."

"I'll kill you first."

Granby laughed, and Padrig felt a quick flush of
shame. If he were any kind of man at all . . .

"If you were going to kill me," Granby said, "you'd
have done it when you woke up and discovered you'd lost
everything to me, or when you found Maeve had bought
you a six-month reprieve." He straightened his neckcloth,
not even bothering to pretend to be concerned for his
safety. "All you're going to do now is hie yourself back to
England and attempt to correct your mistake."

⚈ CHAPTER 12 ⚈

W hy won't anyone listen?" Beau paced across her brother's library, flexing her hands, nearly overcome with the urge to smash something. She veered toward the fireplace. The Meissen shepherdess on the mantel was perfect for her purposes.

The sound of her father clearing his throat brought her up short, and she spun about to face him. "Boudicea, sit down," he said, his tone brooking no disobedience.

Beau threw herself into the window seat, staring resolutely out at the lawn. Her elder brother had fled the moment that her parents had arrived. Her sister-in-law was playing least in sight, and her parents were driving her mad. Her mother was planning a wedding, while her father was planning a funeral. It had got so bad that the two of them had stopped speaking to each other. Beau couldn't remember her parents ever disagreeing about anything to this extent.

"I don't want to hear any more of your stories, my dear. As I've already told you, I'll make up my mind about what's to be done when I've spoken to Mr. Sandison." He drummed his fingers on the desk. Beau turned her head to find him studying her with a resigned look on his face.

"Perhaps your mother's right," he continued, "and a quick marriage under the aegis of your family would be best. But I want you to think—truly think—about whether you really want to tie yourself to such a man. He's a rake, my dear. And everyone knows it. He's been playing fast and loose with Lady Cook these past few months, and the pair of them have been none too sly about it. Think about that. He's been debauching another man's wife while seducing you. Is that really the kind of man you want to marry?"

Beau let her breath out in a long sigh. Though her father's facts were faulty, the sentiment wasn't. Sandison had been having an affair with Lady Cook, and before that it had been Mrs. Langley, and before her, some blond girl from the opera house—one could hardly have missed the way they flaunted themselves about Rotten Row. Beau might only have been on the marriage mart for a few years, but she could tally at least a score of Gareth's conquests, and no doubt she'd missed just as many.

He never stayed loyal to any of them very long. Like a stallion with his harem of mares. Would she be any different? Perhaps she was mad to believe so, but she did. Once given, Sandison's loyalty was steadfast.

"Would it be indelicate of me to say I don't care, Papa? Or rather, that I might care, but not so much that I'd rather spend the rest of my life in quiet obscurity, paying penance for my supposed sins."

"So you really want to marry him?"

"I do, *a'dhadaidh*," Beau said, using the Gaelic of her childhood rather than the English *father*.

"Well then, *mo cridhe*, we'd best hope your brother hasn't killed him."

Gareth reined Monty in and studied Dyrham in the moonlight. The house was quiet. Every window was dark. He was late. He'd ridden all night, but it was the morning of the third day. No getting around the fact that he'd failed to meet Leo's deadline by several hours. He only hoped Beau hadn't been worried that he'd fail her . . . and that she still wanted him to follow.

That niggling doubt had been torturing him the entire ride. What might have seemed a good idea under one set of circumstances might look very different after a couple days apart, or after her family had had a chance to formulate an alternative.

Monty's hooves fell heavily on the gravel of the drive, overly loud in the quiet of the predawn morning. As he rounded the house and entered the stable yard, a light appeared in a window, followed by a pale face. Gareth raised a hand in greeting, but whoever he'd seen was already gone.

Perhaps he was wrong about the likelihood of a few hours' grace and Leo had been waiting to pounce.

Gareth unsaddled Monty, twisted a handful of hay into a wisp, and rubbed the gelding down. The layer of sweat that Monty had built up on their race to Dyrham had already begun to dry, leaving the gelding's coat stiff and hard. Gareth was just about done when the unmistakable sound of footsteps caused him to pause.

"You're late."

Gareth smiled into the darkness at the sound of Beau's voice. The teasing tone of her opening salvo told him everything that he needed to know. Whatever her family's sentiments, she hadn't changed her mind, and that was all that mattered.

"If you're holding me to the letter of the law rather than the spirit, yes, I am." Gareth continued to work his way down Monty's side. Beau went to the gelding's head and rested her forehead against the animal's cheek. Monty nickered softly and tossed his head. Beau ran a soothing hand down the horse's neck.

Gareth watched her, transfixed. Her hair was a dark coil spilling over her shoulder, the plait standing out against the pale fabric of her nightrail. It was all he could do not to wrap it around his hand and drag her to him.

"Had to fetch Mountebank?" she asked.

Gareth nodded, took one last stroke down the gelding's rump, and let the wisp fall to the ground. "Couldn't have him eating his head off in Neville's Cross with no idea of when I might be free to retrieve him. Besides, if your brothers are going to murder me, I want Monty somewhere safe when I'm gone."

"And there's nowhere safer than your prospective killer's stable?"

Gareth could feel rather than see the mocking little smile that accompanied the quip. He smiled back at her, and her lush mouth expanded into a visible grin of white teeth.

"For Monty?" he replied. "No. For me? That remains to be seen."

Her smile faded, and her brows pinched worriedly. She let go of the gelding and reached for him, hands locking onto the lapel of his coat. Warmth leaked through the layers of their clothes where they touched, licking like lightning through every nerve in his body.

"You're mine," Beau said fiercely, giving him a little shake for emphasis. "And Leo shan't be allowed to take you away. That is, if you still want to be."

"I wouldn't be here if I didn't, brat. Your brother's threats to hunt me down and kill me aside, it's a big, wide world, and I'm not a pauper. I could have easily made a run for it."

Beau's answering smile was everything that he could have hoped for. It lit her up and made him almost dizzy. Gareth locked his hands behind the small of her back and kissed her. Just a quick meeting of the lips. The rush of blood through his veins was deafening. Beau wilted against him, into him, and Gareth pulled himself back from the precipice.

Leo really would kill him if he caught Gareth tupping his sister in the stables like a milkmaid. "Shall we put Monty up and go await your family's verdict?"

Beau drained the dregs of her second cup of tea and set the thin porcelain cup back onto its saucer. The clatter of the servants beginning their day below stairs made her jump.

Sandison raised one brow and drank from his own cup. The elegant cup looked ridiculously small in his hand. Like a child's toy, or something offered to Gulliver by the Lilliputians.

"What version of events have you told your family?" he asked, setting his cup aside.

Beau sank back into the embrace of her chair. "The truth. Or at least that's what I've told my parents. Leo didn't arrive until after dinner last night. He looked right through me, like I wasn't even there, and went straight upstairs."

Sandison nodded, not looking at all surprised. "And did it serve?"

"No," Beau replied baldly. "I found myself getting somewhat tangled when attempting to impart it."

"And now they don't believe a word of it."

Beau shook her head, wishing she were a more eloquent storyteller, or a far better liar. "I think Mamma wants to, and I think the duke will warp the story to suit his purposes, whatever they may turn out to be."

"So you think your father may want to kill me as well?"

"I think he hasn't made up his mind."

"Which is more than I could hope for, under the circumstances."

"Exactly," Beau said, glad that he understood.

"Don't look so surprised, brat. I may not be a wily MP or a noted wit, but I am the son of a dangerously conniving earl. A younger son to boot, which means I was born to serve and be of use. I was raised on intrigue and politics. They were just of the petty familial kind."

"So you know what to expect from my family?"

Sandison shook his head. "Not at all, but I know enough to expect them to make the most expedient use of me. And I know that I should be careful—very, very careful—of all of them. Especially Her Grace, who is, if you don't mind my saying so, by far the most intimidating member of your family."

"Mamma most certainly means for you to live," Beau said, pouring herself another cup of tea. "She's been planning the wedding since she arrived. I think she even forced Papa to apply for a license, so we can be married quietly from Dyrham."

"Oh, I'm sure Her Grace wants me alive at least long enough to plight my troth and give you my name," Sandison said, his tone wry. "I rather imagine my neck might not be worth much after that, however."

❧ CHAPTER 13 ❧

This is not the first time our daughter has had to be rescued from the jaws of scandal."

Beau could feel her cheeks burning with indignation as her father continued his litany of her failings. She and Sandison were both still as they'd been found: she in her bedclothes and he in his muddy boots and dusty traveling gear. Her father had launched his first salvo from the doorway and had continued, unabated, for nearly an hour now.

Pointing out that she'd never meant for any of it to happen would get her nowhere. Attempting to defend herself, or Sandison, was a losing proposition.

"But it's to be hoped this will be the end of such nonsense from her," the duke continued, twisting the knife as he went. "I'm prepared to force the issue if I have to, but I'm hoping neither of you will make that necessary. Her Grace wants a wedding, and my daughter has voiced her willingness. I assume, young man, that if you were anything less than willing you'd have fled rather than turn up here."

Beside her, Sandison nodded, seeming almost absurdly at his ease. Beau's hands ached with clenching them, her teeth felt as though they might crack each time she swallowed down an angry retort. Sandison was simply taking it all in, nodding occasionally. He was disgustingly calm, which made her burn all the more with the urge to defend them both.

"No force or coercion will be necessary, Your Grace. But then you knew that from the start. Any man, especially one such as myself, would be lucky to be given Lady Boudicea's hand."

Her father sucked in one cheek as he watched them, his eyes keenly searching for weakness. "Quite," he said dryly. "Though I'm not at all sure *given* was the word you were looking for, Beau." He rounded on her. "You'd best run and get dressed, then go and find your mother. You can be the one to tell her she may have her way and set the wheels of your marriage into motion. Sandison, you'd best stay. You and I still have many things to discuss."

Beau nodded, not trusting herself to speak, and strode from the room. Feeling petty, but unable to stop herself, she shut the door with enough force to communicate her annoyance but not so much as to cause her father to upbraid her for insolence.

She found her sister-in-law in the corridor outside her room and nearly burst into tears when Viola silently hugged her. After a moment, she shrugged out of the other woman's embrace.

"Come along," Viola said, the coaxing note in her voice nearly causing Beau to baulk. "I've got something for you."

Once inside her room, her sister-in-law pulled a small book out of her pocket and held it out. Beau took it from her and stared down at it dumbly. The simple cloth cover was worn and somewhat grimy. No title or author appeared anywhere on it. She flipped it open: *Aristotle's Masterpiece* stood alone on the third page.

"Philosophy?" Beau said, allowing the cover to fall shut. What the hell was she supposed to do with a book of philosophy?

Viola smiled slyly. "Of a sort, but not the fusty old kind that your father and I favor. This is of a more practical nature, especially for a new bride."

Her sister-in-law crossed the room, took a seat at the small vanity table, and began straightening Beau's myriad assortment of bottles, boxes, trays, and brushes. Beau cracked the book open again.

It is strange to see how things are slighted only because they are common, though in themselves worthy of the most serious consideration. This is the very case of the subject I am now treating of. What is more common than the begetting of children? And what is more wonderful than the plastic power of Nature, by which children are formed? For though there be radicated in the very nature of all creatures a propension which leads them to produce the image of themselves, yet how these images are produced after those propensions are satisfied, is only known to those who trace the secret meanders of Nature in her private chambers, those dark recesses of the womb where this embryo receives formation. The original of which proceeds from the Divine command—increase

and multiply. The natural inclination and propensity of
both sexes to each other, with the plastic power of Nature,
is only the energy of the first blessing, which to this day
upholds the species of mankind in the world.

Beau shut it again with snap. She glanced across the room to find her sister-in-law laughing silently.

"I know it's not the most traditional bridal present," Viola said, "but it's far more useful, I promise. Keep in mind that it was writ by a man, but in among all the scientific and anatomical pedantry, there's a great deal of useful information. Especially if, by chance, you might already be with child." The slight upswing of her voice almost made the last sentence a question. "Or if you might want to prevent yourself from becoming so long enough for it to become clear that you didn't *have* to marry."

Beau looked down at the unproposing little book again. "No worry on that front. Mr. Sandison was adamant that there be no possibility of a pregnancy."

Viola bit her lips, half-containing her smile. "You sound put out, Beau. Didn't you want him to be a gentleman?"

Beau wrinkled her nose and sat down on the bed. "No, I don't think I did. Anymore than you wanted my brother to be one."

"Our circumstances were somewhat different, my dear," Viola said repressively. "Besides which, a Cyprian and the daughter of a duke have entirely different definitions of what constitutes gentlemanly behavior."

"I would prefer he had to marry me, that he had no choice, and that it was at least partially his fault. As it is, I can't help but feel I've trapped him into something he'll regret. He's done nothing wrong, not to me anyway, and I've turned his entire life topsy-turvy and set his oldest friend at his throat."

Beau flung herself back onto the bed and stared up at the ruched canopy of the bed curtains. "I know none of you believe me, but Sandison wasn't the villain of this piece. He really was trying to save me."

"Well, he had an awfully strange way of going about it."

"That was all me. You know us both. Does this seem like the kind of thing he would do? I was ruined either way, and I knew it. I saw a chance to save myself, and I took it, and I truly am afraid he'll hate me for it in the end."

Her sister-in-law made a dismissive tut-tutting sound with her tongue. "You saw a chance to save yourself, or you saw a chance to acquire something you wanted?" Viola's question hung in the air like a bird of prey hovering over a hare.

Beau let her breath out in a long, resigned sigh but didn't reply. Viola always did seem to see things a little clearer than one might like.

"Because I've always wondered about you two," Viola said, appearing beside the bed, staring down at her with something a little too close to pity. "Your brother thinks I'm mad. You and Sandison may bicker and poke at one another and avoid each other most of the time, but you always seem to circle back to each other. You might take a moment to wonder if his motives are any purer than yours."

Beau pushed herself up on her elbows. Viola stared her down, her expression suddenly somber.

"And you should read that little book," Viola continued. "Most especially the sections pertaining to conception, the pleasures and duties of the marriage bed, and the prevention of moles—which serves just as well to prevent conception, as do several other techniques you might want to avail yourself of. If you have any questions, come and find me."

❦ CHAPTER 14 ❧

Gareth allowed the duke's homily to crash over him unchecked. If there was one thing that his father had trained him to do over the years, it was to take a dressing down in silence. Protesting, attempting to provide excuses, or anything else that might be interpreted as whining all served to make things worse.

Besides, he'd earned this. It was a small price to pay when the prize at the end was Lady Boudicea. And he'd much prefer the duke rail at him than at Beau. She hadn't done anything to deserve such treatment. She was the victim in all this.

"I've written to your father," the duke said, changing topics with his usual facile alacrity.

"And what have you told him?"

"The same plausible lie we'll tell everyone else: The two of you have had a long-standing affection. You applied for permission to address her and were denied. Being young and impetuous, you took my own example and eloped. No need to hide the smile, boy. I'm well aware

of the irony of my lecturing anyone on the inadvisability
of eloping with an heiress. So too will the world be."

"Yes, Your Grace."

The duke harrumphed, the side curls of his wig shaking. Gareth couldn't begin to guess if it was with rage or
repressed laughter. The duke was impossible to read.

"Needless to say," Beau's father went on, "her mother
and I have had a change of heart and are now prepared to
allow Beau to have her way." He looked sour as he said it,
as though swallowing a dose of some vile sickroom potion.

"Is there anything else, Your Grace?"

The duke's expression brightened somewhat. "Just the
mercenary details. Knowing your father as I do, I assume
you're in no position to support a wife."

Now they'd come to it, and Beau's father seemed to
understand the matter perfectly, and he clearly enjoyed
pointing it out. "Certainly not one such as Lady Boudicea.
I've nearly a thousand a year—"

"Which would barely pay for her fripperies."

"—and I live in bachelor quarters on Halfmoon
Street."

"So no house in town, no estate in the country, and no
expectation of such. Correct?"

Gareth gave a snort of laughter. "None whatsoever,
Your Grace." Not a chance. Everything was to be kept
whole and inviolate for the heir. Breaking up an estate or
frittering away a substantial sum on a younger son was
anathema to his father. Unconscionable.

The duke grumbled under his breath and rifled
through the stack of papers on his son's desk, before setting them aside, as though he'd just remembered that he

wasn't in his own home. "Well, we'll have to see what can be done—"

A preemptory knock presaged the sudden appearance of Gareth's father. The earl appeared to be more than a bit perturbed. He was spewing invective at Leo's butler and demanding to know just what his younger son's folly was going to cost him.

Gareth grit his teeth. It was so like his father to think only of himself, the inconvenience, and the cost.

The duke greeted him far more civilly than Gareth could have managed under the same set of circumstances. The duke's calm sangfroid stood out in sharp contrast to the earl's agitated demeanor.

Gareth nodded to his father, even as the earl continued to ignore his presence. Gareth struggled to keep his expression impassive as the two noblemen squared off like cocks in the ring.

"Is your countess with you?" the duke asked, rounding the desk and extending a hand. "No? A pity. But I'm sure she can be fetched for the wedding."

Gareth watched his father's face flush from red to purple. "We shall see, Your Grace," the earl ground out. "My wife's very delicate, and all this bother our younger son has caused has left her quite out of twig."

"Yes, very troublesome, our children," the duke replied. "But I'm sure something can be contrived. We wouldn't want the world to get the wrong idea, would we?"

Gareth's amusement at his father's discomfiture fled. They were both going to be raked over the coals before the duke was done with them. And the old devil looked as though he meant to enjoy it.

The earl glared at Gareth before swinging his attention back to Lochmaben. The two were political enemies of the first order, the joining of their two houses couldn't be particularly desirable to either of them, especially when neither party to the marriage brought their prospective in-laws anything they'd value. Both families had money. All that was left was power.

"Not to disparage your daughter, Lochmaben, but it seems damn outrageous to me that she should throw herself away on a younger son. She's an heiress, I presume? Everything locked in by settlement?"

Gareth winced inwardly as his father cut to the chase in the crudest way possible. Trust the earl to slight them all in a few short sentences. He'd all but called Beau fast and his son a worthless fortune hunter. The edge of annoyance that said the fortune wouldn't be joining the Sandison family coffers was starkly evident.

"I think you forget, my lord—as many have before you—that my wife and I also eloped. Therefore, there are no settlements guaranteeing anything to any of our children. However, *Lady Boudicea*"—the duke stressed her name and title—"has a dowry of fifty thousand pounds, invested in the three-percents. I shan't be so petty as to renege on that simply because she's behaved poorly."

His father's expression flew from startled to disgusted to conniving in an instant. It would have been easy to miss, but judging by the sudden tick in the duke's jaw, he'd seen it clearly enough.

"You hear that boy?" the earl said, not bothering to look at Gareth. "A fortune stripped away from the main estate. Some might call it folly, especially under circumstances such as these."

"Circumstances that her family is taking pains to hide," Gareth said in a burst of annoyance. What would his father have done if he had daughters of his own? Would his mercenary sensibilities have been more offended by having to provide a proper dowry, or by welcoming Cits and mushrooms into the family who would be pleased enough with the noble connection?

"Just so," Lochmaben said, his eyes flinty and trained on the earl. "Everything shall be done properly, if quietly. All speculation and scandal will wither away once they're married, as it has with so many other couples. Though it would hurt our cause if the groom's family were to be seen as opposing the match."

The earl smiled, a lazy, self-satisfied expression that Gareth knew only too well. "I wouldn't say I oppose the match, Your Grace, but I'm not sure I can condone their behavior by contributing to their support."

And there it was. A ready excuse to avoid doing what the world would expect. They'd made their bed in haste and must now lie in it. That's what he would say, and many would agree.

The duke raised his brows, his mouth pressed into a hard, thin line. Gareth watched the two older men glare at one another. Tension crackled between them. If they'd been younger, they'd have come to blows already.

"I'll throw my support behind the canal project you keep proposing," the duke said, "if you provide your son with an estate of at least five thousand a year."

Gareth's jaw sagged open. He snapped it shut. His

father had been trying to get that canal project pushed through for several years. Cheap, easy access to market for the coal on his Newcastle estates would make them far more profitable.

"I have a small estate in Kent, gets its value from hops. The market's volatile. Some years it's five or even six thousand. Some years it's nearer to two."

"With an additional annuity of a thousand then," the duke countered.

"Payable only in years when the estate's income drops below three."

"Done," said the duke, slapping his hand down on the desk as though ending an auction. "We'll have the settlements drawn up by tomorrow, and the wedding can take place just as soon as my eldest returns with the license."

❧ CHAPTER 15 ❧

Beau skulked at the top of the stairs until she heard the library door open. Being excluded from something that so clearly concerned her merely because of her sex was vexing in the extreme. Not even her sister-in-law's intriguing little book had been able to fully distract her, though she now knew words for body parts that she barely even dared to think about.

Sandison's distinct footsteps followed the shutting of the door, and she hurried down the stairs. "Well? What happened?"

Sandison's head snapped up. He looked somewhat dazed. "I rather feel like a horse at Tattersall's at the moment."

"Sold you off, have they?"

"Sold *us* off, you mean. Your father bargains like a gypsy horse trader. I feel as though I should count my fingers and toes."

Beau grinned. "I've never seen anyone get the better of the duke."

"My father certainly thinks he did."

"And that's a good thing, right?" Beau gave Sandison's arm a squeeze, the hard muscles beneath the fine wool of his coat flexed beneath her fingers. The knowledge that he was hers sang through her blood, pushing away the ever-present bubble of guilt. "Come out to the folly with me," she whispered, tugging him toward the door.

"Do you think that wise?" Sandison's pace slowed, and Beau pulled him along, hands encircling his wrist. She fumbled with the door and led him outside.

"We're well past *wise*, don't you think? Besides, I have something to show you."

"I don't trust that smile of yours, brat."

Beau's smile grew until her cheeks almost hurt. "Walk me to the folly and tell me what our illustrious fathers have cobbled together."

Sandison's thumb circled inside her palm as they wove through the garden. All around them the gardeners were busy mulching the beds and trimming the plants back for the approaching winter.

"More than I would ever have expected," he said. "Fifty thousand pounds from your father and a small estate somewhere in Kent from mine." A subtle smile curled up one corner of his mouth. "It must have killed my father to make such a concession."

"Really?"

"Oh, yes, brat. You've yet to be introduced to the feudal ways of the Earls of Roxwell. The earl himself comes first, his son and heir second, and everyone else exists only to serve them. Breaking off a profitable estate for a younger son goes quite strongly against the grain."

"Younger sons are not allowed to marry?"

"They're certainly not encouraged to do so. Tradition-
ally, the earl uses a pocket borough to put them into the
House of Commons."

"Where the son is expected to support whatever views
his father and brother dictate."

"Precisely. If the eldest seems unlikely to produce an
heir, then—and only then—would any of the younger
sons be encouraged to marry. The fifth earl was just such
a younger son, and he didn't marry until his late fifties.
I've no doubt that I'll spend the rest of my life being
reminded that everything I have is essentially food stolen
from the mouths of my brother's children."

"If any of your family ever dares to express such sentiments in my presence, he'll rue the day," Beau said, anger
flushing though her.

"Going to protect me, are you?" Sandison said with a
chuckle.

"If need be, yes. Lord knows you deserve it, having
already done the same for me."

A slightly pained expression flashed across his face.
No more than a pinch about the eyes and a tightening of
the lips. Gone almost before Beau could recognize it.

It could mean anything. Could be interpreted in multiple ways. She really didn't know him well enough to
be sure that she could plumb the depths of his soul, but
that brief hint of unhappiness made it suddenly hard to
breathe.

Beau pulled Sandison to a stop at the base of the tower
folly. He leaned back against the stone wall, stooping so
they were eye to eye. His hands settled about her waist,

fingers overlapped in the back, thumbs only scant inches apart.

She felt almost delicate. It was an alarmingly feminine sensation. Sandison tugged her closer, hands holding her against him, arms encircling her.

Not willing to wait for him to overcome whatever gentlemanly sensibilities might constrain him, Beau tugged him to her and kissed him.

Sandison kissed her back, his mouth hot and urgent as it covered hers. His hands moved lazily down to her hips, fingers kneading her flesh through the layers of petticoats.

"Come upstairs," Beau said, catching one of those roving hands and pulling him after her. "The view from grandmother's folly is enchanting."

"It certainly is," Sandison said as he followed her up the winding stairs.

Beau grinned over her shoulder, allowing the compliment to burn through her blood. Her heart was hammering, and not with exertion from the climb. Words and ideas from her little book swirled inside her head.

The stairs ended at an artfully toppled battlement, with a sweeping view of a meadow and stream and the wooded section of Leo's estate in the distance. Beau watched the sheep in the meadow, pretending that she hadn't led Sandison up there with an ulterior motive thoroughly unbecoming of a daughter of the *ton*.

Sandison stood just behind her, his body touching hers from shoulder to hip, feet braced on either side of hers. His mouth traced a line down her neck from her ear to the edge of her bodice. Beau sagged back against him, bracing herself with her hands on his thighs.

"My brother might come looking for us."

Sandison chuckled, one hand slowly drawing up her petticoats, fingers inching it up bit by bit. "Leo is currently enjoying his own interview with your father. The duke sent a footman to fetch him when he was done eviscerating me."

The tips of his fingers found the bare flesh of her thigh, and Beau fought to stay upright as her knees turned watery. She put more of her weight onto her hands, letting him hold her up. The muscles in his thighs hardened under her grip.

"Besides," he said, lips at her ear, "isn't this why you brought me up here, little libertine?"

Beau's *yes* caught in her throat as Sandison's hand slipped between her thighs, the tip of his finger circling the peak hidden just inside. Clitoris. Seat of passion. Throne of desire. All the terms in her new book fluttered past the back of her eyelids.

Sandison's fingers pressed harder, stroking, grinding, and then he stopped. "What did you say?" His tone was almost shocked.

Beau's breath shuddered out of her. "Nothing. I didn't—"

"You most certainly did, brat." His fingers swirled, making her gasp and grind back against him. "Clitoris? Seat of passion? Just what has your sister-in-law been telling you?"

"Gave me a book." Beau's breath hitched as he continued his rhythmic assault. "And I've read Rochester—just didn't know what the words meant."

"No? Poor little frustrated libertine. Those poems must have made no sense at all."

Beau's knees gave out as her climax took her. Sandison held her up, one arm securely about her waist, his wicked hand still teasing her slick, throbbing flesh.

After a moment, she drew a shuddering breath and locked her hand about his wrist, forcing him to stop. "They make more sense now."

"I'll just bet they do," Sandison said with a self-satisfied chuckle. "Now show me this book of yours."

Gareth flipped through the small book that Beau pulled from her pocket after she shook out her skirts and caught her breath. Leo's wife was full of surprises. As was his wife-to-be. *Throne of desire*, indeed.

"*These amorous engagements should not be often repeated*," he read aloud, "*And it may not be amiss to remind the bridegroom that the fair lasts all the year, and that he should be careful not to spend his stock lavishly, as women in general are better pleased in having a thing once well done than often ill done*. What say you, little libertine?"

Beau gave him a wicked, coquettish smile, which did nothing to help subdue his clamoring cock. "I'd hazard that most women would be better pleased to have the thing done both well *and* often," she said with a bit of a purr.

Gareth smiled back at her and handed back the book. Beau thrust it into her pocket with a conspiratorial grin. "Viola said something when she gave me the book."

Gareth raised his brows. Lord only knew what Beau's former courtesan sister-in-law was capable of.

"She-she-she said I might not want to fall pregnant too

soon. Otherwise it might look like you had to marry me. Or that I had to marry someone, at any rate."

"Lady Leonidas is correct. I told you much the same thing that first night."

"But she also said there were ways to prevent conception."

"Well," Gareth said, feeling something of a fool for trying to explain such a thing, "there are methods to make conception far less likely, but the only sure way is for us to put off consummating the marriage."

"No." Beau shook her head, sending her dark curls bouncing. "To be a virginal bride for months on end? No."

Gareth laughed and pulled her to him, wrapping his arms about her. "I'm forced to agree with you, brat. Ours may be a marriage of convenience, but there's nothing convenient about celibacy."

"Is that what it is?" She looked surprised and slightly crushed. "A marriage of convenience? I-I-I guess I hadn't quite thought it through. Not in that way."

Gareth felt a flicker of guilt. He shouldn't have said that. A girl—even such a one as Beau—didn't want to be told such a thing. "It's the common parlance, yes. But like celibacy, there's nothing convenient about you either."

Doubt and hurt scuttled through her eyes. She swallowed hard. Gareth took a deep breath. He was making it worse with every word. "That came out wrong, brat."

"Stop calling me that," Beau snapped. "I'm not twelve anymore."

∼ CHAPTER 16 ∼

A marriage of convenience. Beau couldn't get the phrase out of her head. It swirled inside her brain, twisting around her sister-in-law's observations about her and Gareth, and always circling back to one another.

The curate droned on, and Beau parroted back the marriage vows, hardly even aware that she was doing so. Gareth stood beside her, gaze holding hers, a hint of a smile on his face. For once in his life, his brows didn't seem to be begging for her to sooth away some hurt.

Viola was right. The realization struck her an almost physical blow. What they'd been doing was their own special brand of flirtation. And it certainly wasn't one-sided. He'd been flirting with her too. For years now.

Gareth slipped a simple posey ring onto her finger, and the curate pronounced them man and wife. *Man and wife.* The words echoed through her mind as clearly as the clarion call of the church bells that followed them back down the aisle and outside into the crisp autumn air.

Beau took a deep breath as their families joined them.

Only their female relatives looked truly happy. Their mothers were wreathed in smiles. Viola was keeping a firm hold on Leo's arm, but she looked pleased. Their elder brothers hadn't even bothered to bring their wives, a point that clearly annoyed the duke.

"Shall we return to Dyrham for the breakfast?" Leo said, not even bothering to try and sound as though he were happy to be hosting it.

"We shall," his wife replied, pulling him away toward the carriages before he could make a scene. Viola threw Beau an apologetic look over her shoulder, and Beau forced herself to smile back.

Leo hadn't softened in the slightest. He was still too furious to speak to either of them. Glennalmond had moralized over her that morning, saying he wished her happy in her marriage in a tone that clearly implied that he believed she would regret it.

Beau raised her chin and smiled. She was going to be happy. She was already happy. And so would Gareth be, as soon as he realized what she already had: that he loved her, just as she loved him. It might be an unconventional, uncomfortable, disarming sort of love, but it was there all the same.

There was no need for her brothers to be angry, for her father to worry, or for Viola to pity her. She was going to be happy.

Both families fled the scene as soon as the breakfast was over. Beau's family was returning to London, Gareth's to their estates in the north. Gareth's mother hugged her like she genuinely meant it before she was hustled out the door by the earl. Her own family made a bit more of a fuss, her parents promising to send her things to her new home, her brothers both hugging her fiercely, and Viola whispering, "I've left something for you beside the bed. Sandison will know what to do with it."

Gareth watched them all go with a disturbingly blank expression. Beau squeezed his hand, and he came back from wherever his mind had wandered off to. He laughed and squeezed her hand back.

"I rather imagine that's the last we'll be seeing of any of them for quite a while. The estate my father gave us is as far away from either family seat as possible, without actually being in France or Ireland."

"Have you ever seen it?" she asked as he led her back to her brother's now-vacant library.

Gareth shook his head. "I never knew it existed."

"So it could be anything? A rundown farmhouse. A glorified ruin."

"All I know is it's in Kent, produces roughly five thousand pounds a year, and that my father swore it was habitable. I pressed him on that point before the duke and I signed the settlement. He assured me it was furnished, and that the couple installed to see to its care would serve handily as butler and housekeeper should we see fit to keep them on."

"It seems odd, having an estate so far from the others that is not a hunting box or London retreat." Beau wandered across the room, trailing her shawl after her. She was nervous now that they were alone. No, not nervous exactly. She was simply at a loss about what to do next.

"Apparently," Gareth said from where he knelt, stoking the fire, "he won it at faro in his youth, and being as avaricious as a dragon, held on to it until now. I expect we'll find it somewhat old-fashioned."

Beau circled back and claimed one of the chairs near the fireplace. "The Lochmaben family seat is more castle than house. It can hardly be more old-fashioned than that. I swear to you, the house still has garderobes, though we don't use them, thank heavens."

Gareth set the poker aside and stood warming his hands. "The earl said it was not dissimilar to Dyrham."

"Bah," Beau said, exasperation winning out over her nerves. "What the devil are we supposed to *do* all day alone in Leo's house?" Especially when all she could think about was what would happen tonight. Her stomach was full of butterflies, and her hands were tingling with anticipation and the slight hint of worry.

"We could make use of your brother's exceptional bathhouse?" Gareth said with a wicked waggle of his brows.

"Or we could simply scandalize the servants and retreat to our room," Beau suggested, rushing her fence.

Gareth's smile grew. "Yes, we most certainly could. Or…" He drew the word out. "I could lock the door and seduce you here."

Beau's heartbeat lodged between her thighs, a heavy, throbbing ache. She shook her head. "The gardeners might see."

Gareth shrugged, and Beau shook her head a tad more vigorously, a blush burning its way up her chest and flooding over her cheeks. "They'd tell Leo."

"The servants might just as well tell him I dragged you upstairs and debauched you as soon as he was out the door."

Beau smiled and shook her head one more time. "Is debauchery really possible with one's spouse?"

"It is if you do it right, little libertine," Gareth said with a grin.

~ CHAPTER 17 ~

The best guestroom was flooded with late-afternoon sunlight. Beau stood beside the dressing table, carefully removing the pins that held her gown shut. The bodice fluttered open, revealing the pink silk of her stays.

Gareth stood rooted to the floor. She was his. Irrevocably. Body and soul. There was something humbling—and slightly terrifying—about it.

She smiled, looking a bit lost. "I can't get out of this gown without assistance," she finally said.

Of course she couldn't. How many women had he undressed over the years? Too many to remember, and here he stood watching her as though she were a pantomime.

"A man would rather unwrap his own present anyway," he said, tugging the sleeves down and easing the bodice off her shoulders. Beau loosed the tapes that held up her petticoats and the gown fell to the floor with a whisper of silk. She stepped out of the sea of fabric and Gareth reached for the lace of her stays. He kissed the nape of her neck before tugging the knot loose.

"Do you know how much I wanted to do that in the woods?" He swiftly unlaced her, letting her stays join her gown on the floor. He slid his hands over her stomach and brought them up to cup her breasts, weighing them in his hands. "How much I wanted to touch you."

Beau turned her head so that their eyes met. Her nipples ruched beneath his palms, nothing but a gossamer wisp of a shift covering them. With a heady moan, she twisted about in his arms, slid her own arms about his neck, and dragged him down for a kiss.

Gareth scooped her up, tossed her onto the bed, and shrugged out of his coat. Beau propped herself up on one elbow and watched him. No maidenly modesty. No blush. No averted gaze.

His cock was already hard, the confinement of his breeches almost unbearable. Gareth yanked off his shirt and kicked off his shoes.

Beau was smiling now. She sat up and pulled her shift over her head, tossing it to the floor. There were clear marks of mishandling on the pale skin of her arms.

"You've got bruises."

"So do you," she pointed out, bending to unbuckle her shoe. She tossed both shoes after her shift and reached to unhook her garter.

"Don't," Gareth said, nearly choking. "Leave them."

Beau looked at him quizzically, but did as he said. "Part of unwrapping your present?"

"Oh, God yes."

The beam of light washing across the bed sparked off a jar on the bedside table. Gareth smiled. A handful of small sponges floating in amber liquid. Beau followed his gaze. "Viola said she'd left us something, and that you'd know what to do with it."

"That I do, sweetheart," Gareth replied, shucking off his breeches and drawers and putting one knee on the bed. Beau knelt in the center, still watching.

She grinned. "*Husband rampant, pizzled.*"

Gareth shook his head. "You are the oddest girl. *Bride ravissant.*" And she was, ready to spring—eager and inquisitive.

She reached for him, hand sliding over his shoulders. "Not *couchant*?"

"No." Gareth tipped her under him. "*Passant.*"

He kissed her hard, cupped her breast, and rolled the already peaked nipple between his fingers. Beau threw her head back, wrapped one leg around his hip, and slid a hand between them, fingers brushing lightly over his engorged cock.

Gareth pulled her hand away, and she made a small sound of protest. "You'll have me going off like a green boy. And you don't want that, I promise you."

She smiled wickedly and rocked her hips against his. Gareth ignored her teasing and slid his mouth down her neck, over her chest, and captured a nipple between his teeth.

Beau's hand locked in his hair, tightening slowly, a sweet, exquisite pain. Gareth bit a little harder, sucking as he did so. She gasped and loosened her grip. Gareth let go as well, stretching to reach the jar by the side of the bed. The lid hit the floor with a hollow clatter, and the scent of brandy rose up. He plucked out a sponge.

Beau raised one brow, eyeing him quizzically. Gareth trailed the hand with the sponge down across her stomach, leaving a trail of brandy across her pale skin. He followed the trail with his mouth, down her belly, over her mons, to the already rigid peak at the top of her slick folds.

The warmth of the brandy mingled with the sweet, earthy taste that was simply Beau. She bucked, gasping out an incoherent phrase. Gareth flicked his tongue over her and slid the sponge inside, pushing it up against the mouth of her womb with his finger.

He carefully worked a second finger inside, holding her down, his free hand splayed across her torso. He'd never deflowered a virgin, but logic told him the odds of her finding any pleasure her first time were low. Most of the women he'd bedded over the years had nothing pleasant to say about their first time, or their husband's clumsy initial efforts.

Better to bring her to her climax first.

Beau shut her eyes and gasped for air, concentrating on the deep throb of her release. It pulsed through her, spreading outward from her womb all the way to her fingertips and toes.

Gareth withdrew his hand, and her mumbled protest turned into a gasp of surprise as he entered her with one, swift thrust. She gripped his hips with her thighs and held tight. Gareth rested motionless above her.

Having his—her mind stumbled over the words, *cock, penis, yard*—inside her was entirely different from his fingers. And not just because it was larger. The burn of invasion faded, leaving behind a sensation of satiety, of rightness.

Gareth bent down to kiss her, lips soft, tongue teasing hers until she responded in kind. He flexed his back, pressing into her, easing out, the slight motion a sharp, sweet agony against her already enflamed flesh.

"Gareth, I-I—" She what? She wasn't entirely sure what she meant to say, just that it needed to be said.

"Did I hurt you?" The question was soft, his breath warm across the skin just below her ear.

"Yes. No." Beau took a shuddering breath. "No," she repeated with more authority.

"Good." He kissed her again, hands sliding along her thighs until they caught in the crook of her knees. He used his weight to gently push them farther apart, increasing the ratio of pull and thrust as he did so.

"Don't think, little libertine." His teeth scraped along her jaw, his tongue traced over the pulse point in her neck. "Thinking's bad for this."

Beau pushed her questions, her thoughts, aside and concentrated on the raw sensation of their joining—the powerful thrust of Gareth's body into hers, the liquid reception of her own body, the tortuous grind where his pelvis rocked against her swollen, inflamed flesh.

Gareth let go of her legs, and she pulled her knees up, hugging his rib cage with them. He propped himself up on his elbows, weight crushing her into the bed, every thrust pushing her closer to the bright edge that she'd already come to recognize as the cusp of climax. She tumbled over with a cry that Gareth quickly stifled, his mouth covering hers. He broke off the kiss to seek his own release with unrestrained abandon.

Beau clung to him, giddy, restless, enraptured. He growled, grasped, and pulsed hotly within her, before collapsing onto her chest, hair spread over her in a silver wave.

❧ CHAPTER 18 ❧

Beau stretched and ran a possessive eye over her husband. He might call this a marriage of convenience but she was afraid that she was half in love with him already. Always had been. Just one small push from tumbling all the way...It would be so easy.

It might even be easy to convince herself that he felt the same way. He was certainly prodigiously interested in bedding her. He rolled over and reached for her sleepily. Beau plucked a sponge out of the jar, slipped it inside her, and slid her leg over his hip to straddle him.

His cock was trapped between them, hard, straining, ready. Beau rocked her hips slowly, waiting for Gareth to open his eyes. He was smiling, hands on her thighs, but she wasn't entirely sure that he was awake.

She leaned forward, breasts brushing across his chest, nipples pebbling. She ran her lips along his jaw, gripped his shaft, and guided him into her. Gareth's eyes flew open, shock quickly replaced by gratification.

Their hips met, and Beau moaned as he flexed upward, filling her. "Finally awake?" she said.

He groaned in response, hands moving up to grip her hips. Beau splayed her hands across his chest for balance and began to move, barely. Really, it was enough to take in the sensation of having him inside her, the slight friction of her swollen clitoris against his pubic bone. There was something delightful about going from nearly full to almost too full and back again, over and over and over as her body adjusted and took him deeper with every thrust.

"Have a little mercy," Gareth said.

Beau ignored him, not altering the pace. Her hands and feet were tingling. Her pulse had spread outward to encompass her womb. She spread her thighs wider, reaching for the last infinitesimal inch of him.

Her climax was soft, just like their joining. Gareth ground himself against her as her body pulsed around his. His hands gripped her, forcing a new, harder pace. Beau bit the heel of her hand as she came a second time, and Gareth spilled himself into her with his own release.

"Good morning, wife."

His hands were on her bottom, holding her firmly in place. His lips found her nipple, and he flicked his tongue over it. Beau arched in response, the sensitive, swollen flesh between her thighs throbbing almost painfully with every tiny motion.

"We leave for London in a few hours," he said, one hand trailing up her body to cover her other breast. He found her nipple again and sucked hard, drawing her breast into his mouth until she could feel the slight abrasion of teeth.

"Yes." Her answer came out in a breathy gasp, the one word all that she could manage.

"Shall we see how many times I can make you come before then?"

"Yes."

His thumb slicked over the tight peak just above where their bodies joined. "How about on the road? Shall we carry the game over to the trip itself?"

Beau moaned, unable to speak.

"Was that a yes?" Gareth lifted her, pushing her up until only the head of his cock was still inside her, holding his place, driving her mad.

"Yes."

He pulled her back down, hard, bodies colliding with enough force to make her quake with the need to do it again. She pushed off the bed, slammed back down. Gareth bit her breast hard enough to almost distract her, but the shiver of almost-pain merely tipped her ever closer to her release.

Gareth let go of her breast and wrapped his arms around her, hands curled up over her shoulders. She pushed up, and he yanked her back down. She came sobbing his name.

"Again?" he said, withdrawing from her, hand replacing his cock, fingers delving inside her.

"Can't."

He tumbled her onto her back. "Of course you can."

"Can't. Impossible."

"One more time, love." He pushed in another finger,

hand working rhythmically between her legs. "Once more."

"Bastard," Beau said, having trouble getting her tongue around the word. Gareth grinned and kissed her, his mouth covering hers as her breathing hitched and her climax roared through her.

✒ CHAPTER 19 ✒

Granby finished Nowlin's letter, dropped the sheet of foolscap into the fire, and swept everything on the mantle onto the floor with one clean motion. Porcelain shattered into dust. The expensive, ormolu clock broke apart on the fender. The branch of candles splattered wax all over the hearth.

"Bitch!" Granby let the single word carry him along. Lady Boudicea was married. Married to the son of an earl, no less. His plans were in ruins.

At the sound of a strangled sob, Granby spun around. Nowlin's stupid sister leapt off the settee and fled the room in a welter of tears. Granby slammed the door behind her. The girl had gone from tiresome to annoying. It wasn't even any fun to bed her. And if he had to look at her whey-faced countenance for weeks to come...Well, he wasn't sure that he could.

Married. His hand shook. She'd led him to believe she'd loved him once. He touched the patch that covered his eye. She'd flirted and fawned and all but offered herself to him, only to change her mind when he'd done what any man would do with such an offer on the table.

The clipping of the announcement began to char atop the coals and then went up in a flash. Granby watched it burn, taking his plans for revenge with it.

He toed the coals, and the blackened paper broke apart, disappearing completely. This couldn't stand. She couldn't be allowed to buy her way out of ruin so easily. She owed him—an eye for an eye—and he had every intention of collecting that debt, one way or another.

~ CHAPTER 20 ~

Beau had expected to enjoy their time in London. There might be scandal attached to them, but a marriage had a way of cooling even the hottest scandal broth. What she hadn't counted on was Leo's continued pig-headedness.

While she and Gareth had been cavorting at Dyrham, her brother had been blackening Gareth's name with their mutual friends. And he'd done a thorough job of it.

Gareth came home to her family's house in Pall Mall with a black cloud hanging over him the very first afternoon. Beau let the book of furniture patterns that she'd been poring over drop to her lap.

"Gareth?"

He nodded and went to pour himself a drink. He tossed it back and then refilled the glass.

"That good a day?" she said, guilt flooding through her. He looked miserable, and that was her fault. She'd done this to him.

"I'm no longer welcome at The Red Lion." He gave a

derisive laugh and sat down in the window seat, staring out at the square. Weak afternoon sunlight played over his face, the edge of his high cheekbones cutting sharply down to the frown that curled the corner of his mouth. "I was shown the door in no uncertain terms."

Beau caught her lip between her teeth, a bubble of sorrow blooming behind her sternum. Her brother and his friends were quiet about the club that met at the coffee shop they all frequented, but it was impossible not to know about it if you paid attention. And it was equally impossible not to be aware of just how much they all valued it.

"Leo?" she said, knowing it must have been.

Gareth nodded and took a drink, light refracting through the glass like a prism. Beau tossed the book aside and stood, stalking across the room. Leo was still in town, and this estrangement had gone far enough.

"Don't," Gareth called after her, clearly aware of what she was about to do. "Your brother has a right to be angry."

"No, he doesn't," she said through gritted teeth. "He deserves to be flogged. And I think today might be the day I track him down and make the attempt. At least he'll be able to vent his annoyance on the proper target."

"He has every right, brat. I don't think you quite grasp the full import of my transgression."

Beau rolled her eyes. "You didn't do anything I didn't force you into."

"*Force* is an awfully strong word," he said, twirling his now-empty glass between his fingers. Beau's breath rushed out of her with a shudder. She could almost feel his hands roaming over her... worse, she wanted to, now. He called her a libertine, and it was true. She was wanton as a cat in heat.

She plucked the glass from his grasp and refilled it. Once for herself, and again for him. The fiery burn of the brandy merged with the steady smolder of desire that never seemed to abate.

"Is *tempted* a better word?" She handed the glass back to him, and he gave her a hint of a lopsided smile. Even so, she could feel it like a caress. She wanted to crawl into his lap, to demonstrate in the most primal way that he'd made the right decision.

"It's a damn accurate one," he said.

"Bah." Beau made a rude, dismissive sound in the back of her throat. "My brother is begging to have some sense beaten into him."

A lock of hair slipped from Sandison's queue as he shook his head. "Give him time, he'll come round."

Beau nodded, not believing it any more than Gareth did. She pushed the stray lock back into place, lingering with her fingers in his hair. Leo had been getting worse, not better. Only her sister-in-law's intervention had kept him even vaguely civil.

"Was Leo there?"

"No. It was Thane who ejected me."

"Doing Leo's dirty work, damn them all."

Gareth smiled again, clearly appreciating her annoyance on his behalf, even if he didn't want her to act upon it. He slipped deeper into his chair, crossing his ankles and sinking his chin down to his chest.

"I knew this was the likely outcome when I agreed to your madcap plan."

Beau nodded and sank down onto the footstool next to Gareth's chair. She rested her head on the arm, and he twisted one of her curls around his finger.

"I guess I'd expected more from him," she said after a moment. "It seems so petty."

Gareth chuckled softly. "It is, I suppose, but it's a petty I can understand. He's not yet willing to forgive us. Me for acting the scoundrel with his sister, and you for tempting his best friend into such a betrayal."

Beau sighed. "Are men always this stupid?"

"You'd never noticed?"

She sat up, laughing, her hair trailing across his hand. "Well, yes, but not the men in my own family."

"Glennalmond?" His voice held utter disbelief.

"Fine," Beau said. "The men in my own family as well. What are we going to do about it?"

"Nothing," Gareth said, blue eyes weary, brows slanting down in exactly the way that always made her most wish to offer comfort. "We're going to enjoy ourselves while we purchase the most obvious of necessities and then we're going to decamp to our new home and let things settle down. We'll come back in spring when the Season starts and see if our scandal has blown over enough for us to be received back into the arms of the *ton*. Perhaps someone else will eclipse us by committing an even more entertaining folly."

Beau smoothed her thumb over one of his eyebrows, hand cupping his cheek. "You're half hoping our exile will be permanent, aren't you?"

He captured her hand in his own and kissed her palm. "It would mean keeping you all to myself, brat."

The frisson of awareness flooded through her, making her breasts ache and her heart beat unevenly. "I expect that come spring, you'll be glad enough to share me."

"Don't be too sure, love."

The sound of a door closing in the distance made her sharply aware of the danger of remaining closeted with him. It was her parents' home they were in, not their own. Being discovered *cavorting* in the drawing room was the last thing either of them needed.

Holding his hand in both of hers, Beau stood. "Come for a ride."

Gareth waggled his brows, and she made a face at him. "I mean it. I can't stand being cooped up for the rest of the day."

A cold, dismal fog swirled about their feet, obscuring the pavement and muffling the ring of the horses' metal-shod hooves. Beau shivered, wishing they'd gone earlier, when the day was crisp and clear. Thin of company as London was at the moment, late afternoon was still the most popular time for a ride along Rotton Row. There were already a good number of people shuffling along the wide path that cut through the park. Far too many for her to be able to shake out her gelding's fidgets with a quick gallop.

Beside her, Gareth reined Monty in and gave her a lazy, seductive smile. Heat crept up her cheeks as Beau attempted to force her mind away from the reason for his sleepy state. It was just cold enough that an observer might mistake her blush for a rosy glow. Might, but probably wouldn't.

"Explain to me again why we couldn't simply retire to your chamber for an afternoon of sport?"

Laughing, Beau brought Gunpowder up to the bit and urged him into a canter. Muscle, bone, and pure spirit surged down the sandy track, carrying her along. The steady tattoo of the gelding's hooves was the only thing that existed in the moment. The simple pleasure of motion, the rush of cold air across her skin, the feeling, almost, of flight.

She flashed by a group of women, eliciting a shout of annoyance from one of them. A rumble of masculine laughter chased after her. At the end, she slowed to a walk. Gunpowder's ribs went in and out like a bellows, and he snorted his displeasure.

Beau clapped him on the shoulder and ran her hand soothingly along his neck. The bit jangled as he shook his head in protest, mouth yawning wide.

"One of these days that animal is going to bite you."

Beau turned her head to find Roland Devere trotting toward her on a chestnut hack with a piebald face. "Not a chance." The gelding swung his head toward Devere, teeth snapping. "Stop that," she said to the horse. "But he may bite you, nasty beast."

She turned Gunpowder in a sharp circle and fell in beside Devere. "Had a pony like that as a boy. It was always biting someone." He grinned suddenly, clearly enjoying the memory.

Beau gave him an amused glance. "I assume the *some-one* was mostly your brother, Segrave?"

Devere's grin widened. "Gingerbread—my sister named him—never could stand poor Segrave. So he went from Margo to me. Ancient thing is still alive, a doted pet, and it still can't stand my brother."

They skirted past a group of slightly raucous blades, moving slowly back toward the entrance of the park. The fog had begun to thicken, so that people materialized out of the shadows like ghosts.

Beau put her hand tentatively on Devere's arm, and he reined in beside her. "How bad are things, really?"

Devere's expression went slack for a moment, his dark eyes shuttered. "Bad enough." He thrust his fingers under his hat and scratched his head, pulling hair from his queue.

"Damn my brother." Beau removed her hand from his sleeve and gave Gunpowder a sharp correction, pulling his head away from the vicinity of Devere's knee.

Devere's response was a cackle of laughter worthy of the witches from *Macbeth*. "A worthy sentiment, I'm sure. And one you can express to its fullest should he choose to show up for our cricket match tomorrow."

Beau found herself smiling back at him. Devere had that effect on people. He had a talent for making one see the amusing and absurd side of things. Things couldn't be as bad as she feared if he was still thinking of cricket.

"I just don't understand what Leo finds so objectionable," Beau said.

Devere's face drained of merriment. "Well, perhaps the tableau awaiting us might make your brother's concerns clearer."

Beau froze, yanking Gunpowder to a stop. Gareth had dismounted and was standing beside a lady mounted upon a small bay, locked in heated conversation.

Lady Cook. Flushed and obviously unhappy. Her blond curls trembled as she shook her head. She sawed at the reigns, trying to yank them from Gareth's grasp. An audience was building up, hazy in the fog, but clearly growing by the minute.

Gareth cursed loudly, hands falling away from her, as Lady Cook brought her crop down across his face. "I hate you, Gareth Sandison." Her horse minced in place, as agitated as its rider. Sand sprayed up from its hooves.

Lady Cook stiffened as she spied Beau, and her expression hardened. Her eyes bored into Beau. They'd never got on, but Lady Cook's palpable dislike was new.

Beau stared her would-be adversary down, the moment pregnant with the promise of violence. She knew hatred when she saw it. Beau urged Gunpowder forward, and Lady Cook shrank back, eyes wide, full of impotent rage.

"Don't you think you've humiliated yourself—and your husband—enough?" Beau said. It wasn't kind of her, and it probably wasn't wise, but she couldn't help herself. The sight of Gareth with his hands so familiarly on his lover had turned her blood to ice.

Lady Cook straightened in the saddle, shaking her hair back over her shoulder and raising her chin. "Not as much as your husband is likely to humiliate you," she said with a flash of satisfaction.

Gareth swung up into the saddle as Lady Cook rode off, his expression hard to read. It could have been anything from anger to disgust, perhaps even regret. The crop mark on his cheek stood out in sharp, brilliant relief.

Devere tipped his hat and disappeared into the slowly dispersing crowd. Beau's stomach churned, fighting against the constriction of her stays.

✁ CHAPTER 21 ✁

Gareth spun the cricket bat in his hand and then tapped it on the ground. The clouds parted momentarily, and he squinted at the bowler as the sudden shaft of sunlight nearly blinded him. He dug his feet into the ground and waited.

His own side didn't want him here. Their icy welcome when he'd turned up had been one more slight to bear. Vaughn wasn't even here to witness it, which meant it was utterly genuine. His friends despised him, and the feeling was beginning to be mutual.

The dull roar of those gathered beyond the boundary filled his ears like the din of an orchestra tuning up. It diminished to a hush as the Etonian's new bowler toed the line. Behind him, the wicketkeeper snickered. Harrow had been having quite the day of it so far, a run of luck Gareth fully intended to end here and now.

Beau was standing at the boundary, hands gripping the rope, her scarlet redingote unmistakable in the sea of dark-coated gentlemen. She shouldn't be here, but she'd refused to stay home, threatening to make her own way if he refused to bring her. He'd left her in the care of Devere's father, who'd promised to see that she wasn't trampled by the crowd.

The ball came at him with a wicked spin, and Gareth sent it flying back, high and long. Gareth sprinted down the pitch, passing Devere as the nonstriker did the same. Gareth reached the crease and reversed, shoes sliding on the grass.

Devere was no longer running; he was smiling, standing stock-still midpitch, hair down around his shoulders. Gareth skidded to a halt, attention riveted to the still-standing wicket.

"Boundary," the umpire called. "Six."

Devere stopped to clap Gareth on the shoulder as he made his way back to his wicket. The very public gesture wasn't lost on him. "One more like that," Devere said loudly, "and the umpire could call stumps."

Young Crawley screwed up his face. He caught the ball as it was returned by one of the fielders, turning it about in his hand as though examining it for defect.

Gareth took his place before the wicket and flicked his eyes to Beau. He could make out the flash of her smile from here, as well as those of her circle of admirers. She was surrounded, the center of attention in her own little island.

His chest felt suddenly heavy. Who would she have chosen if her hand hadn't been forced? Not him, certainly.

"Shouldn't even be here," the Etonian keeper said to his back, his animosity clearly not confined to the game.

Gareth grimaced as what little enjoyment he'd managed

to squeeze out of the day evaporated. Devere was right. One more over the boundary and they could go home.

The Etonian's bowler sent the ball hurtling toward Gareth, but it was wide. The boy was shaken. He'd knocked out the opposition one by one, but Gareth had been hitting—and scoring—steadily since coming up to bat.

The boy bowled again, and the crack of the bat made Beau jump. Gareth and Devere, both stripped to their shirts, dashed across the length of the pitch, scoring again. Lord Moubray cheered, elbowed her gently, and held out a flask.

"You must be freezing, my dear," he said, rubbing his hands together to fend off the cold.

Beau tipped the flask carefully into her mouth and let the slow burn of the brandy warm her from the inside out. "I'm fine, truly, my lord."

"Your ears are turning pink, and you're not one for blushing," he said with a sly grin so reminiscent of his son's that Beau nearly burst into laughter.

She tugged her fur-lined hat down. "No, blushing was never a talent of mine."

He nodded, eyes darting back to the match. "Don't start now," he advised. "Take your mother as your example. The duchess could ride through the streets of London naked as Lady Godiva and no one would dare to sneer at her."

Beau stared at the earl's profile, surprised by his advice. After a moment he turned back to her, brows meeting in a frown. "Don't ever let them cow you," he said earnestly. "No one speaks of it, of course, but we've all born witness to many a girl who could have saved herself by demonstrating a bit of pluck in the face of adversity."

He placed her hand on his arm, and Beau squeezed it. She knew full well that once you let the *ton* snub you, it was nearly impossible to claw your way back in.

Some, like her sister-in-law, didn't even try. Viola was comfortable, happy even, living on the fringes just as she had before marrying Leo. Beau couldn't quite see herself accepting such constraints with equal equanimity.

Out on the field, Gareth struck the ball again, sending it flying over their heads to a victory.

❧ CHAPTER 22 ❧

The steady clip of the horses' hooves was like the ticking of some fantastical instrument, measuring both time and distance, taking Beau farther away from her life as Lady Boudicea and London both. Lord only knew when she'd next see Scotland. It hadn't seemed daunting until today. Until she'd said good-bye to her parents and actually left to go to a home of her own.

Of their own.

It didn't help that Gareth was clearly miserable. He'd been unusually withdrawn since their encounter with Lady Cook, and he'd barely spoken to her at all once they'd returned home from the cricket match, except to express his desire to be on their way immediately. Whatever Lady Cook had said to him, it had stung worse than her crop, though the livid mark still stood out across his cheek.

The thousandth green hill, studded with sheep and trees, rolled past the carriage's window. Beau sighed and stretched until her spine popped. She sagged back into the seat.

"What exactly does a gentleman farmer do?" Beau said, breaking the silence.

Gareth's eyes snapped open, and the side of his mouth cocked up in a familiar, welcome way. "I believe he wears gaiters and talks of nothing but bullocks. And perhaps pigs," he added contemplatively.

"So you don't know either," Beau said with an attempt at a laugh. It felt easy, but there was an underlying constraint. She couldn't stop picturing the horror and heartbreak on Lady Cook's face.

Gareth shook his head and fiddled with his cravat. "Haven't the slightest idea, and not entirely sure I wish to find out. Though perhaps I could be persuaded about the pigs."

"I'm sure there must be a home farm. You can keep your pigs there, alongside the milch cow and chickens."

"Very sporting of you," Gareth said with a grimace.

"Even the queen of France does so at her little farm."

"Have you seen it?" Gareth moved to the seat opposite her, drew her feet up into his lap, and began to unbuckle her shoe.

"No. I haven't been to France since I was a little girl. The queen did pat me on the head and tell Mamma I was *très jolie* though. Have you seen it?"

"Me? No." He stroked her foot, pushing his thumb into the tender underside. "Never seduced my way into the right bed, though the Princess de Lambelle was a tempting option. I've heard the stories of perfumed lambs and pet chickens though."

"No sheep," Beau said. "Perfumed or otherwise."

"No sheep?"

"I've dealt with enough sheep to last a lifetime. Scotland has more sheep than people, and each of them is dumber than the next."

"The people?" Gareth said with a grin.

"Them too," Beau replied.

"You are severe today. First you attack my pigs, and now the queen's sheep."

"You don't *have* any pigs."

"Yet. I don't have any pigs *yet.*"

"Be careful, or I'm going to get you pigs as a wedding present." Beau narrowed her eyes and poked him with her stockinged foot for emphasis. "And I'll make you wear gaiters too, over a pair of old brogues."

"Witch."

"Popinjay."

Gareth studied her with an evil glint in his eyes and then yanked her into his lap. Beau landed astride him, knees on the seat, skirts riding up in a froth.

A rush of damp heat liquefied her core. Gareth's knuckles brushed over the sensitive skin of her inner thighs and slick folds between them as he freed himself from his breeches.

Beau bit down on the collar of his coat to keep from crying out as he entered her. Glorious and familiar, she struggled to take all of him, rocking her hips, need almost frantic. Whatever he was thinking of now, it certainly wasn't Lady Cook, and that was triumph enough.

Gareth held her down by the shoulders and thrust upward. Beau gasped as their bodies met. He ground against her, holding her down, and she nearly came on the spot. He'd never been so precipitous, or so rough, but her body responded with what should have been humiliating swiftness.

Should have been. Beau could find no such emotion in the swirl of things running through her. There was shock, mingled with excitement, and the thrill of possession. It was no wonder unmarried women were strictly warned not to bestow their favors. Who could stop once they started?

Beau arched her back, and her nipples pressed almost painfully into the hard wall of her stays. Gareth's mouth was on her neck, lips and teeth surely leaving a mark. Beau locked her hand in his hair and pulled him away.

Gareth nipped at her again, and she gripped his queue with both hands, holding his gaze with her own. He let go of her shoulders and slid his hands up her thighs until his thumbs rode over the hard peak of her clitoris as she rocked against him.

"Make me come," he said. "All on your own. No help."

"I'm to do all the work now?" she asked.

Gareth just smiled.

"Bastard."

His smile grew, and he slid slightly forward so she had better leverage against the narrow seat.

"You've done this before!"

"And you haven't," he said provokingly. Beau sank down, rose up until he was barely inside her, and then rocked down hard again. Gareth inhaled sharply, his hands tightening their grip. Beau found her rhythm, set her pace, and bent her every action to the challenge. He was hers, and she meant to keep him.

The smirk slid off Gareth's face, and his breathing

went shallow. He flexed beneath her. Hands starting to lift her away.

"Don't you dare," Beau said.

"But—"

"Wait." She was so close. If he finished without her, she was going to kill him. "Just, one, more . . ." Her release rushed through her, leaving her deaf, blind, and dumb.

Gareth groaned and attempted to unseat her again. Beau held on. "You could get pregnant."

"So I could." Beau clenched herself around him.

A deep growl was his only answer.

~&~ CHAPTER 23 ~&~

L ooks like someone beached a galleon and put a roof on it," Gareth said with a hint of disgust.

Beau stood gaping at the Magpie quatrefoils that made up the façade of her new home. The branching *L* to the right was half-timbered in the same black and white, the color scheme broken only by the large windows that ran along both floors, all of them made up of a dozen or more tiny panes.

A welcoming wisp of smoke curled up out of the middle bank of chimneys that rose from the heavy slate roof. Beau shivered in the damp, watching the smoke disappear into the wet, gray skies.

"I think it's beautiful," she said, meaning every word.

"I think it looks cold and drafty," he continued sourly, "and I'll bet you a year's pin money that it still has a turn-spit in the kitchen."

"Lochmaben house certainly does. Though mother says she's taking it out and replacing it with a French range next spring."

A spatter of rain hit her as the door opened and an elderly couple stepped out to greet them. Gareth waved them back inside and pushed Beau into the house before him, abandoning the coachman to find the stables on his own.

"Mr. Sandison?" the man said with a thick, musical accent that moved letters from one syllable to the next. "Peebles. And this is my missus. We've made the house as ready as can be and hired on staff, as instructed by your father."

The woman curtsied and hurried to take their coats and hats. "I've water on for tea, my lady. Come this way, through the Great Hall. When you're warm and rested, I can show you the house."

Beau smiled at her husband, and Gareth raised his brows mockingly, daring her to continue liking the place. "Tea would be wonderful, Mrs. Peebles," she said. "Thank you."

The housekeeper, her arms still overflowing with their coats, led them through an enormous, vaulted hall, down a paneled corridor, and into a smaller parlor that boasted a fireplace that was merely large and a smattering of furniture, including a settee flanked by tiny, spindly looking chairs.

"I'll be back in a tick," Mrs. Peebles said as she disappeared out the door on the other side of the room.

Beau spun slowly around, trying to take in all the ancient glory and then went to warm her hands by the fire. The logs crackled, sap popping, spitting tiny embers out toward her skirts. "Don't say it."

"Don't say what?" Gareth said, all innocence.

"I know what you're thinking. It's a Tudor pile, with a leaking roof, and the ghosts of murdered wives haunting the halls. I don't care. I like it."

"Why not husbands?"

"Tudors and Elizabethans were always murdering their wives. Or didn't you study history at Harrow?"

Gareth broke into laughter and dropped onto the settee, which squealed alarmingly and sank a bit closer to the floor. Beau held her breath as she waited for it to give out, but it held. Gareth's eyes roved over her. Beau caught his gaze and held it. They'd been married a fortnight, and they'd hardly left the bedchamber except to travel from Dyrham to London, and thence to Morton Hall.

The things you could do in a carriage . . . Just thinking about their trip set her pulse racing. And he was smiling again, though the welt across his cheek remained to taunt her.

"You can stop thinking *that* too," she said, half to herself, but mostly to Gareth. "We're not going to scandalize the servants by being caught with your tarse up my petticoats just as we've arrived."

"My what?"

"Shakespeare," Beau replied with a laugh. "I know you must have studied *him*."

Gareth sputtered for a moment, looking highly aggrieved. "Thoroughly, but I don't remember any such language in the Bard's work." He paused, eyes quizzing her. "Are you suggesting that we wait to scandalize the servants at some future date, my little libertine?"

"I fear it's inevitable," Beau said, well aware that what

he was saying was true, joy at the prospect singing in her veins. "You're very badly behaved, you know."

"I know." Gareth smiled as he said it, shaking out the cuffs of his shirt like a bird fluffing its feathers.

Beau rolled her eyes and carefully took a seat beside him, brushing her lips hurriedly over his as she did so. Lady Cook be damned, he was hers.

"The house has a fairy-tale quality," she said, smoothing her skirts over her knees, pushing their absorbed warmth down into her skin. "I can imagine Sir Lancelot bringing Guinevere here. Or Sir Gawain and his tusked-bride. It needs tapestries and suits of armor and a great stag's head over the mantle."

"It needs chairs I'm not afraid to sit in," Gareth replied, eyeing the chairs scattered about the room askance. "And very likely every amenity invented after Elizabeth's reign."

"Are you determined to be dour?" Beau asked, starting to feel perturbed. "This is our house. Our home. I command you to find at least one thing to like."

Gareth screwed up his mouth thoughtfully and turned his head about, studying the room. Beau widened her eyes and refused to smile. A flash of dimple caught her eye. Yes, he liked it too, loath as he was to admit it.

"I can find three. One"—he ticked it off on his fingers—"my wife likes it. Two, it's far, far away from my family. Three, did I already say my wife likes it?"

"Yes, but your wife *does* like it. And so shall you once we've settled in and the shock has worn off. Think of the parties. The Great Hall is practically large enough to play cricket in, and just picture the size of the Yule log we could burn in that fireplace. I swear it looked big enough to cook an ox."

"It was probably designed to do just that," Gareth said.

"Then we shall throw a fancy dress ball and roast an ox. I think your friends would find that terribly amusing. I know mine would."

Gareth smiled back at her, but his eyes were bleak again. Beau mentally cursed herself. She knew better than to bring up his friends. Their desertion was an open wound, just as her father and brother's refusal to accept the true version of events was for her. They should have been falling over themselves with thanks.

Beau shoved the thought away. She was not going to let them spoil this. And she was not going to let any of it hurt Gareth if there was anything she could do to alleviate the sting. Anything short of sharing him with Lady Cook, that was.

"We could invite the neighbors," Gareth said with forced cheerfulness. "As the new arrivals, we'll be expected to do something. Especially as the house has been unoccupied for some thirty years or more."

Beau nodded her head, grateful that Mrs. Peebles chose that exact moment to return with a well-laden tea tray. Beau ate one Naples biscuit after another, suddenly ravenous. Outside, the rain had begun to fall more heavily, the darkening sky leaving the room as gloomy as her husband.

"Garderobes," Gareth said with horrified awe as Mrs. Peebles pointed out the two small doors just off the master's bedchamber.

His wife gave him a slightly exasperated look, and Gareth let the topic go. The house was worse than he'd feared, but Beau seemed determined to like it, and to force him to do likewise. The dark paneling she called *cozy*. The beds, raised up on daises and engulfed in ancient, rotting curtains, were *impressive*. But even she could find nothing better than *historical* for the intact garderobes.

There was an impressive long gallery on the first floor, lined with tall, empty bookcases separated by caryatid columns. It ran over the entry, its windows looking out on a sweeping view of the lane leading up to the house and the lawn that led down toward the chalk cliffs and the road to Kingstown.

Beau wandered away from him and Mrs. Peebles, running her fingers along the windowsills. Her lips were moving, as though she were talking to herself.

"Cursing my father?"

She shook her head. "Making a list. Every house needs books. I'd never thought to create a library from nothing though. It's a bit daunting."

"It does give one the option to leave out fusty sermons and improving tracts," Gareth said. Mrs. Peebles shot him a scandalized look before dropping her eyes. Gareth snorted. It was best that she know right from the start whom she was working for.

"We never had many of those at home," Beau said. "We had a Bible, of course. Several in fact, but the duke is not fond of religious treatises. Unless they're Roman and advocating the proper way to worship Mithras or the like, that is. Those he'd display with glee."

Mrs. Peebles hands were clenched into tiny fists, the knuckles burning white. Gareth bit his tongue and let Beau continue to rattle on about pagan deities and just what sorts of books they should send for. He gave the Peebleses a month at most before they gave their notice.

After a few minutes, the housekeeper excused herself to check on the preparations for dinner, and Gareth gave into the amusement that had been slowly overwhelming him. His guffaws echoed back from the barrel-arched ceiling, making it sound as though the room were filled with laughing men.

"What?" Beau said, looking adorably confused. "You're not allowed to say you don't want a library. And you're certainly not allowed to laugh at my penchant for novels."

"Buy all the novels you like, brat. But for heaven's sake, don't start the library out with your sister-in-law's donation. I think that really would be the last straw for poor Mrs. Peebles."

"Oh," Beau said with dawning understanding. She caught her lower lip between her teeth as she always did when worried or perplexed. "Do you think she's packing at this very moment, or might we simply be on notice?"

"Definitely on notice, the both of us. I thought it was going to be just me, but then you had to go and talk about filling the house with odes to pagan gods."

"And novels. Don't forget the novels. Surely those are every bit as bad."

"If not worse," Gareth agreed. "Shall we see if we can find our way back through the rabbit warren to the parlor? I'm beginning to lose all sensation in my fingers and the night isn't going to get any warmer." He rubbed his hands briskly together for emphasis.

After several false starts and roundabout journeys, a somewhat startled maid led them back to the parlor. "Is it me," Gareth said, "or have the chairs shrunk since we were last here?"

"Perhaps you've grown," Beau said, reclaiming her seat on the settee.

"Those," he waved his hand at the chairs, "are going to have to be banished to the nursery, assuming we have one. We must, mustn't we? All old piles do. Can you imagine Thane attempting to balance his great carcass on one of them?"

Gareth cringed as soon as the words left his mouth. Beau blinked, clearly afraid to respond. Damn it all. They'd been on tenterhooks ever since their encounter with Lady Cook in Hyde Park. His former mistress had waylaid him with a plea for help with her stirrup, and things had deteriorated from the moment he'd swung out of the saddle.

She and Vaughn were both busy portraying him as a villainous seducer. Vaughn out of anger, Lady Cook out of a thirst for revenge. She'd accused him of slighting her. As though he were somehow her possession.

Bad enough that he was *persona non grata* with the League. He'd expected problems there, though perhaps not quite such serious ones. Lady Cook was bent upon reminding the *ton* of his every misstep. She wanted his transgressions fresh in their minds.

And no one was going to give him the chance to explain, except perhaps Devere, who seemed as blasé about this as he did about everything. The fact that almost every member of the League had known Beau since she was a girl thundering about behind them on her pony could only have served to make things worse.

Sisters were sacrosanct. Everyone knew that.

~ CHAPTER 24 ~

T he first three days of their life at Morton Hall took place in a deluge. It was like living inside a goldfish bowl. By the time the storm broke, they'd explored every inch of the house, from the attic to the kitchen.

Gareth had claimed one of the smaller parlors on the ground floor for his study, and Beau had left him there, poring over the spider scrawl in the account books while she went outside to explore the remains of the gardens.

The very formal pathways were all still intact, but the herbal borders had died away, and the beds contained nothing but a deep layer of straw mulch. Some distance from the house, the geometric pathways and beds gave way to a lawn, the transition marked by a long line of untidy yew sentinels.

Beau pulled the hem of her gown up through her pocket slits to shorten it and headed for the cliff's edge. The ground squelched underfoot, sinking beneath every step. Her half boots were soaked through by the time she caught her first view of the sea, but the view was undeniably worth wet feet and ruined stockings.

The tide was rolling in, dark, white-capped waves crashing on the beach, slowly working their way closer and closer to the base of the cliff. Down along the shore, she could make out the village of Kingstown. Tiny gray houses with dark roofs and the occasional curl of smoke. Utterly different from the thatched cottages scattered about her father's estate.

The wind whipped her hair into her eyes and pulled at her skirts as though they were sails. Beau braced her feet and took a deep breath of the salty air. A deep, loud bark caught her attention. Down on the shore, a huge black-and-white dog was running along the narrow strip of beach. A man on horseback spun about, cantering back toward the village. The dog stopped, shook, and lay down, apparently content to have the beach to itself once more.

Beau turned back toward the house. From this angle, it really did look like a galleon. Like the storm that had wrecked the Spanish Armada had swept one of the boats up, deposited it atop the cliff, and someone planted a garden all around it. Clip the yews to look like dolphins, and the image would be complete.

Beau pushed her hair out of her eyes and let the wind push her back up toward the house. She found Gareth still poring over the household ledger, a look of disgruntled annoyance on his face.

"It can't be that bad," she said, leaning in to look over his shoulder. Gareth sat back with a sigh. Beau perched on the edge of the desk. She cupped his face, smoothing her thumbs over his brows, the thrill of having a right to do so still strong. "It's nothing money can't fix."

"Your money," he said, the frown returning in full force.

"Legally, it's *your* money now," she replied.

"Said with the perfect nonchalance of someone who's never fretted over an account or bill in her life."

Beau jerked her hands back, anger flushing through her. "It's unfair to behave as though you wished me to have been a penniless bride."

Gareth raised one hand and rubbed his eyes. "I'm sorry, brat. That's not what I meant at all. It's just these damn columns of numbers are making my head ache."

Beau bit the inside of her cheek to keep from snapping back at him. She'd sworn to make him happy. Fighting over money, especially a surplus of it, was ridiculous. "Leave them alone then and come back to them tomorrow," she said, forcing a light tone.

The only reason that he was trapped here slaving over that ledger in a house he clearly hated was that he'd married her. And she'd done everything in her power to leave him no choice. She'd got what she wanted, but she wasn't entirely sure that Gareth could say the same. The memory of his hand on Lady Cook's ankle skittered through her brain. He'd given up a lot of things to save her.

"Have the horses arrived yet?" he asked, his tone conciliatory.

Beau shook her head. "I don't know. I don't think so. Why?"

"I was thinking we could go for a ride. Maybe tour the village. Introduce ourselves to the vicar."

Beau forced a smile. His comment still stung, but he was trying. "I would like to know who our neighbors are. Whom to call upon."

"So, a frontal attack? Before Mrs. Peebles brands us as heathens and we have to turn Methodist?"

"Yes," she said, accepting what she knew to be an olive branch. "We should begin as we mean to go on. And I've no intention of hiding."

"Newlyweds," Mr. Tillyard said, his tone somehow implying that there was something suspicious about such a state. "And taking up residence at Morton Hall."

The statement hung in the air as though it were a question. Gareth found himself nodding, afraid to reply verbally to the ancient vicar, lest he say the wrong thing. Beau was frozen beside him, her eyes a little too large, as though she too were barely able to restrain herself.

"Yes," Gareth said. "My father gave it over to me upon my wedding to Lady Boudicea."

The old man nodded, the side curls of his wig bobbing in time with his head shakes. "Lot of work, setting a house like that to rights. Been vacant as long as I've held the living here."

"Yes," Gareth said and nodded back. He was beginning to sound like some kind of parrot. Only able to reply with a single word. And the vicar was right. It was going to be a great deal of work. Not to mention expense.

The estate might have a decent income—thank God that the hop fields hadn't been left to go to rack and ruin like the house—but they wouldn't see any of it for nearly a year. The harvest had taken place only a few months previous, and his father had sold the crop before bestowing the estate. He was going to have to broach the principal of Beau's dowry to restore the house and grounds to a livable state in the meantime. He didn't have any choice.

The thought made him slightly sick. Fortune hunter. Like it or not, that's what he'd been reduced to. He'd gone from philanderer to this. At moments like these, he was almost certain that his father had chosen this particular property as some kind of punishment. Step out of line, boy, and you'll see what happens.

And step out of line he had. He was never supposed to have married. Never supposed to have caused his family any unexpected expense. And now that he had, he was being forced to pour his wife's dowry into an estate that might never be truly habitable if the state of their bedroom was any indication.

Between the hole in the sheets that he'd caught his toe in, the smoking fireplace, and the abysmal damp, they might as well be living in a crofter's cottage on his father's estate. No, all the crofter's cottages there had good, thatch roofs. There were leaks aplenty at Morton Hall.

The rattle of his cup on its saucer snapped his attention away from the horrors of his monetary predicament and back to his present surroundings. Beau took the cup from him without a word and set it aside. The amusement dancing in her eyes warned him that he was moments away from her foisting another cup of the vicar's awful tea on him. There wasn't enough sugar in the world to mask the moldering flavor of whatever it was the vicar had served them.

"What sport is there to be had locally?" Beau asked, smoothly moving the conversation on just like the duke's daughter that she was. She might have preferred to rub elbows with the squirearchy and Corinthians, but she'd still been trained to be a proper hostess. It was easy to forget that fact when she was cursing like a jack tar and throwing her horse over fences that most gentlemen preferred to avoid.

Mr. Tillyard gave them both the fishy eye. "Neither of you from Kent?"

"No," Gareth said, not sure if they were further damning themselves. "Neither of us has ever lived so far south."

The vicar harrumphed noncommittally. "Good shooting. Pheasant, mostly. Some grouse." He rubbed his chin. "Rather poor hunting, but good beagling. Morton Hall had a fine pack of beagles at one point, or so they say. And there're the annual races at Ashford. Nothing like the Oaks or the Derby, of course, but a good day all the same."

"I've never been beagling," Beau said.

"I would hope not, my lady," the vicar replied, bristling with outrage.

Gareth watched as his wife took a deep breath and held it, batting her lashes in a way that he knew spelled trouble. She was practically shaking as she held herself back. Clearly, whatever reply she wanted to make was only going to further scandalize the old man.

"Is that your dog I always see running on the beach?" Beau finally said, her color still high.

The vicar made a face, as though discovering mice nesting amongst his stockings. "The great black-and-white beast?"

Beau nodded. "I saw him in your garden and thought—"

"Not mine, my lady. Not anybody's really. Only survivor of a shipwreck some years back. Swam ashore with the first mate clinging to his neck, but the man died a few days later. Just roams about the village now and harasses the fishermen."

"Oh." Beau glanced over at him, her expression forlorn, clearly at the end of her rope when it came to making nice.

"We should be going, sir," Gareth said, rising from his chair. "I'm sure you have things to do."

"Yes, yes," the vicar said. "Get you home while it's still light. We'll see you again on Sunday. I'll have them reserve a spot for you in the first pew."

Once they were outside, Beau fastened her hat down securely and slipped her arm through his. "Still enamored with the Hall?" Gareth said.

"Yes," Beau replied, "though turning Methodist is looking more and more appealing."

"I don't think they'd smile upon your going beagling any more than Mr. Tillyard."

Beau narrowed her eyes and glared. The wind pulled at her curls, swiping them across her eyes, and she blinked them away. "I'm going to start my own pack just to annoy him."

"We could get you a pack of duc de Noaille's spaniels. Nothing like foreign dogs to set off a good Englishman."

"Since that's clearly my intent." Beau squeezed his arm and sighed. "I do *try* to behave myself, but it's very hard sometimes."

~ CHAPTER 25 ~

"I t makes me nervous when you're this quiet for the entire day," Gareth said as he entered the small chamber that Beau had claimed as her sitting room. Beau looked up, momentarily startled. As she took in his countenance, a smile pulled at her lips.

Mud-spattered and windblown, in a buff-leather shooting coat that had seen better days, there was not a bit of the elegant London gentleman about him. And she loved him this way. Preferred it, even. This Gareth was hers, and hers alone.

"I've been finishing the last few invitations for our party." She set her quill aside and flexed her cramping fingers. She licked her thumb and rubbed at an ink spot on her finger. When the stubborn stain remained, she held up her hand for inspection. "I hope you don't mind being married to a woman with hands like a clerk."

Gareth bent with a flourish and kissed her hand. He retained it in his own, thumb circling in her palm. "Not at all. But if you prove yourself good at sums, I shall force you to manage the household accounts. They're a nightmare. I've been trying to get them to balance for days now."

Beau laughed and shook her head. "Mathematics was never my strong point. I always seem to flip the numbers around, and my tallies never come out right. Father was always wondering how I could be so stupid in that one subject."

"I suppose I'll persevere then," he said with a dramatic sigh. He squeezed her hand and let it go, moving deeper into the room.

"You carry on with the household accounts, and I'll carry on with the invitations." She picked her quill up again and caught the feathered tip between her lips. Gareth wandered to stand beside the fire. He pushed the log with his foot and bent to add another, causing a small whirlwind of sparks.

"I've already sent invitations to both our families," Beau said.

He turned to look at her, one brow raised mockingly. He pushed a loose lock of hair behind his ear. "You don't actually expect any of them to come, do you, love?"

"No." She shook her head, worrying the tip of the quill with her teeth again. "Even if we were all on speaking terms, it's a week's journey for any of our parents to reach us, and that's with the roads dry and easily passable. There's a reason everyone stays home and makes do with their neighbors for Christmas and Boxing Day."

"Or goes for a long visit," he said.

"Yes, or that. I don't expect we'll have above ten families though. Less if the weather turns foul."

"Are we being high in the instep?"

Beau burst into laughter. "Not at all, I've invited the curate, the doctor, even the local solicitor. Our little corner of the world is simply very sparsely populated. Oh, and the Miss Ackeroyds. They're very genteel."

"Even if their mother isn't," Gareth said, rolling his eyes heavenward.

"Even if their mother isn't," Beau echoed back, giving him a reproving stare. "If any of your friends come—Mr. Devere, for example—they'll be happy we've some pretty girls for them to dance with."

"There's to be dancing, now?"

Beau felt a hint of a blush burn her cheeks. She raised her chin. There was no reason to be embarrassed simply because she wanted their first party to be a success.

"Only informally. I'm not attempting to bring in musicians or anything grand. Did you find us our Yule log?" she said, switching the subject.

Gareth grinned, face lighting up in a way that made her suddenly lightheaded. "I did. The men are arranging it in the fireplace as we speak. I'll lay you a pony it burns for a week. I've a surprise for you too."

Beau bit back an answering grin and stared at him skeptically. "A good surprise?"

"You'll have to come and see." He held out his hand.

Beau put the cap on the ink and set her quill aside. Gareth led her through the house and into the grand hall. Two footmen and three of their tenants were in the final stages of wrestling a massive log into the ancient fireplace. Piles of greenery were spread across the long table in the center of the room, where Mrs. Peebles was directing the maids as they tied it into swags. Peebles himself was busy tucking bits of mistletoe into a large straw ball. The heavy berries nodded and shook as he worked.

"All the proper frills and furbelows," Gareth said with a perfectly serious expression that nearly set Beau off laughing. "Just like at Lochmaben."

Beau sniffled, blinking away tears. It was just like Christmas at home. Or as like as it could be. "I've something for you too," she said, glad that her surprise had arrived that morning after he'd ridden out. "Come down to the home farm."

Gareth tilted his head like a distrustful horse. "The home farm?"

"Yes, the *farm*." She emphasized the last word menacingly. "Your present arrived while you were gone."

Gareth followed her into the entry hall and helped her with her redingote. "You didn't actually get me a pig, did you?"

Beau grinned at him. He made it sound as though a pig were some kind of royal death warrant. "You'll have to come and see."

She headed out, not bothering to check that he was following. He was insatiably curious by nature. She knew he would follow. He couldn't help himself.

When she reached the home farm, she stopped and leaned against the railing of the newly erected sty. Gareth's piglet grunted and climbed up, begging for attention. Beau leaned over and scratched him on his fuzzy black-and-white-spotted head.

"It looks like a rotund carriage dog." Gareth eyed the piglet with trepidation, much as he had the house upon their arrival.

Beau smiled and continued to scratch the little pig, who was grunting and ugging with delight, its enormous ears flipped back to show their pink lining. "Mr. Moreland breeds them. He says it's a Gloucestershire Spotted Pig. The most English of pigs. I couldn't resist when I saw them."

Gareth reached out and scratched behind its ear, just as he would a dog.

"There are apples in the bucket," Beau said, repressing a smile. "Carrots too."

Gareth fished out an apple. The piglet took a noisy bite, dribbling drool all over Gareth's hand. Gareth's face crumpled into something between disgust and amusement.

"What shall you name him?" Beau said.

Gareth looked at her as if she were mad. "Does one name pigs?" He held out the apple so it could take another bite. His queue fell forward over his shoulder, and Beau swept it back for him before the piglet got hold of it.

"All pets should be named."

"That"—he gestured with the dripping remains of the apple to the piglet—"is a pet?"

"Of course it's a pet. If I'd wanted to give you a ham, I would have."

Gareth laughed and tossed the last of the apple to the loudly chewing animal. "He does put me strongly in mind of Lord North," Gareth said with a wicked, ingratiating grin. "I shall call him Frederick. And we shall eat his children."

Beau clapped her hand over her mouth. The piglet's tiny eyes and fat cheeks were more than a little reminiscent of the former prime minster, unkind as it was to say.

Gareth leaned his hip against the sty and crossed his ankles. "Please tell me I'm not to be condemned to gaiters too."

Beau caught her lips between her teeth to keep from grinning. She'd already put a pair in his clothes press, much to his valet's horror.

~ CHAPTER 26 ~

Gareth waited for Beau to curtsey to Roland Devere as their set concluded before stepping in and claiming her. "Go and flirt with someone else," he said, waving his friend away.

Devere wrinkled his nose at him, bowed to Beau, and then wandered away to turn the pages at the pianoforte for the youngest of the Ackeroyd girls. The stripling that he displaced glowered with displeasure before stalking off. Miss Alice, all of twelve, glowed with pleasure.

"Do you know," Beau said, smiling up at him, "I don't think you've ever asked me to dance. Not once. We must have been at dozens of balls together every year, and you never came near me."

"I was purposefully avoiding you, brat," Gareth responded with perfect truth.

"Really? I always thought you just didn't like me."

"Ha!" Gareth steered her in a circuitous path through their tiny throng of guests. "You never in your life thought for a moment that any man alive didn't like you."

"Is that really what you think?" Her forehead wrinkled, and her eyes looked almost hurt. "Because I assure you, plenty of gentlemen have disliked me over the years. And even more have disapproved of me."

Another set began and the majority of their guests circled to the middle of the Great Hall. Even the vicar and the doctor were dancing. Gareth stopped beside the roaring Yule log, under the giant ball of mistletoe.

"But did you ever think you couldn't bring them to heel if you truly set your mind to it?" He'd seen her twisting men around her little finger since she was a girl. It was an innate talent.

Her cheeks flushed pink under the layer of powder dusted across them. "I only ever tried it once," she said.

"And?"

"And you raised one supercilious brow and stalked off without a word."

"When was that, brat?" he said, though he already knew the answer. He could still see her outraged expression, could still remember the gown she'd been wearing. Peach-and-green chine silk with matching feathers in her hair.

"At the hunt ball when I was sixteen."

"And if you'd had your way and I'd run tame behind you, what would you have done with me?"

"Done with you?" She blinked as the impossibility of the scenario hit her. Grown men with no fortune of their own didn't pay court to underage heiresses.

Gareth chuckled. "You were best avoided entirely." He reached up, plucked a berry from the mistletoe, and held it out to her.

"I suppose I was," she said as though still thinking it

over. She took the berry from him and stared at it, turning it between her fingers. "Show me what you would have done if I hadn't been. If I'd been one of your string of married conquests, or that yellow-haired opera dancer."

Gareth's cock twitched rudely, immediately in favor of her suggestion. "We have guests."

"They'll keep," Beau replied with a hint of a wicked smile curling up one side of her mouth. "The set has barely begun and it will take half an hour or more. Are you really telling me you couldn't have concluded an assignation in half that time?"

Gareth smiled back at his mad wife. "Meet me in the long gallery."

"The gallery? Why not your room?"

"When debauching a lady at a ball, you don't generally have access to a bedchamber. You have to make do with something public, but unlikely to be in use."

"Someone could see us."

"The risk is part of why you do it." Gareth bowed, plucked the berry from her fingers, took the chaste kiss to which it entitled him, and walked off. He circled the room, smiling to himself when Beau slipped out. He stopped to talk to Mr. Howley, the largest landowner in the neighborhood, for a moment. Howley was smiling indulgently as his son danced with one of the younger Misses Ackeroyds.

"Miss Julia?" Gareth nodded toward the couple.

"Miss Hester," Howley said with a grin. "Though it was a good guess. The Ackeroyd girls are all very similar, and Julia and Hester are twins, just to add to the confusion."

"Half the people I know can't tell my brother Souttar and me apart, and he's several years older and several inches shorter. I feel for them. As boys we were always getting blamed for something the other did."

Howley chuckled. "Young Thomas has no such luck. No one to blame but him when his mother's Chinese vase was broken or a plate of biscuits went missing."

"That's why every boy needs a dog," Gareth replied before bowing slightly and slipping out of the room in pursuit of his wife.

He found her pacing the unlit, long gallery. She started like a frightened doe when he shut the door behind him. "Never sneaked off to a dark corner for a kiss?" he said, burning to know the answer, jealous already of whoever it might have been.

He pushed her up against the wall, covering her mouth with his. She was pliant, nearly boneless in his arms.

"Never," Beau replied, breaking off the kiss. Her eyes were wide, wild, the whites reflecting the moonlight spilling through the tall windows.

"And here I thought you quite the hoyden." Gareth opened the fall of his breeches, hauled her skirts up, and lifted her, so she was splayed open, feet off the floor, legs around his hips.

"On the hunting field, yes." She gasped and dropped her head back against the wall as he probed for entrance. "But aside from my lamentable talent at being abducted—oh, God—I conducted myself with a great deal of decorum."

He found the proper angle and thrust in. Her legs tightened around him. One shoe fell to the floor with a clatter. "Well thank heaven that's at an end," he said. Gareth gripped her buttocks and ground into her, pushing them both toward climax as quickly as he could. She stiffened in his arms, gasps turning to mewls, and her body pulsed around his cock, triggering his own release.

He leaned hard against her, pinning her to the wall with his body, savoring the tiny contractions of her sheath. She let her breath out in a long, satisfied sigh.

"Is that really what people do in dark corners?" she said.

Gareth laughed softly and kissed the pulse point just below her ear. "Some variation thereof, yes."

"Is that what you did with Lady Cook?"

The question caught him off guard, punching the air out of his lungs. She sounded hurt by the very idea of it. He let her slide to the floor.

He took a rattling breath. "With Lady Cook, and others." Many, many others. He'd lost count. It wasn't important. They weren't important.

Beau's chin wobbled. "I think she loved you."

Gareth would have laughed at the preposterousness of that statement if he couldn't see that Beau utterly believed it to be true, or at least feared that it was.

"Lady Cook loved the idea of rubbing me in her husband's face. Nothing more."

"And you liked it too," Beau said with a hint of resentment.

Gareth tipped her head up with his knuckle under her chin. "Yes, brat. I liked it too. But Lady Cook isn't in love with me, and I certainly wasn't in love with her."

"No?" Beau stared up at him, a tiny frown line between her brows. "You're sure about that?"

"I'm sure, Beau," Gareth said before kissing her again, hard, fast, and hungry.

• • •

"Where did the two of you disappear to last night?" Devere said as he piled a rasher of bacon on top of the steak and kidney pie and eggs that he'd already loaded his plate down with.

Gareth gave him a repressive stare, but Devere merely smiled, showing his teeth in a wolfish grin, and sat down. No one else was up and about yet, but it still didn't make for polite conversation for the breakfast room.

"No one else noticed," Devere said before taking a large bite. He chewed happily, a smile still lurking in his eyes. He swallowed and reached for the cup of coffee that Gareth had poured for him. "But I've had years of experience watching you cut your fillies from the herd."

"Have you?" Beau said from the doorway, voice heavy with interest and amusement.

Devere choked and snatched up his napkin. He wiped coffee from his chin and went off in a fit of coughing.

"Imbecile." Gareth shook his head and refilled Devere's cup.

Beau smiled at him before filling a plate for herself and sitting down beside Devere. "So, what's my husband's usual method?"

"Beau," Gareth said, hinting her away from the topic. Beau blinked innocently at him as she heaped marmalade atop a wedge of toast. He'd as good as told her he loved her last night, and the same pleased half-smile was still lurking at the corner of her mouth.

Devere grinned, and Gareth prayed for patience. "Well, he's always liked the assignation. Do you remember the time I walked in on you and Lady Ligonier in the bathhouse at Dyrham?"

Gareth glared at him. He most certainly did. Very awkward it had been, too. And far too recent for comfort, seeing as it had been at a party only a few months ago.

Devere shrugged, eyes full of devilment. "Or the time the innkeeper caught you and his daughter in the taproom at The White Horse? I thought you were a dead man for sure." He leaned closer to Beau. "Man was screaming his head off and waving a cleaver around like a sword. Sandison's lucky he's not a capon."

"I was sixteen!"

"And already a bad piece of work," Devere said, nodding as though he were pronouncing a home truth.

Beau burst into laughter. "He's learned a little something since then," she said.

"I would hope so," Devere said.

Gareth ground his teeth. "Come on, you," he said to Devere, rising from the table. "Come and meet Frederick."

"Frederick?" Devere looked baffled.

"New pet. I can't even begin to explain. You just have to see him for yourself."

Devere swallowed the last of his eggs and followed him out. Beau's laughter chased them down the corridor and into the hall.

"You don't have to encourage her, you know," Gareth said as he led his last remaining friend across the lawn to the home farm.

"Not sure I can help myself," Devere said. "She always was a delightful little beast of a girl. Who knew marriage to one of us could improve upon that trait."

Gareth tamped down the urge to laugh. Devere didn't need any encouragement, and it shouldn't have been funny.

They reached the sty, and Frederick came bolting out, jumping up against the fence in a frenzy of excitement. Gareth obligingly scratched behind his ear.

"What the devil is that thing?" Devere said, staring at the little piglet with horrified fascination.

"The brat's idea of a joke, I think," Gareth replied. "I'm a gentleman farmer now, and Lord North here is my prize pig."

"Kind of runty for a prize pig, isn't he?"

"He'll grow."

"Kind of..." Devere waved his hands about as though shaping a pig in the air. "Spotty too."

"I'm assured that he's supposed to look like an obese carriage dog. It proves he's the most English of pigs or something."

A low wuffle from beside the sty drew their attention. "Well, there's your answer," Devere said, gesturing to the giant black-and-white dog. "Its mother is a Newfoundland."

Frederick abandoned them to run to the fence nearest the dog. The dog licked the pig's nose through the slats. Gareth shook his head. "Beau's been trying to lure that dog to her for weeks."

"Taking after her sister-in-law, is she?"

"What?" Gareth said. "Oh, yes. Giant strays. You have to admit, Pen is hard to resist. And this beast here, should he ever allow himself to be captured and tamed, would make an impressive conquest." Gareth snapped his fingers, and the dog cocked its head and backed away, never taking its eyes off them. "But not today, and alas, not for me. I suppose that's for the best. Beau would never forgive me if I took her dog."

"Laid claim to it, has she?" Devere leaned on the fence, calling the piglet back over with dangling fingers.

"Along with everything else," Gareth said with a chuckle. "Beau does tend to suck everything into orbit around her."

Devere turned his head and slanted his gaze so their eyes met. "Any regrets?"

"About Beau? Good Lord, no."

"About Vaughn?"

Gareth nodded. "I keep hoping he'll come around. He can't stay mad forever, can he?"

"We are talking about Leonidas Vaughn," Devere said with a sad shake of his head. "He's got a talent for holding a grudge."

≈ CHAPTER 27 ≈

Beau gripped her husband's arm as Devere's coach rolled away. He'd stayed with them an extra three days and was now off to Dover to meet their friend the Chevalier de Moulines and carry the Frenchman back to London. She rested her head on Gareth's shoulder for a moment.

"It seems odd that Devere of all people would be the only one to stand by me," Gareth said. "I'd have expected it to be Thane."

"Nonsense," Beau said, giving him a little shake. "Come spring, this will all have blown over, and we'll have a full house for the beagling, or the races, or both."

Gareth smiled down at her, his expression clearly saying that he didn't believe a word of what she was saying. Beau shook him a bit harder, knocking him off balance. She didn't like his sad, reflective mood.

"Come and help me spy on my dog," she said. "I've been leaving food out for him near Frederick's pen all week." She looped her gown up through her pockets, exposing the intricately quilted petticoat beneath it.

"Haven't named him yet?" Gareth took her hand and crossed the lawn with her.

"You have to know a dog before you can name it. For example, if you called my sister-in-law's mastiff Petunia, it just wouldn't work. And de Moulines's greyhound simply isn't an Angus or a Jemmy."

"And you wouldn't want to get used to calling your beast Gulliver when he's more of a Crusoe."

"Precisely," Beau said with a laugh, amused that he so clearly understood.

Upon approaching the sty, they found Frederick lazing in the midday sun on one side of the fence, and the dog doing the same on the other. At the sound of their footsteps, they both raised their heads. The piglet scrambled up and cavorted madly about the pen. The dog heaved itself up and stood watching them, warily.

Gareth scratched his pig while Beau attempted to lure the dog to her with a bone that she'd brought down wrapped in a handkerchief. The dog took a step toward her, and Beau waggled the bone.

"Come here, boy," she said softly. She tsked the way she would to a horse, keeping the dog's attention. The dog inched close enough to sniff the bone, and Beau held perfectly still. After a moment's hesitation, it carefully took the bone and went to lie on the far side of the sty with it, keeping an eye on them while it ate.

"Success?" Gareth said, giving Frederick a final, hearty slap on the side.

"It's closer than he's ever come before," Beau replied. "I just wish he was more the trusting type, poor thing.

There's something about a stray that breaks my heart. A stray dog has had a covenant broken."

"Every stray?" Gareth said, looking horrified.

"Every last one." Beau looped her arm through his as they wandered back up to the house. "I had a scraggly terrier with a broken tail and a missing ear as a little girl. His name was Grendel. I found him running wild in Hyde Park. I was quite upset when the portrait painter my father hired prettied him up."

Gareth stopped for a moment, staring down at her with a slightly stunned expression. "You mean the little dog in the family portrait in the duchess's sitting room?"

Beau nodded.

"That is the singularly ugliest dog I've ever seen. Worse than my grandmother's pop-eyed pug or the Duchess of Richmond's lantern-jawed spaniel."

Beau grinned. "You should have seen him in all his raggedy glory. Ugly doesn't even begin to sum it up. But my point is that even Grendel, ugly as he was, didn't deserve to be abandoned. He'd obviously been someone's dog. He was trained to sit, to lie down, and he was a magnificent ratter."

"Are you warning me that you mean to turn Morton Hall into a home for abandoned dogs?"

"No." Beau shook her head. "But I think in order to make Morton Hall into a home, we should have a dog, and the village's shipwrecked giant would seem to be a perfect choice."

"Definitely Gulliver then," Gareth said, starting back toward the house. "Unless we want to change Frederick's name to Friday."

~ CHAPTER 28 ~

L ord Souttar has arrived, sir," Mr. Peebles said with a
sniff as he held open the massive, iron-strapped front
door. "I've put him in the drawing room."

"My brother's here?" Gareth handed over his greatcoat and hat. His butler was looking distinctly offended,
which was not at all his normal mien. Souttar had a way
of doing that to people. Toplofty. That's what all Gareth's
friends always said about him, at least when they were
being kind.

"Yes, sir. Been waiting an hour or more. I told him we
didn't know when you'd return, but his lordship made it
clear the *matter* was pressing."

"Is Lady Boudicea with him?"

"No, her ladyship went for a walk, sir. Down to the village to visit the Misses Ackeroyd, I believe."

Gareth nodded and hurried through the Great Hall,
boots ringing on the floor with every step. Good Lord,
Souttar was going to be in a rage. He hated to be kept
waiting. But what the hell was he doing here?

He burst into the drawing room to find his brother looking very much the worse for wear. "Mother?" Gareth said, expressing the only real worry he had about his brother's unexpected arrival.

Souttar made a dismissive face and shook his head. "Mother was fine when I left Ashburn." He held up a hand, forestalling Gareth's next inquiry. "The earl too, in case that was your next question."

Gareth looked his brother over more carefully, taking in his disordered hair, crumpled coat, and dirty boots. The fact that he hadn't even asked for a room or bothered to tidy himself spoke volumes. And there was a haunted look about his eyes. Something was very, very wrong.

"So, what brings you to Kent?" It couldn't be anything good. Souttar would never have traveled all this way without a damn good reason.

"Same business I needed you to take care of weeks ago when I wrote and asked you to come home," Souttar said in an aggrieved tone. "Been a deal of work taking care of it myself, I can assure you."

"Oh?" Gareth raised his brows, staring his brother down. Anyone else would have flinched or fidgeted or at least had the decency to look contrite. Souttar stared right back, clearly secure in his belief that it was Gareth's duty to be at his beck and call.

"You might at least have asked why I'd sent for you when last we met."

"When last we met," Gareth said, trying to keep the annoyance out of his voice, "I was getting married. I had other things on my mind."

His brother waved a dismissive hand and then flinched

as a loud wail split the air. Gareth made a questioning gesture toward the writhing, crying bundle on the settee.

"What the hell is that?"

"It's a baby," Souttar replied with perfect aplomb.

Gareth peered past his brother. A dark-haired child of about two was struggling to escape the confines of the greatcoat it was wrapped in. "I can see that. What the hell is it doing on my settee?"

"You need to take care of him. Keep him here."

Gareth found himself momentarily unable to reply as his brain ground to a halt like a clock with a missing gear. "Are you mad?" he shouted, trying to be heard over the child. "Whose baby is it, and why the hell would *I* keep it?"

"It's mine, and father can't find out."

"Father? The earl won't care that you'd sired a bastard. He wouldn't care if you had an entire regiment of them. He's got one of his own that he supports. Even mother knows."

"You don't understand," his brother said, chin jutting out stubbornly, just as it had when they were boys and being dressed down for some infraction. Gareth got a sinking feeling in the pit of his stomach. "He's not a bastard. Or at least, I don't think he is."

There was panic in his voice. Panic, and something very close to fear. Gareth rubbed at his eye, which had begun to throb. "What the hell have you done, Souttar? He's either one or the other. There's no middle ground."

"No one needs to know," Souttar said, his tone pleading. "Not father. Not Olivia. If you'll just claim him. Raise him. I rarely ask you for anything... You've got to help me.

It's your duty. He's family." He picked up the crying child, plucking it out of his coat, and held it awkwardly. The little boy sobbed anew, repeatedly asking for his mamma.

Gareth could feel his resistance weakening. He'd pulled his brother out of any number of scrapes over the years, and Souttar had done the same for him…the two of them united against the earl, deflecting his anger, protecting each other. It was second nature to do so. Even if, once again, Souttar's needs were paramount to his own.

"What would I tell Beau?" Gareth asked in a bid to force his brother to understand just what he was asking.

"What would you tell me about what?" Beau's question broke over the room like a wave, forcing the air right out of Gareth's lungs. Gareth watched in horror as his brother's eyes flashed triumphantly and his expression went sly.

The room went suddenly quiet as Beau caught sight of the child and stopped in her tracks. The smile slid right off her face.

Gareth could almost feel the anger whip through her. Beau's head was up, her eyes wide, like a horse about to shy, or strike.

"It's Gareth's," Souttar said, thrusting the child at him, nearly dropping it in the process. "The child's mother died a few weeks ago, and he was sent to us by her family."

Gareth ground his teeth, opened his mouth to contradict him, and shut it again as facts and dates spun through his head.

"A few weeks ago?" Gareth said with dawning horror. Souttar flinched. The boy thrashed in his arms, hiccupping pitifully.

"What does it matter?" Beau said, voice tight with repressed rage. "Through no fault of his own, he's here." She scooped the child out of his arms and settled him on her hip. "We can decide what's to be done later. After such a journey, I expect he's exhausted. And you two yelling at each other is clearly not helping him calm down one bit."

She spun on her heel and marched out, skirts rustling with agitation. The boy watched them over her shoulder, his eyes the same familiar blue as all the men in their family.

"You bloody fool," Gareth said as soon as the door shut behind them.

"I know. I know."

"You married Olivia *knowing* you already had a wife?"

"No. I mean, yes, but..." He swallowed hard, hands opening and closing in frustration. "It wasn't a real marriage. Not the kind with a church or a license. It was just a bit of fun one summer in Scotland. I'd forgot all about it."

"Go on." Gareth repressed the urge to cuff his elder brother. What kind of a man forgot he was already married?

"It all started a month or so after the wedding. I got a letter—well, you did, really—asking me to take the child."

"What do I have to do with it?"

"I may have used your name," he replied offhandedly. "Or at least, I didn't use all of mine."

"You may have..." Gareth took a deep breath, struggling with his temper. Fratricide didn't seem out of the question at that exact moment. "You set up house with a girl in Scotland under my name. Abandoned her and your child. Married another girl—the only child of the Earl of Arlington, just to make it all the more disastrous—and now you're proposing to abandon your son a second time, because it's better to ruin my marriage than yours. Have I got that all straight?"

"It's not as though it would just make Olivia angry. It would ruin her. Our marriage would be invalid. Mary's dead. What's the purpose of letting it all come to light now?"

Gareth barely repressed the urge to strangle Souttar then and there. "You're perfectly right. There's no reason to ruin Olivia's life just because you're a selfish bastard without so much as a shred of honor."

"There's no need—"

"There's *every* need, damn you. We'll keep this quiet. Between only the two of us. But you'll sign something here and now pledging to support that child when it's grown."

Souttar stiffened, clearly not enjoying being dictated to.

"You're taking away his birthright," Gareth said, gripping his brother's arm hard. "Instead of being the future Earl of Roxwell, he's going to grow up as my bastard. You're going to make that up to him as best you can, even though he'll never know why."

"He's the son of a tradesman's daughter," Souttar said dismissively, as though that made the deception alright.

"My help, my terms."

❧ CHAPTER 29 ❧

Beau stormed up the stairs and marched through the winding corridors until she came to the suite of rooms that were devoted to the nursery. Everything was draped in Holland covers, and the windows were filmed with dust.

It hadn't seemed a priority to get the nursery in order. She still couldn't quite wrap her head around the idea that it was now, even with a squirming little boy in her arms.

She flipped the cover back from a chair and sat down hard, legs nearly giving out from under her. The child pulled out of her arms and worked his way to the floor. "Want mamma," he said decisively, his forehead puckered with confusion.

"I'm sure you do, moppet. But mamma isn't here." Beau pulled her handkerchief from her pocket and wiped his runny nose. She looked around the room. There must be toys somewhere. Something to entertain him with. She got up from the chair to explore the room.

Gareth's son—Beau took a deep breath at the

thought—toddled after her. She knelt down beside the window seat and lifted the lid. Inside, there was a very battered stuffed monkey, a box of blocks, and a broken leather cockhorse, just the head with a few inches of stick protruding from the neck.

She handed the little boy the monkey, and he clutched it to his chest, holding on as though it might come to life and escape. "Monkey," she said, pointing at it.

"Mokee."

Beau nodded. It was close enough.

"Mokee, mokee, mokee." He said the new word over and over, wrapping his tongue around it. "Up!" he demanded, pointing to the window seat where she was now sitting. Beau lifted him up and set him down beside her on the unpadded wooden bench.

He was still snub-nosed and unformed in the way of all small children. It was hard to say if he looked like his father. But there was certainly something very like Gareth about the eyes and chin.

Beau let her breath out with a shudder. It felt as though there was a bubble behind her breastbone, and it ached. Anger, resentment, disillusionment, annoyance, betrayal. She could feel them all swirling inside that bubble. What would she do if it burst?

She'd known what Gareth was. A rake. A seducer of other men's wives. A man who consorted with opera dancers and Cyprians. She had assured her father that she knew and understood. Had sworn that she didn't care.

It was a very inconvenient time to discover that she did. The *idea* of marrying a rake hadn't bothered her. Seeing him with Lady Cook—wondering if he still desired her, if he resented having to give her up—that had been painful enough in the moment, but easily dispelled. The reality of having her nose rubbed in his past on a daily basis was nearly impossible to choke down.

The little boy sat quietly beside her, monkey in his lap, as though he hadn't the slightest idea what to do now. At least he'd stopped crying. Beau swallowed hard. She wasn't entirely sure what to do either. It wasn't quite the same as being left to play with her nephews for an afternoon.

"My lady?" Mrs. Peebles stood in the doorway, nose wrinkled up as though something stank. Behind her, one of the grooms was hefting a small, battered trunk in both hands.

Beau sat up straighter as annoyance overtook everything else. *She* was the only one who had a right to be offended. Mrs. Peebles could take it in stride, or she could give her notice. She waved them both in. The groom deposited the trunk, tugged his forelock, and fled as though he knew full well there was about to be a reckoning.

"Mrs. Peebles," Beau said, using the same tone she would have when dealing with an overly familiar buck at the opera. "We'll need to set the nursery in order. Can you send up something for the child to eat and one of the maids to look after him?"

"I'll send Peg up to prepare the nursery," the housekeeper said with chilly hauteur before sweeping out, her ring of keys jangling with every step.

"Well," Beau said, addressing herself to the boy, "it appears that you may well be the straw that breaks the camel's back."

The child blinked, his large eyes ringed with sooty lashes just as his father's were. "No camel. Mokee."

Gareth stared at the cold food on his plate before refilling his wine glass. The meat had congealed in its sauce, the fat turning opaque. He'd foolishly thought his wife would join him. He'd held off eating, waiting for her to appear.

What the hell was he going to say to her?

He shoved the plate away and took another drink. Damn his brother. It was one thing to believe the world was your oyster. When you were the heir to an earldom, it was, more or less. But Souttar's utter belief that none of life's rules or England's laws applied to him was maddening.

How could you save such a man from himself? How could you control the damage he did? Everything he touched was in danger of exploding in his face like a mortar heaved over a castle wall and just lying there, smoldering.

If anyone ever found out what Souttar had done, what the two of them had conspired to cover up, it would be disastrous. Hell, it already was for one small boy, and quite possibly for his own marriage.

He'd seen Beau angry, offended, upset, but he'd never seen her hurt. Not like she had been today. This was a thousand times worse than the day that they'd encountered Lady Cook in the park, and Lord knew that had been awful enough. Something vital had been crushed right out of Beau today. Trust perhaps? Faith that she'd made the right decision? And it was all Souttar's fault.

Gareth finished the wine and went in search of his

wife. It wasn't as if he didn't know where to look. He found her down on her knees on the worn Turkey carpet in the nursery, surrounded by open trunks, sorting through a sea of clothing, toys, and linens.

The floor creaked beneath his foot, and she looked up from her trove. "Shhhh." She crossed her lips with her finger. "He's finally asleep."

Gareth searched her face. Nothing. She was carefully blank. Devoid of any hint of emotion. Was it mad that he would rather she railed at him? He stepped closer, careful to walk on the balls of his feet.

He looked down at the various stacks of garments. "What are you doing?"

"Sorting through all the things that Peebles brought down from the attic." She shook out a small blue gown, its long sleeves and large cuffs clearly from an earlier generation.

"Why?" Gareth stared down at the clutter. Very little of it appeared salvageable. It was just the ghosts of children past, remnants of unknown childhoods boxed up and forgot.

Beau shrugged and shook out the next garment, tossing it aside when she found it badly moth-eaten. "Someone has to. There was little enough in the boy's own trunk. Some of this can be made over for his use. It will at least get us by until more suitable clothing can be procured."

"Leave it to the maids then," he said, holding out a hand to help her up.

Beau's shoulders stiffened, and she pointedly ignored his hand. She held up a tiny yellow gown and then tossed it into what appeared to be the discard pile.

"Really, Beau. We'll hire one just for the boy. She can deal with all of his. With him. You needn't bother yourself. In fact, I'd prefer if you didn't." He felt like a monster the second the words were out of his mouth, but it was true nonetheless.

Beau's hands dropped to her lap, fingers clutching a small, padded pudding cap. She nodded her head, but she was biting her lips, holding them shut. Gareth looked away, sure she was about to cry.

"I don't know what else to say, Beau. Come downstairs and eat something."

"I'm not hungry." She tossed the pudding cap back into the trunk, her head still lowered, face averted.

Gareth tiptoed back to the door. She didn't want him there, and he had no desire to stay. He was unwelcome, unwanted, and utterly superfluous. In his own home. All because of a child who wasn't even his.

"What's his name?" Beau asked with a sniffle that clearly presaged tears.

"Jamie. James Gareth Sandison."

~≪ CHAPTER 30 ≫~

Jamie toddled through the ruins of the garden, trailing his leading strings behind him. Beau clutched her shawl about her shoulders to keep it from trailing likewise and followed him down the path.

Gareth had ridden out before she'd risen. Peebles said something about the master wanting to look over the oast houses where the hops were dried and stored. Beau had a vague understanding that the crop was valuable and had something to do with brewing, and she found herself resenting the fact that Gareth hadn't asked her to accompany him.

Not that she'd given him a chance to do so. For the first time since their marriage, she'd slept in her own bed. It had been cold, and slightly musty, and she'd lain awake half the night waiting for Gareth to storm in and carry her back to his bed.

But he hadn't done so.

Jamie tripped over his skirts and tumbled to the ground, his monkey flying out of his grasp and landing in the dirt. The boy lay there for a moment, quietly, before looking back at her. The moment he saw she was looking, he began to cry.

Unlike his pleas for his mother, this she knew how to deal with, having seen her nephews do the same any number of times. With a shake of her head, Beau scooped him up and put him back on his feet. She dusted him off and wiped away his tears with her thumbs.

"Little faker," she said, ruffling his dark curls. "We should put you on the stage."

Jamie blinked at her and then shook his head *no* quite decisively. One of the stable cats slunk by, and Jamie darted after it, abandoning his toy where it lay.

Beau picked up his monkey and shook it off. One of its eyes was lolling off to one side, and its rag stuffing was leaking out of a split seam along its side. It looked thoroughly disreputable, and like some child had likely loved it to death.

Before Jamie made it even halfway to the stables, the cat made good its escape by darting into the shrubbery. Jamie stopped and turned back to face her. His expression of confusion and consternation made the bubble inside her chest expand until her lungs felt crushed between it and her stays. She knew that look. Those brows. Jamie spotted his toy and ran stiffly back to her to reclaim it.

At the sound of hooves on gravel, they both turned toward the stable block. Jamie clutched her skirts and buried his face in them. Gareth swung out of the saddle and stood staring at them, disapproval leaking off him in waves.

Beau squared her shoulders and dropped one hand to

stroke Jamie's head. The boy was here. Pretending otherwise was simply ludicrous.

Gareth's expression hardened. Beau's pulse was racing. Her knees wobbled. Whatever it was that her husband expected of her—wanted of her—mothering his bastard wasn't any part of it.

After a long, pregnant moment, Gareth spun on his heel and marched toward the house, pale queue stark against the dark-fabric coat. Beau let out a breath that she hadn't realized she'd been holding.

"Shall we walk down to the cliffs and look at the ocean?" Beau said, loosening Jamie's grip on her skirts. The child didn't answer, but he clutched her offered hand and followed along as she led him down through the garden.

It seemed simple enough when she looked at it dispassionately. All she had to do was acquiesce to Gareth's command. Just let the servants take care of Jamie. Leave him upstairs. Pretend he didn't exist. Pretend nothing had changed.

It's what most women would do, after all. It was the sensible thing. But she didn't feel sensible at the moment. Mostly, she was angry. Angry at herself for being so easily upset by something that she should have known was a distinct possibility. Angry at Gareth for being exactly who everyone had always said he was, and angry at the world in general for disrupting her plans so thoroughly.

As they approached the cliff's edge, Jamie dropped her hand and Beau snatched up the leading strings of his gown, wrapping them securely around her hand. The tide was in, the water lapping directly at the cliff base.

Beau studied the spit of sand that twisted off toward the village. No sign of the shipwrecked dog today, just a fisherman dragging his boat up onto the beach.

The idea of writing to her mother for advice was risky. Too high a chance of the duke reading it also, and Beau simply wasn't prepared to face down her father again quite so soon. None of her friends would understand, and if their parents or husbands found out the topic of her letter, they'd be furious and scandalized. The virginal daughters and young matrons of the *ton* did not need to have their minds sullied with topics such as surprise bastards and questions of how best to care for them.

There was her sister-in-law, but what if Viola told Leo? Her brother was already furious and more than ready to murder Gareth given even the flimsiest of excuses. The last thing that was needed was more fuel for that fire.

Beau gazed out at the ocean, feeling suddenly very small and very alone. They might as well be living on a desert island. There was no help anywhere.

⊰ CHAPTER 31 ⊱

Riotous laugher spilled down the corridor, followed quickly by a giggling, muddy child running full-tilt, cockhorse between his knees. Jamie didn't even pause as he passed Gareth, and Gareth made no attempt to catch hold of him. He'd learned quickly enough that while the boy adored Beau, he was very much still under suspicion.

Their nursery maid, Peg, came rushing after him, hair straggling down around her face, mud smeared liberally across her apron. Gareth pressed himself to the paneling as the girl attempted a curtsey without stopping.

Beau appeared last of all, face rosy with mirth. She lurched to stop when she saw him, and the laughter went out of her eyes. Gareth did his best not to frown. Jamie had only been with them a week, and in that time, he'd found himself becoming a glowering beast. Everyone, including his wife, had taken to avoiding him, which didn't make him any more inclined to look upon the boy favorably.

"He slipped out of the house and went to visit Frederick,"

Beau said, wiping at the mud on her own skirts. "And he seems to have got into the sty itself this time."

"Likes pigs, does he?"

"Not as much as dogs or horses. Gulliver won't let me touch him, but he allows Jamie to hang upon him, pull his ears and tail. He's even started to follow the boy about. Yesterday, Jamie climbed on top of the poor thing and tried to ride him, which is rather what I think he might have done to Frederick today."

"Sounds like poor Frederick to me," Gareth said with feeling.

Beau tilted her head, studying him as though she were about to ask for something. Gareth's pulse repeated upon itself unevenly. He wanted back into her good graces, back into her bed, but he hadn't been able to work out how to effect such a turn.

"The boy needs a pony," she said, putting her hand on his arm.

Squeals erupted from the nursery, followed by a long wail and a clearly audible protest about being forced to bathe. Beau's smile flared back to life. Gareth felt a sudden stab of envy. How had he been displaced so thoroughly? She should have been smiling for him, at him. He missed being the cynosure of her world. Once a man had experienced that, had been that, how could he be happy with anything less?

"Isn't he too young for a pony?" If the boy got hurt, it would be him that she would blame. And all boys got hurt when they got their first pony.

"I was put into the saddle at about his age."

"Put there?" Gareth said with a snort of disbelief. "Or

you climbed up and refused to give your brother's pony back?"

She grinned, and he felt it all the way to his toes. He hadn't seen her smile at him like that since the boy's arrival. "It's not fair that you know my brother well enough to be privy to all my childhood escapades."

Gareth shrugged. "Horse theft is a serious offense. Even when the horse in question is a pony the owner has outgrown. And as I remember it, you were riding that very pony the first time we met."

Beau bit her lip, white teeth sinking into the rosy flesh in a way that made his hands itch to touch her. She looked chagrined, but a wicked twinkle lurked in her eyes.

"A boy's not ready for a pony until he's breeched," Gareth said, staving her off.

"Those are just the clothes he came with. Jamie's out of diapers. We're going to have to replace them soon enough anyway, and there's no reason for him to continue being dressed as a baby."

She took a step toward him, breasts swelling above her bodice as she leaned against him. The scent of her made him dizzy. The electric shock of her touch had his cock flaring to attention.

"Find him a pony, Gareth. Teaching him to ride is something a boy's father should do. Every boy deserves that."

Gareth's delight in the moment drained away, and Beau must have sensed the change in him, for she stepped back, hands moving to fidget with the closure of her bodice. Another wail of protest sent her scurrying toward the nursery without so much as a glance in his direction.

Gareth leaned back against the wall, cursing under his breath. Teaching a boy to ride *was* something his father should do, but he wasn't Jamie's father. And nothing so far had made the pretense that he was one jot more real.

~ CHAPTER 32 ~

Granby put his collar up to ward off the damp of the coming storm. Far above, at the top of the cliff, Lady Boudicea stood staring off toward France. As beautiful as ever. And she should have been his. Her and her fortune.

He swallowed down the bitter taste that flooded his mouth. He'd been sure she'd loved him. Sure she'd see the romance in their flight. Instead, she'd ruined his life.

He stared up at her, watching her skirts flap like sails in the wind. He'd traveled all the way from the Scottish border, the thirst for justice as strong now as it ever had been. How to achieve restitution and satisfaction had been the question. It wasn't cheap, financing an abduction. If Nowlin and his friends hadn't practically thrown their fortunes at him in the gaming hells of Dublin, he'd have had no chance at his revenge.

His options had dwindled. Killing her wasn't enough. It was too easy. He might enjoy the headiness of the moment, but it would be over too quickly.

Lady Boudicea deserved to suffer for what she'd done

to him. Being made an early widow wasn't nearly punishment enough. Especially when widowhood came with the security of fortune. At her age, she'd recover from the loss.

He wanted her alone. Ruined. Hopeless. He wanted her to understand exactly how he'd felt when she betrayed him.

"Who's the child?" Granby asked, narrowing his eyes to better see the tiny figure in Lady Boudicea's arms.

"Village gossip says it's her husband's bastard," Nowlin said.

"Really?" Granby replied, an idea flaring to life. "I'd say it was just as likely—based on her behavior, both previously and now—that we are looking at the true parent."

Nowlin stared at him stupidly.

"A fast, sporting girl, known to flirt and stray beyond acceptable behavior. A girl like that is capable of anything. Even foisting her bastard upon a husband who was bought and paid for. Don't you think?"

Nowlin mumbled something, and Granby snapped, "What? Speak up."

"I said I wouldn't know, sir."

"Well, I rather imagine the world will think so too. Or at least enough of them to scandalize both their families and set them all to fighting."

"Why?"

Granby shook his head. "Because a united front is impenetrable. That was our mistake. We need them all at each others' throats. Full of hatred and distrust. We need them fighting, not talking. And we need to find out more about the origins of that child."

"How? Where do we look? The mother could be anywhere."

"You said his brother brought it here?"

Nowlin nodded. "That's the story the maid told anyway when I bought her a pint last market day."

"Very well, we start there. Somewhere there's a witness. A story. Perhaps even a scandal. Don't look surprised. Fathers make arrangements for bastards all the time. Foster them out with a tenant family. Dump them in a charity school. What they don't do is take them into their homes. Not without a compelling reason, and certainly not hot upon the heels of their marriage."

✺ CHAPTER 33 ✺

The pane of glass was cold against his forehead. Gareth leaned harder against the window, trying to keep his wife in sight as long as possible. She was taking advantage of a break in the dismal weather that they'd been having to consult with a few of the older tenants about what the gardens had looked like in their prime.

The ancient advisors were slowly meandering about, hands sculpting visions in the air. Beau was busy taking notes, pausing occasionally to sketch. Whatever her feelings about him—and at this point, he wasn't entirely sure what they were—she clearly wasn't planning on running home to her parents.

That fact should have been a relief, but he couldn't seem to take comfort in it. Beau was making Morton Hall hers. Laying claim to it. Building a life for herself here that didn't necessarily include him. His face seemed to always be pressed to a window of one sort or another, the demarcation of his world and hers becoming more and more concrete.

Beau had set up her own little fiefdom in the nursery wing. She ate her meals there. Spent her days there. Never seemed to go anywhere without Jamie clinging to her skirts like a barnacle.

He'd never seen anything like it. Most mothers were more than content to leave their children in the care of their nursery maid or governess. His own certainly had. They'd been lucky to see her a few times a week. And even then only for a few minutes. A kiss, a scold, very occasionally a slice of plum cake. That is what his mother had been. A magnificent visitation.

There was no reason at all for Beau to expend so much time and energy on a child who wasn't even hers. No reason other than the fact that it gave her an excuse to avoid seeing him. And whenever he crossed their path, the resentment in her eyes was enough to stop him from joining them.

They had barely spoken in days. Not a word since she'd asked him to get the boy a pony. Something had shifted in that moment, hardening within her. It was as if she'd realized that her vision for their life wasn't a shared one, and she'd decided to forge ahead with her own regardless.

Beau continued to sleep in her own chamber, and he simply didn't want to know—couldn't bring himself to find out—if she was barring her door against him. It was better not to know. Better to live in ignorance, imagining himself free to join her, even if it wasn't true.

Beau and her guests rounded the corner of the house, and Gareth pulled himself away from the window, returning to the open ledger on his desk. Mathematics had been a strong point at Harrow, but he'd never had to keep track of so many disparate streams of revenue and so many petty outlays. It was no wonder his father employed stewards, land agents, *and* a secretary. One estate was a great deal of work. Multiple estates, most much larger than this one, must have been the devil to keep track of.

He was struggling to get the household accounts to balance—there was something seriously wrong with the receipts for candles; they couldn't possibly use so many at such a pace—when the door opened and Beau wandered in. She had her nose planted in her sketchbook, and Jamie was blissfully absent. She bumped into one of the chairs near the fireplace and stopped with a thoroughly unladylike curse.

Gareth chuckled, and her head snapped around. She blinked and looked about confusedly, like a sleepwalker unceremoniously awakened.

"Lost?" he said, drinking in the sight of her. Her hair was tumbled from the wind, dark curls falling in a riot all around her face, making the green of her eyes almost glow.

"Turned about, certainly," she replied, tucking her sketchbook under her arm. "I could have sworn I was headed toward the kitchen block."

"Took the wrong door out of the drawing room. I've done the same on multiple occasions. The house is a damned labyrinth."

Beau nodded, arm locked tight over the sketchbook as though she didn't want him to see it. "I wanted to ask Mrs. Peebles about the kitchen garden. See if there was anything needed there."

"Show me what you've been working on." Could he

keep her talking? Keep her with him for even a quarter of an hour? Make her remember that he wasn't a villain and didn't deserve to be treated like one?

She hesitated, one cheek sucked in as she weighed her answer. Gareth raised his brows questioningly, hopefully. Her shoulders sagged slightly, and one corner of her mouth twitched as though she were fighting a smile.

"I've no idea what it will cost," she said, stepping toward the desk and laying her sketchbook down atop the ledger. She flipped it open, revealing a diagram of the beds, all the sections clearly labeled with letters that corresponded to lists on the opposite page.

She traced her fingers over the sketch, smudging it slightly. The poesy ring on her finger glinted in the sunlight. A bolt of pure possessiveness lanced through him. His wife. His. He was making a muddle of it, but that fact remained unchanged.

Gareth put a hand on her hip and leaned forward to study the plan. "Do you really want to keep it so formal?"

She pressed a little closer as she bent over her sketch. The soft tuberose scent she wore addled his brain. It worked its way through his bloodstream, coiling painfully in his groin.

"We've enough real wilderness all around us," she said. "It seems silly to create a false one. And such a garden wouldn't suit the house."

"There is that." Gareth nodded his head in agreement. Beneath his fingertips, he could just make out the wales of her stays through the fine linen of her gown. He spread his hand wide over her ribs. Beau's small intake of breath set his pulse drumming loudly in his ears.

She started to pull away. Gareth held tight, swinging her about so she was facing him, trapped between him and the desk. He put his knees on either side of hers, hemming her in.

"You've been avoiding me," he said, holding her perched on the edge of the desk.

Beau just looked at him. Her gaze dropped to his lap, where the tented fall of his breeches left no doubt of his desire.

"I've been giving you time to think," she said, voice tinged with repressed excitement.

Gareth smiled slyly up at her and slid his hands up and under her skirts. When she didn't pull away, he maneuvered his knees between hers and pushed them apart, hands riding up the soft skin along the inside of her thighs.

"Oh, I've been thinking," he replied.

Beau's breath hitched, and her hands locked on his shoulders. Gareth continued his slow path north until his fingers slipped into the already slick folds at the apex of her thighs.

Her grip tightened. "Clearly," she said, the word breathy, as though she'd been running.

Gareth smiled. There she was. His little libertine. She just needed reminding of what was waiting for her in his bed, reminding that she missed him, wanted him, needed him.

Gareth freed himself from his breeches and stood, taking her back onto the desk. He fit himself to her and thrust in, filling her with one hard stroke. Beau cried out, wrapped her legs around him, and threw back her head, hair tangling in the inkwell and quills.

"Don't thrash about," Gareth whispered against her ear. "You're in danger of making a mess."

Beau strained beneath him, pushing back, matching the rhythm that he established. Gareth let all thought go, a series of frantic thrusts taking him irrevocably to his release. Beau pulsed and throbbed, close but not yet done.

Gareth stilled, concentrating on the delicious feeling of being inside her. Beau made a small sound of protest and rocked against him. Gareth had a sudden wicked thought. What was his opera dancer's advice for controlling a lover? Always leave them wanting more?

He propped himself up on his elbows and began disentangling her hair. Beau's legs gripped his hips, and she ground against him. Gareth kissed the side of her neck as he freed the inkwell from one last curl.

"Gareth." The note of protest, of entreaty, was clear.

"You want your turn?" Gareth's grin turned into a chuckle at the sight of her indignant expression. "Good."

He stood and buttoned up his breeches. Beau just lay there, staring at him. He traced one finger along the inside of her exposed knee, playing idly with her garter.

"You've got two choices, Beau." He tugged down her skirts and pulled her to her feet. "You can go upstairs, put your hand between your thighs and think of me, or you can come to me tonight and let me finish what I started."

Beau snatched up her sketchbook, threw her husband one last aggrieved look, and marched out of his study. Her hands were shaking with anger, but her knees were wobbly for an entirely different reason.

Her thighs were wet and sticky. The ache of frustrated

passion redoubled with every step. She could throttle him! She would throttle him. He deserved nothing less for such a trick.

She reached her room, where her maid was busy reattaching a flounce to one of Beau's gowns. Lucy looked up, needle paused in the air like a moth.

"Lucy," Beau said, doing her best to appear calm. "Please fetch me a basin of hot water."

The maid wove the needle into the fabric and set her sewing aside. "Yes, my lady. Would you like me to send tea up as well?"

"Yes, but have it fetched to the nursery. I'll be going there as soon as I've washed the dirt from my hands."

Lucy nodded, sketched the kind of half-hearted curtsey only a servant of long employ could ever hope to get away with, and departed. Beau dropped into the chair that her maid had just vacated. She could almost feel Gareth's hands on her skin, almost still feel him inside her. Her body pulsed weakly, and she let out her breath with a shuddering sigh.

Damn him. No matter what she did for the rest of the day, she'd be thinking about him. Thinking about going to him, about how much she wanted him, how she craved his touch...

Damn him. Damn him. Damn him.

❧ CHAPTER 34 ❧

Granby caught the eye of the innkeeper and raised two fingers, calling for more ale for himself and the man sprawled across from him in the inglenook. Drunk, loquacious, and full of gossip. Exactly what he'd been hoping to find when he'd traced the child's path back to the Earl of Roxwell's estate in Yorkshire.

There was only one inn within easy reach of the estate so it hadn't been hard to track down a likely source of information. All he'd had to do was wait and stand a few rounds to the likeliest candidates. When a groom in the earl's employ had broached his third pint and begun loudly talking about his recent trip south, Granby had paid and invited the man to join him by the fire.

"What prompted such a trip at this time of year?" Granby said. "The mud alone must have made the journey quite dismal. I wouldn't be traveling myself, except that I got word my mother is very ill."

"Some Scot," the groom said, ale sloshing off the edge of the newly arrived mug. "Showed up with a brat, claiming it was Mr. Sandison's. You should have seen Lord Souttar." The man paused and glanced around the taproom before adding sotto voice, "Desperate to keep his father from finding out."

"Why would Lord Souttar care if their father found out his brother had a bastard?"

The footman grinned and downed half the mug of ale. "Wasn't the babe that caused the stir. It was the mother."

"The mother?"

The footman frowned into his beer. "Not su'posed to tell anyone. Hs'lordship made me swear."

Granby signaled for another mug. The man finished what was in his current one and reached unsteadily for the next.

"His lordship made you swear to keep it from the earl?" Granby prompted.

The footman nodded. "Big secret. Mother's not dead. Makes Mr. Sandison a bi—a big—a—a something terrible."

"I think bigamist is the word you're looking for."

∽ CHAPTER 35 ∽

"My sister's what?" Lord Leonidas struggled to contain his temper. The banked coals of betrayal that he'd been carefully maintaining flared into open flame.

"Bastard," Roland Devere said grimly, mouth pressed into a hard line. "That's the latest on-dit. Heard it from several people last night at Lady Dalrymple's. Everyone claiming not to believe it, but whispering about it all the same."

"Where do these kinds of rumors come from? It's ridiculous. When would Beau have had time to accomplish such a feat without the entire world witnessing it?" Leo raked both hands through his hair, gripping his skull hard. This was madness. Pure and simple.

"Proof is hardly needed." Devere shook his head slightly, his own annoyance clear. He'd been the only one to stand by Sandison, and this was his reward. "And she does disappear for months every year. She spends the entire winter out of sight in Scotland."

"*Everyone* spends months in the country," Leo protested.

Devere leaned in across the table, his expression utterly serious. "Beau's sudden marriage to a younger son with no fortune or prospects. That alone was enough to set tongues wagging. And now there's a baby always at her knee. People are saying Sandison was bought and paid for. And that you had a hand in it. Helping your closest friend to a honey fall, and your sister out of a horrible predicament."

"That's absurd." Leo ground his teeth, repressing the urge to take his frustration out on his friend. Coming to blows with Devere wouldn't help anything.

"Agreed," Devere said. "But just because it's absurd, doesn't mean it can be laughed off. What the hell is Sandison thinking? It's not surprising that he might have a bastard—"

"Or four," Leo interjected sourly.

"—tucked away, but even Sandison wouldn't be fool enough to try and house it with his wife. Least of all when he and Beau were already drowning in scandal broth. Lady Cook was in alt as she spoke of it."

"I'm going to kill him," Leo said, rising quickly enough that his chair scraped loudly across the floor, drawing the attention of the rest of the room. Leo stared out at them. His friends. The League. Sandison's friends, too. Or they had been, until Leo had blackballed him. His gaze locked with Anthony Thane. He could tell by the man's expression that he'd heard the same ugly rumor and felt just as powerless to do anything about it.

Leo turned and strode toward the door. Anthony Thane caught up with him in the vestibule as he struggled into his greatcoat.

"Don't make it worse," Thane said, putting a restraining hand on his arm.

"It couldn't be any worse," Leo replied. Trust Thane to want to attack the issue calmly. With Thane, everything could be conquered with logic and wit. All those years in the Commons had deafened him to the call to action.

Thane shook his head. "It could *always* be worse. If life's taught me anything, it's taught me that simple lesson."

Leo arrived home, Thane's warning still ringing in his ears, to find his wife pacing the length of the carpet in their drawing room, a letter clutched in her hand. She spun about and held out the piece of foolscap as though it were a snake.

"This came while you were out."

Leo turned the letter over. It bore no name. Just their London address. He unfolded it and scanned its contents. His blood went from boiling to icy cold by the time he reached the final paragraph.

"I don't believe a word of it," Viola said. "Sandison wouldn't do such a thing. Not to Beau. Not to *you*."

Leo crumpled the letter in his fist, the sound satisfying in the moment. "I'm beginning to wonder if I know Gareth Sandison at all."

Viola shook her head, took the note from him, and tossed it onto the fire. The flames licked over it, slowly turning it to char. "I shouldn't have shown it to you. I should have burnt it the moment I read it."

Leo pulled her into his arms and rested his chin on the top of her head. She was the one solid, trustworthy thing in his world. "Not showing me wouldn't have helped. If Sandison really did already have a wife—"

"Then I'll kill him myself," Viola said. "But I can't believe it of him. I simply can't."

"Won't."

Viola gave him a little shake. "Can't," she said with single-minded determination, as though willing the tale to be false could make it so. "And you don't believe it either. You're just too angry to think at the moment."

"Just for you, I'll hold off killing him until we have proof, but if a similar note has been sent to the duke..."

"It will take your father at least a week to get here from Lochmaben. And another day or two beyond that to reach Sandison."

"So we have our deadline," Leo said, feeling a chill run up his spine. A week. Seven short days to find proof of innocence or guilt. And no idea where to start, except with Sandison himself.

❧ CHAPTER 36 ❧

The winter sun broke weakly through the bed curtains, barely diffusing the shadows where it trailed across the bedclothes. Beau lay still, Gareth curled around her, and watched the light move slowly toward them as the minutes passed. Any moment it would hit Gareth's eyes and wake him.

It had taken two days for her to reconcile herself to his machinations and return to his bed, but she couldn't even pretend to regret that she'd done so. Sleeping alone had punished her every bit as much as it had him. And to no real purpose, except that she'd been feeling prideful.

He nuzzled sleepily into the back of her neck, fingers playing almost idly with her nipple. His hips rocked against her, his erection riding the cleft of her buttocks.

After a moment, his hand left her breast, sliding down to lift her leg, hooking her calf back over his knee. Fingers between her thighs, cock now riding the valley between them, Gareth kissed his way up her shoulder. His mouth was hot on her neck, teeth scraping lightly over her skin.

Beau twisted her head just enough so she could kiss him. Gareth curled his body against hers, and then he was inside her, the shallow penetration just enough to make her crave more. His hand cupped her sex, holding her in place for his thrusts.

She pushed her knee higher, opened herself wider. Gareth's fingers found her clitoris, riding slickly over the swollen peak with every rock of their hips. Beau's release washed over her like a wave—soft, sudden, utterly different from the wild crash engendered by a frantic coupling.

Gareth held still long enough for the small tremors to abate, and then rolled her under him, his knees on the outside of hers, and found his own release with long, slow strokes that left Beau shattered and boneless.

"Morning, love." He kissed her on the shoulder, his weight still pressing her down into their newly arrived mattress.

Beau stretched out her neck, utterly content. "It can't be morning yet."

"I heard the clock chime eight some time ago," he said as he slid off her.

Beau made a wordless sound of disgust and buried her face in the pillow. They'd been up half the night. She had no intention of getting out of bed until at least noon.

She heard the floorboards creak, and she cracked one eye open just in time to see Gareth pull on his banyan. The heavy silk slid around him, masking the long, lean lines of his body.

Hers. Beau smiled to herself. Whatever he may have done previously, he was hers now, and she had every intention of keeping him. He glanced over, caught her watching him, and smiled. She knew that smile. Had seen it often enough on his face when he looked at other women. Lazy, self-satisfied, possessive.

It was madness to feel warmed by it, but it was impossible to resist.

Beau kept Jamie well back from the cliff's edge as they took their afternoon walk. He pointed excitedly to the roiling whitecaps racing toward the beach.

"Waves," Beau said. "Waves on the ocean."

"Jamie go ocean."

Beau shook her head. "Not today, little man." She tugged back on his leading strings, wrapping them securely around her hand when he tried to pull away. "Today Jamie will have to make do with the garden before he goes with Peg to take a nap."

Jamie wrinkled his nose, his expression remarkably like his father's when Gareth was feeling disgruntled. Whatever Gareth's reason for ignoring the child, questionable paternity wasn't among them. Jamie was clearly a Sandison.

"Mokee go ocean?"

"Monkey most certainly does *not* want to go to the ocean. Monkeys don't like water."

Jamie's face fell and then his eyes lit with clear intent. "Mokee take nap. Jamie go horses."

Beau laughed and knelt down beside him. There was a child after her own heart. Horses were far better than naps. "Would you like to go see the horses?"

Jamie nodded, dark curls bouncing all about his head.

"Then go to the horses we shall." She scooped him up and turned toward the stable, only to find her path blocked by two very familiar faces. Granby and Nowlin.

Granby's smile didn't hide the malice in the eye she'd left him. Beau took a step back and let Jamie slide to the ground. She glanced at the house. Not a servant in sight.

"Good afternoon, Lady Boudicea," Granby said, bowing formally, as though he were paying a call.

"Jamie," Beau said, not taking her eyes off the men. "Go back to the house. Back to Peg."

Jamie's grip on her hand tightened.

"No need for the little mite to cause alarm." Granby snapped his fingers and pointed from Nowlin to Jamie. The Irishman reached for the boy, and Beau lashed out with a fist, landing a lucky and unexpected hit that sent him sprawling onto the wet grass. Jamie clutched her skirts and shrieked at the top of his lungs.

Nowlin scrambled up, wiping mud from his breeches. He and Granby moved in from opposite sides. Granby grabbed hold of her arm while Nowlin plucked Jamie up.

Beau struggled free but tripped as Granby caught her by the skirts and yanked. She pulled away, stumbled, and then she was falling.

The water felt like stone when she hit it, knocking the air from her lungs. It took a moment to realize that she wasn't dead, another to recognize the sensation of sinking and to combat the overwhelming urge to scream.

Her skirts dragged her down, making it nearly impossible to kick. Beau fought her way toward the surface, clawing at the water. Her lungs burned. The pain—the need to breathe—growing more intense by the second. She broke the surface, swallowing air and water both, and sank back under, choking.

Something hard and sharp caught her arm, and this time she did scream, losing what little air she'd managed to inhale. She was pushed up. Borne up. She gasped for air, hands disconcertingly full of fur.

Beau took another breath, and the panic started to recede. Gulliver circled, whining softly, pushing her up whenever she started to sink. Beau looked about frantically. No tiny body bobbed in waves. No toy monkey either.

The dog nudged her as a wave broke over her, thrusting her down. Beau grabbed ahold of him, arms around his neck. He turned about and swam powerfully toward shore.

Men splashed into the water as they approached the beach. Beau struggled to her feet, using Gulliver as a crutch. Someone threw a blanket smelling of fish and smoke about her shoulders, and Beau clutched it to her, teeth chattering as the wind raised gooseflesh all over her body.

She pushed her hair from her face and looked up at the top of the cliffs. She could see no one peering down. Had they taken Jamie? Left him alone on the cliffs? Had they watched as she was rescued? Or had they fled the moment that she'd tumbled over the cliff?

"My lady?" one of the men said, face puckered with concern.

"Poor woman's lucky to be alive," another one responded.

The dog sat at her feet, pressed close, rumbling low in the back of its throat whenever any of the men got too close. Beau put a hand on its head, and it quieted.

"Don't growl at me, beast," the second man said, wind-chapped face stern. "Get her ladyship back to the vicar's house, John. You, Henry, run up to the Hall and tell them we've got her safe. Have them send a coach and a change of clothes."

"Henry," Beau said through chattering teeth, "tell them to look for Jamie. He was with me. He's up there by himself now." Or she hoped he was. Better that than with Granby.

Men darted off in several directions. The man who seemed to be in charge offered his arm, and Beau took it, shushing the dog again as she did so. Gulliver protested softly all the way to the vicar's cottage and then flung itself down across the doorway when the vicar refused to allow it inside.

The vicar's housekeeper chased Beau into her own quarters and ruthlessly stripped her wet garments off. "You can wear my flannel wrapper, ma'am. I mean *my lady.*"

"Either is fine, Mrs. Batey," Beau said, reaching for the proffered robe. "I'm not about to stand on ceremony. Not today."

"You tuck in by the fire. And I'll be back with something hot for you to drink quick as a cat can lick its ear."

"Thank you. Have they come back from the Hall yet?"

"No, my lady. It's a steep hill, and they were on foot. They'll be a while yet."

Beau huddled by the fire, toes and fingers cold on the inside, skin painfully hot as she held them near the flames. The numbness in her extremities gave way to full-fledged pain as she slowly warmed up. Everything ached. Every joint. Her head throbbed as though it had been used as an anvil.

Mrs. Batey returned with a pot of tea, Gareth hard upon her heels. Beau flung herself into his arms, and he held her tight. "What the devil happened?"

Beau opened her mouth and nothing but a sob came out. Gareth forced her back into the chair, pulled a flask from his pocket, and dropped down beside the chair, his expression harried.

"Brandy," he said. "Drink it."

Beau took the flask and drank, the fumes nearly choking her.

"All of it," Gareth said, pushing her hand back to her mouth with his own. He tipped it up, so she had to either drink it or wear it. Beau pushed his hand away and drained it.

"Jamie?" she said when she'd finished, knowing to expect the worst. Granby. Her past come back to haunt them this time. Hers, not Gareth's.

Gareth shook his head. "No sign of him. No one seems to have known either of you were missing until Mr. Dobbs showed up claiming they'd fished you out of the sea."

"They had nothing to do with it." Beau clutched the robe tighter around herself as the brandy burned inside her belly. "It was the dog. Gulliver. I'd have drowned if he hadn't swum out and pulled me in."

"What happened, brat?"

"Granby. Granby happened," she said bleakly, tears leaking uncontrollably down her cheeks, so hot that they stung. "It's been him all along. Nowlin was his, and now this. I think he's taken Jamie. What could he possibly want with him?"

❧ CHAPTER 37 ❧

W hat the hell did you bring that along for?" Granby asked, staring with revulsion at the squalling child clutched in Padrig's arms.

Padrig looked down at the little boy. He'd wrapped him in his coat and chased after Granby's coach on horseback. "You said grab them. I thought you wanted him."

Granby rubbed his temples. "A misstatement. Clearly. I wanted Lady Boudicea. That," he said and waved one hand dismissively at the boy, "you could have chucked over the cliff after her. Should have, as a matter of fact."

Padrig's mouth fell open. "You can't just drop a baby over a cliff, sir."

"Why not? Once we'd lost Lady Boudicea, there was no reason to keep the child. I'm certainly not going to cart it all the way back to London. You took it. You get rid of it."

❧ CHAPTER 38 ❧

Beau's breathing steadied as she dropped off to sleep. Gareth loosened his grip and let her slide down beside him on the bed. She'd been disturbingly quiet until they'd entered the house, but once she'd started crying, she'd been unable to stop.

She'd sobbed until she'd begun hiccupping, face buried in his chest, the child's toy monkey locked in her hand. Gareth hadn't the slightest idea what to say to comfort her. She'd been flung off a cliff. Had nearly drowned. And Jamie was gone, perhaps forever.

Granby could be anywhere by now, though there were a couple of options more likely than the rest. Gareth wiped a thumb over his wife's tear-stained cheek. Whatever he was going to do, he had to do it now. Every minute put Jamie further out of their reach.

He slipped out from under Beau and tucked her in, twitching the bed curtains closed behind him. The best thing he could do for her at the moment was let her sleep. From beside the fire, the giant Newfoundland silently wagged its tail. Gareth crouched down and rubbed its head. Gulliver had earned his place, and he'd seemingly decided to transfer his trust of Jamie to the rest of them.

Dover was the most immediate concern. If he could get there before the next packet left, he could at least rule out a flight to France. If they'd fled to London, there was no catching them now anyway and finding them would be next to impossible.

Gareth left the dog to guard his wife and went to order Monty saddled. He dashed off a quick note for Beau and instructed Peebles to give it to her should she wake while he was gone. He claimed the reins from a groom, checked the girth out of habit, and swung into the saddle.

It was getting dark already. He was in for one hell of a dismal ride. Gareth loosened the reins and gave Monty his head. The gelding lengthened his stride, breaking into a flat-out run.

He reached Dover well after dark. Monty was slick with sweat and breathing like a bellows. Gareth reined him in, and the gelding dropped into a walk.

By the time they reached the docks, the horse had cooled. Gareth handed him over to an ostler at the largest inn and went inside to question the innkeeper. The man shook his head. No one-eyed man, and no one with a small boy in tow. The results were the same at every other inn.

All the same, Gareth waited at the quay and watched as the passengers piled aboard the morning packet. No sign of Granby, Nowlin, or Jamie.

Bloody-holy-fucking-hell.

Dover had been his best hope. They could be any-where. Traveling to anywhere. They could have run for

London, the largest city in the world. A city rife with almost impenetrable slums. Or they could be bound for Nowlin's own country. Ireland might as well be the moon. He'd have no chance at all of tracing them there. Or they could simply disappear into the English countryside.

A sick feeling roiled through him. He couldn't turn to his family. Souttar had seen to that. Gareth's mouth was suddenly dry. He was trapped in a web of half-truths and necessary lies.

The precariousness of his exile hit him like a physical blow. It had burned like salt in a wound, but he'd convinced himself that it wasn't as serious as it seemed. That there was time to fix it. But there wasn't. He needed The League, and he needed them now, which meant he needed to somehow get Beau's brother to not just forgive him but to stand with him.

When he finally arrived back at the Hall, it was well past noon, Monty being unable to sustain a second mad dash across the countryside. The house was utterly quiet. He handed his hat and coat to Peebles.

"Lady Boudicea?"

"Still abed, sir."

Gareth took the stairs two at a time. He found his wife's maid darning stockings in his room. She took one look at him, scooped up her work basket, and whisked herself out the door. Smart girl. Beau was unlikely to take the news of his failure well.

He pulled the bed curtains aside just enough to peer inside. There was nothing but a lump under the coverlet to tell him Beau was there. The dog was curled up protectively beside her, its giant head resting on top her.

"They weren't at Dover," Beau said, not bothering to emerge. The flat conviction of her statement was like a slap.

"No, they weren't at Dover."

Beau didn't respond. She didn't rail at him or demand what he intended to do next. She didn't declare that she, herself, was going to find them. If anything, she disappeared further into the mattress.

Gareth felt a stab of concern. He'd been expecting to return to the warrior queen, to hell and brimstone and demands for action. Something was very, very wrong, and he hadn't the slightest idea how to go about fixing it.

"Beau?"

"It's my fault. My fault. Mine. All of it. All of this. My fault. Leo warned me."

Gareth put a knee on the bed and attempted to roll her over. She shrugged him off.

"Don't touch me!"

The dog whined, looking at him anxiously.

"Beau." Gareth knew he sounded exasperated, but he couldn't help it. She was being ridiculous. This was no one's fault. Least of all hers.

She flipped over, pushing the covers back as she did so, and glared at him. "I should never have married you."

Gareth slipped into bed beside her, displacing the dog, which got down with a grumpy sigh and went to flop beside the hearth. It was well after midnight, and this was the first she'd seen of him since she'd made her cutting pronouncement. She hadn't gone after him because she'd meant it. She should never have married him. Should never have used him to solve her own problem. But she had, and this was the result. Three lives ruined, and no going back. No fixing things.

She didn't think that she could bear it. She'd wanted to make him happy, wanted to be happy. But happiness seemed an impossibility under the circumstances. A hollow bubble of panic and worry was slowly expanding inside her chest, choking off reason and logic.

He locked her to him, chest to back, arm clamped across her waist as though she might float away. "I don't know what's going on in that head of yours, brat. It's not your fault Jamie's gone. It's Granby's. I'll get Jamie back. Promise."

Beau grasped his hand with both of hers and held on tightly. She wanted to believe him. "You were right," she said quietly. "I should have left Jamie alone. He'd be safe and sound in the nursery if I had."

"That's neither here nor there." Gareth smoothed her hair back from her shoulder and rested his cheek along hers, the faint burr of stubble reminding her what a very long day they'd both had.

"It's me Granby wants, not Jamie." Everything that had happened was her fault. There was no other way of looking at it. It all came down to her.

"Which is why you're not to leave the house. You're going to stay here, with an army of servants guarding you, while I go to London for help."

"I can't stay here and do nothing, Gareth." She'd go mad locked inside the house with nothing to do but fret and wonder what was happening.

"Against your nature to do so, I know. But I'm asking you to all the same. Please, Beau? I can't do what needs to be done if I'm worried that something might happen to you."

Beau pushed his arm away and climbed out of bed. She paced across the room, wincing as her feet touched the icy floor. Why wouldn't he listen? Her fault. Her responsibility. She couldn't sit idly home like a princess in a tower. She'd done enough of that already.

Gareth threw off the bedclothes with a huff and came after her. Beau dropped down into a chair before he could manhandle her back into bed. It would be so easy for him to make her forget everything, at least for a short while. But she didn't want to forget. She'd done enough of that already.

"Do you even want your son back?" Beau said, horrified by the accusatory tone of her own voice. The question had been lurking in the back of her mind all day, and it had slipped out of its own volition.

Gareth's expression hardened, but he didn't answer her, and she couldn't be sure if he was repulsed by her asking, or if it was self-loathing, because she'd come too close to the truth. He just spun on his heel and stalked into his dressing room.

The clink of glass was followed by the distinctive sound of splashing liquid. The squeak of a door was next, and then the sound of his valet's sleepy voice. Gareth's reply was impossible to make out, but the rustle of a man getting dressed was unmistakable.

Beau tucked her freezing feet up under her and worried her thumbnail with her teeth. She'd gone too far. True or not, she should never have said it. Gareth deserved better from her.

Gulliver put his head in her lap, and she smoothed her hand over the tangled fur. Beau yawned and let her head rest on the winged back of the chair. Gareth might not have embraced the addition of Jamie to the household, but he'd done his duty by him. Accusing him of being glad the boy was gone was unjust. Unjust, and unkind.

She woke stiff and shivering in the wee hours of the morning. The predawn glow illuminated the windows, casting hazy shadows across the room. Beau glanced at the bed, but there was no sign of Gareth. She grabbed her wrapper and slippers and went in search of him. She owed him an apology.

Like as not, he'd got drunk as David's sow and was sleeping it off in his study. She hurried downstairs, but when she got to his study, there was no sign of him. He'd not been in the drawing room or Great Hall either, both of which she'd had to pass through.

She ran back upstairs to check the warren of bed-chambers. He was not in her room, nor any of the spare bedchambers. Taking a deep breath, she forced herself to check the nursery. Quiet, dark, and stone cold.

Furious and worried, she was headed to the barn when Peebles, nightcap askew on his bald pate, musket in hand, stumbled into her path. He lowered the gun with an expression of horror.

"My lady? I thought we were under attack."

"No. I was just looking for Mr. Sandison."

Peebles's brow furrowed. "The master left for London several hours ago."

⊰ CHAPTER 39 ⊱

He was going to lose her. Gareth circled the block for the third time, worry over Beau clouding his mind, making it impossible to formulate a proper argument to put to her brother. The wind picked up, and he turned up the collar of his coat.

If he didn't find Jamie, Beau would never forgive him. She'd withdraw even further, cut him out, perhaps even leave him outright. They could never go back to how things had been before.

And Jamie, poor unwanted boy, deserved better from everyone. He certainly deserved better from the uncle who had conspired to deny him his rightful place in the world. If he wasn't to be the future Earl of Roxwell, at least he could be the cosseted son of Gareth's household. Beau hadn't been the one to deny Jamie that—he had.

His circuit brought him back around to Lord Leonidas's house. Still unsure of what he was going to say, Gareth grasped the knocker and employed it several times. The door opened, and the butler's expression slid from impersonal disinterest to unmistakable hostility in an instant. It was a subtle shift. A hardening of the eyes. A downward pinching of the nostrils.

Gareth held out his card. "I need to speak with Lord Leonidas."

The butler took the card and shut the door in his face. Clearly Vaughn had made no secret of his feelings about Gareth and his sister's marriage. To be left kicking his heels on the steps was beyond insult, especially from a household that he'd treated nearly as his own not so long ago.

A long quarter of an hour later, the door opened again. "His lordship is not at home," the butler said, before shutting the door upon him a second time.

Gareth knocked again. Hard. The door opened, and the butler stared at him as though he were a sewer rat. "When Lord Leonidas returns, please tell him I'm at The Red Lion, and that what I have to say concerns Lady Boudicea's safety."

Gareth didn't wait for the door to shut on him a third time. He spun on his heel and marched off. If he was lucky, he'd be able to find Roland Devere or Anthony Thane and run the situation by them. Someone had to listen to him. He couldn't take no for an answer.

The League might think him a villain, but their concern for Beau could only help his cause today. They might not want to help *him*, but they would help for Beau's sake.

When he entered The Red Lion, all conversation stopped. Most of the faces were familiar, but none belonged to his particular set. Damnation. He'd been hoping to find someone to help him tackle Vaughn, though at this time of year, it was impossible to predict who would have returned to town already.

One of the younger members stood up from his card game. "This is a private club, sir," the boy said. "I'll ask you to leave."

Gareth finished shrugging out of his greatcoat and hung it on one of the hooks beside the door. "A private club in a public house," he said, stuffing his hat down on the hook as well. "And I've an appointment with a member."

"We all know what you did." The boy dropped his cards on the table. "You're not welcome here. Not anymore."

"Leave him be, Kettleston," Devere said from a dark corner at the rear of the pub. "If Mr. Sandison is to be evicted, there are others who'd claim the right before you."

"Yes, sir." The boy glared one last time and reclaimed his seat and his cards.

Gareth wove his way through the staring crowd to join Devere. The most jovial member of his set watched him without so much as a hint of a smile. Not exactly the welcome that he'd hoped for. He'd expected it from the others, but not from Devere.

"In your black books too now, am I?" Gareth said, taking the seat across from him.

"Vaughn's likely to horsewhip you in the street," Devere said. "And I'm inclined to let him. No, not just let him." Devere flicked his gaze over him as though picturing it. "I'm inclined to hold you down while he does it."

What the devil? Devere hadn't been nearly this severe the last time he'd seen him. He'd been the person Gareth had thought most likely to stand with him today, in fact. He'd been counting on his help.

"Did you honestly believe nothing has consequences?" Devere said, clearly warming to his subject. "That no one would find out?"

"What are you—"

"It's all over town that you've foisted your bastard on Lady Boudicea. The meaner spirited among the *ton* are even claiming the reverse. That it's Beau's bastard you're housing. How could you have let this happen? What the hell were you thinking? A runaway marriage wasn't enough to contend with?"

Gareth ground his teeth. Explanations were risky, if not impossible. Every detail could lead to a fatal slip. "It wasn't my idea, believe me. Souttar brought the child, and Beau walked in on us. The decision to keep the boy was hers. And you know Beau. There's no stopping her when she has the bit between her teeth."

"Why would Souttar do such a thing? Couldn't he have taken care of matters? He must have known bringing the babe to you would be disastrous."

"You know what Souttar is," Gareth said with a shrug, striving to keep his answer simple. "He'd been inconvenienced as it was, taking care of the matter himself to spare me would be entirely beyond him. And pointless. I exist to serve him, not the other way round."

"You're still alive only to serve my sister," Vaughn said from behind him. "And for no other reason. Souttar be damned."

"Agreed." Gareth met his oldest friend's gaze and saw nothing there to engender hope. "But at the moment, I need your help to do so. Yours and The League's."

Vaughn frowned but didn't reply. He slid into the seat

beside Devere. He hadn't bothered to take off his great-coat, but he did pull off his gloves and stuff them into one of its pockets.

"Help you? With what?" Devere looked leery, as though he were being offered a meat pie of questionable origin.

"To keep Beau safe, for one," Gareth replied.

A derisive snort from Beau's brother was all the reply that he got. Devere shot Vaughn a disbelieving look and shook his head.

"What does Beau need protecting from?" Devere said.

"Besides you," Vaughn added.

Gareth ignored the jibe. "Granby. She needs protecting from George Granby. Because her family didn't take care of the bastard the last time round."

Vaughn shot to his feet, and Devere yanked him back down by his coat. He landed hard enough that the chair squealed in protest. Vaughn shoved Devere's hand off of him.

"What is he talking about, Vaughn?" Devere said, pitching his voice low. "Who the hell is George Granby?"

"The only person Beau needs protecting from is Sandison here. Granby is no one. A ghost."

"A ghost who pitched your sister off a cliff and nearly drowned her not two days ago."

Beau's brother flinched, and Gareth pressed his advantage. "I know you don't believe me, but I really wasn't the one who abducted Beau. It was some creature of Granby's. Beau saw them together when Granby attacked her."

"Was it really?" Vaughn said, his voice shaking with anger. "What do you want, Sandison? I've no time—and no inclination—for your tales."

"From you? I want you to fetch Beau home. Do whatever it takes to convince her. Hate me, disbelieve me, distrust me, just keep her safe."

"Gladly," Vaughn said, rising and pulling on his gloves. "But don't expect me to return her."

"That will be up to her," Gareth said. "Won't it?"

"Not if my family has anything to say about it. And the duke can be very persuasive when he wants to be."

Gareth nodded. If a full estrangement was what was necessary to keep Beau safe, so be it. There were no grounds for a divorce, and he could worry about winning her back once Granby had been dealt with. Assuming he could get near her.

"What did you need The League's help with?" Vaughn asked as he turned to go. "Or were you implying that my family isn't capable of keeping Beau safe without their assistance?"

Gareth shook his head. "It needn't concern you. Just keep your sister safe."

"Done." Lord Leonidas looked down his nose at him, and Gareth swallowed down the sudden urge to simply pound the stiffness out of him. Somewhere behind that icy façade was the man whom he'd known and called a friend for more than twenty years.

With one last disdainful look, Vaughn turned and left.

Devere let his breath out in a dramatic gust. "And what do you need the rest of us for?"

"Tracking down Granby and getting Jamie—the boy, my neph-*son*," he added at Devere's blank look, "back from him."

The lie still didn't come easy, didn't feel natural. The

word *son* didn't fall off his tongue with any grace at all. Damn Souttar for putting him in this position.

Devere sucked in one cheek and nodded thoughtfully. "Your *nephew*, eh? Still covering for Souttar no matter the cost? You're a damn fool, and I'm guessing there's a story there I'm better off being ignorant of."

Gareth nodded, cursing himself for making such a clumsy slip of the tongue. "There is, and it's best left alone."

"So, even if this Granby person did want revenge, why would he take your bastard?"

"That's what I'd like to know," Gareth said. "And what I'm hoping The League can help me find out. If I don't get Jamie back, I'm fairly certain Beau won't be coming back to me. Ever. It's a haphazard family, but it's mine. And it's all I've got."

~ CHAPTER 40 ~

"Get your hand off my bridle, Boaz," Beau said, leaving the threat of recriminations open and vague. He knew better than to stand in her way.

Her footman-cum-groom adjusted his grip on Gunpowder's bridle. "I can't let you go, my lady."

"Because Mr. Sandison ordered you to keep me here?"

Boaz frowned. "I don't work for your husband, but your father would have my hide if I let you ride out like this. And he'd be right to do so."

Gunpowder minced nervously, and Beau forced herself to relax the reins. "Then come with me to Dover where we can catch the mail or hire a carriage of our own."

His grip slackened. "You'll not ride off while I'm saddling Cloud?"

"Not if you're quick," Beau said. "And wake John. He can pony our mounts back to the Hall."

A few minutes later, Boaz and a sleepy John were both mounted beside her. Beau nodded to them, and Gunpowder shot out of the yard.

The first hint of dawn was just coloring the sky as they left the drive and turned their horses west toward Dover. They passed several boys taking their flocks out and sprang past a slow-moving dray loaded down with barrels.

When they reached Dover, Beau handed Gunpowder's reins to John and her portmanteau to Boaz. She fished in her pocket for her purse.

"Wait here," she said. "I think we've beaten the first packet from France, so there should be seats of some kind left."

After a short conversation with the clerk, Beau managed to secure the last two seats on the mail coach. She waved Boaz over. "They're on the roof, but it's all that's available."

"It's more than eighteen hours to London. You'll freeze, my lady."

"Nonsense, Boaz. My habit is kerseymere, and I'm wearing my fur-lined redingote. I'll be every bit as warm as you or the driver."

Her footman shook his head and boosted her up onto the roof of the mail coach. He tossed up her bag and climbed up behind her. Boaz sat down beside her, brow puckered with consternation, clearly uncomfortable with the arrangements.

"It's not fitting, my lady."

Beau didn't answer.

"What if you fall and break your neck?"

"You'll have the satisfaction of telling everyone you warned me."

The coachman bellowed a warning, and they rolled into motion. Beau held tightly to the small railing that encircled the seats. Boaz hunched down beside her, glowering.

By the time they arrived in London, she was frozen, exhausted, starving, and her temper was more than a little frayed. Boaz swung her down and steadied her as she fought to get the blood flowing in her legs again.

They transferred to a hackney, and Beau suffered a moment of indecision when asked for their destination. Her parents were home in Scotland. She hadn't the slightest idea where Gareth's rooms were, or if he even still had them. Which left her with only her brother's house in Chapel Street.

She gave the driver the direction and scrambled into the dilapidated carriage. It creaked and bounced the entire way, but it got her there all the same. While Boaz paid the driver, Beau ran up the steps and knocked.

The familiar face of her brother's long-time butler greeted her when the door opened. "Sampson! It's so very good to see you." She stepped inside and began pulling off her gloves. "Is my brother or Lady Leonidas home?"

"Of course, my lady. Come into the drawing room and warm up while I inform her ladyship that you've arrived."

There was a cheerful fire in the hearth, and Beau stood as close as she could without catching her skirt on fire. She stepped back with a curse when the scent of singed wool caught her attention. She brushed a hand over her skirt, checking for scorch marks. She was still looking when her sister-in-law came running in.

"Beau?" Viola rushed forward to embrace her. "You're cold as ice. Are you hungry? Of course you are. How on earth did you get here?" Viola rattled off one question after another, giving Beau no time to answer any of them. Viola's mastiff pranced excitedly around them, nearly knocking Beau over.

"Yes, hello, Pen," Beau said, fending off the dog with both hands.

Leo came in right behind them. Unlike his wife, Leo didn't say a word. And unlike the dog, he didn't appear to be happy to see her. He just stared at her, arms crossed, an angry frown marring his face.

"Have you seen Gareth?" Beau said, playing with the mastiff's ears now that it had calmed down.

"Yes," Leo said flatly.

"And you still don't believe him. Don't believe me." Beau circled the room, trying to work off the urge to hit him. Pen whined in confusion, and Viola called her over.

"Leo, I've been called a lot of unpleasant things in my life, but *liar* isn't amongst them. Why would I start now? And about this?"

When her brother didn't respond, Beau growled in frustration and flung up her hands. "Do you want the ugly, unadulterated truth? I seduced Gareth, not the other way round. I did it. Me. And I did it knowingly."

Leo drew a sharp breath, and a muscle jumped in his jaw. Behind her, her sister-in-law mumbled something that sounded like *I told you so*.

"Gareth would have brought me safely home, and I knew it. I also knew I was ruined. So I made a choice. A conscious, deliberate, selfish choice." She punctuated each word with another jab to his chest. "I chose my reputation over Gareth's. I sacrificed him in order to save myself. You said last year that maybe you should have left me to Granby. You as good as warned me not to get myself into another scrape."

Leo looked green. The frown was gone, replaced by a wide, horrified gaze. "That's not what I meant."

"Wasn't it?" Beau said, refusing to let him off the hook. "Well, I did find myself in another scrape, so I got myself out. It was me. All of it. If anyone was the victim, it was Gareth. And he's been paying the price for rescuing me ever since."

"Perhaps," Leo said. "But there's also a chance he's not the hero you make him out to be. That you're the victim, whether it was you who did the seducing or not."

Beau raised a brow in disbelief. "You're not making sense, Leo."

"If Sandison already had a wife, then his marrying you would be unforgivable."

Beau caught her lips between her teeth and shook her head. "Don't be absurd."

"We got a letter asserting just that," Viola said, breaking into the conversation. "It said he was already married. That the boy his brother brought was his legitimate son."

"Souttar said the boy's mother was dead." Beau felt suddenly sick. She shook the sensation off. "That her family had dumped the boy on them afterward."

"She may well be dead, now," Leo said grimly. "If so, the question is when did she die? Before or after he married you?"

"No," Beau ground out. "The question is whether or not your mysterious correspondent is lying. And if it's who I think it is, then this is just another attempt to cause trouble."

"Granby?" Leo said.

"I assume Gareth already tried to tell you this?"

Leo nodded. "He did. It sounded as far-fetched then as it does now."

"More far-fetched than your best friend having a secret wife and purposefully ruining your sister? Quit being an ass, brother. Granby showed up at Morton Hall with Mr. Nowlin—my most recent abductor, the one you don't believe exists—in tow. They tried to take me again, but I fell over the cliff fighting them off. They *did* take Jamie, however."

"And you want the boy back?" Leo said.

Beau nodded. She couldn't help it. He was hers now, every bit as much as Gareth. She didn't think that she could face life at Morton Hall without him.

"No matter the cost or scandal?"

"What does it matter anymore?" Beau said. "Either I'm married to a bigamist and I'm ruined, or this is all part of Granby's grand scheme of revenge. My reputation is a house of cards, and it's going to come tumbling down one way or another. But before it's all settled, I intend to have Jamie back and see Granby dead."

⊰ CHAPTER 41 ⊱

A knock at the outer door of Gareth's suite of rooms in Old Bond Street was immediately followed by the sound of the door swinging open. Gareth let the ends of the neckcloth that he was tying flutter loose. He stepped out of his bedroom and into the small front room that served as drawing room, office, and dining room to find Devere, who he'd known was there, bowing over Beau's hand, while Leo leaned against the mantelpiece.

"Beau?" Gareth's pulse leapt at the sight of her. He glanced around the room. Leo shrugged and indicated with his chin that the visit was entirely Beau's doing.

"Were you already married when you married me?" Beau said.

The room spun, nothing but his wife's concerned face remaining steady. Gareth tried to formulate a response, but the words wouldn't come.

"Because someone thinks you were," Vaughn said. "Furthermore, they're purporting that your supposed bastard is, in fact, legitimate, and that his mother is still alive."

"Which is ridiculous," Beau said, her voice begging him to refute the charges. "No one is that stupid."

The word *damn* rebounded through his head like a drumbeat, getting louder with every beat of his heart. Devere glanced heavenward and gave him an exasperated look. Betray his brother or his wife. That was the choice he was left with, and it really wasn't a choice at all.

"No one except, perhaps, Souttar," Gareth said. The statement filled the room until it felt as though the walls were straining to contain it and might fly apart at any moment.

Gareth watched Beau's face as the truth sank in. There was a flash of anger that quickly settled into an expression of sheer hurt that left her eyes looking bruised.

"Souttar? And you didn't tell me?"

"It wasn't my secret to tell. And it's not just about Souttar. His wife—"

"Which one?" Vaughn said with a hint of a drawl. "He seems to have a surfeit."

"Stop helping!" Gareth glared at him, only to be struck by the sudden wicked glint in his eyes. "You would choose such a moment to forgive me, damn you."

"If Jamie's mother is alive, Lady Souttar is ruined." Beau put her hand over her mouth, as though the words frightened her.

"You didn't care when it was you," her brother said, his tone verging on exasperation. "Can't you be happy it's someone else for a change?"

"No, I can't." Beau rounded on her brother. "It's monstrous. I know Olivia. We made our curtsies to the queen together, shared our first season. And if Souttar was—is—married to Jamie's mother, then Jamie is the heir to an earldom. And you"—she turned back toward Gareth—"were going to help take that away from him."

Gareth held up his hand placatingly. "It was for the greater good."

"Not Jamie's greater good," Beau said, face flushed with anger.

"You can't have it both ways, Beau," Gareth replied, stating the bald, ugly truth. "Someone had to lose. I had to weigh Jamie's birthright against my family's good name and your friend's reputation."

Beau nodded, but the set of her jaw was still mutinous. "Granby thinks Jamie is yours and that I'm the one who'll be ruined if the truth comes out."

"So he's probably out looking for Jamie's mother, or proof of Jamie's legitimacy, as we speak," Devere said.

"Then we'd best be doing the same," Vaughn said, sounding as if he was relishing the idea. "Following the same trail is the best way to find Granby and the boy."

Beau sat at Gareth's desk and combed out her hair. It was a tangled mess from her roof-top journey. When she was done, she plaited it and twisted the end several times around her finger so the curl would hold the plait.

"Any idea where to start looking?" she said.

Gareth shook his head. "Nothing more specific than *Scotland*. I was thinking of attempting to trick my brother into helping."

"How so?" She got up and joined him by the fire. He held the toasting fork out to her, and she plucked the piece of toasted bread and melted cheese off with her fingers.

"Well." He settled down beside her on the floor and began toasting another bit of bread and cheese. "If Souttar thinks he's about to be exposed, he might just help us get to the information first so we can cover it up."

"Or he might attempt to do so himself."

"Souttar being a great deal easier to find and follow than Granby."

Beau nodded and blew on the hot cheese before taking a bite. "So you're going to put the fear of God into your brother?"

"Well, the fear of our father finding out what he's done at any rate. I'm fairly certain Souttar is far more afraid of the earl than he is of any member of the Holy Trinity." Gareth flicked his queue back over his shoulder as he leaned closer to the fire.

Beau swallowed the last of her cheese toast and reached for her wine. "Is this really how bachelors live? On toasted bread and wine?"

"And the occasional meat pie."

"Or cup of *blue ruin*," Beau said with a teasing smile.

"Have you ever had gin?"

Beau shook her head. "No, but I should like to try it."

"No, you wouldn't, brat," Gareth said with a laugh. "It tastes like rotting fruit and half the stuff out there will make you go blind."

"Then I'll stick with arrack." She took another sip of wine. "Leo mostly ate at his clubs when he wasn't dining with the family. Don't a lot of men do that?"

"Those who can afford clubs, yes. But I can hardly take you there for supper."

"You could take me to The Red Lion," Beau said.

"No, I really couldn't."

Beau stuck her lower lip out in an exaggerated show of faux petulance. He looked horrified at the very idea, cementing her desire to go. She accepted another cheese toast and blew on it.

"I can't stop worrying about Jamie," she said, staring down at the bubbling cheese, suddenly not hungry in the slightest.

"I know, love," Gareth said, eyes soft and sympathetic. "But Granby took him for a reason. He'll take care of him until we get him back."

"I keep telling myself the same thing, but I have a hard time believing it."

"Money or power. That's what it comes down to. Either he'll want money, in which case we'll manage it, or he'll want to control us—which I think far more likely, given his previous behavior. And if that's the case, we turn his demands against him."

"You make it sound simple."

"It is simple. There are two options. We win, or we lose. And I don't intend to lose."

❧ CHAPTER 42 ❧

Four days later, they were rolling up the long drive of the Earl of Roxwell's seat. Beau took a deep breath, held it, and let it go slowly. Gareth was dozing beside her, long legs angled across the interior of the coach, feet propped up on the opposite seat.

"Gareth?" she said. He opened his eyes, dark brows slanting down. "What if Souttar—or Jamie's mother— wants Jamie back?"

"Souttar? Don't be daft. And if his mother wanted him, she wouldn't have foisted him on Souttar in the first place." He shut his eyes again.

"But what if he does? Or what if she changes her mind when she figures out that Jamie's going to be an earl?"

Gareth sighed but didn't bother to open his eyes. "There isn't the smallest chance that my brother will want anything to do with Jamie, regardless of how this all turns out, and there's even less of a chance of my father allowing some cutler's daughter anywhere near his heir."

"So you think Lord Roxwell might claim him."

"You mean if Jamie really is Souttar's heir?" Gareth turned his head and looked at her. "My father's reaction is likely to be unpredictable under those circumstances. You're correct on that count. But I find it doubtful that the earl will want to be saddled with the living evidence of Souttar's folly and will be content to be guardian in name only."

Beau tucked herself into his side and dropped her head back onto his shoulder. "Good."

Gareth gave her a reassuring squeeze as the coach stopped. "Ready?"

Beau nodded but found herself staring open-mouthed at the house. It was plain. Severe. An enormous three-story box, the front entrance centered and set back, flanked on either side by a column of epic proportion.

"You grew up here?" A cold shudder ran down her spine.

Gareth's mouth quirked into a smile. "It's every bit as charming on the inside," he said, voice dripping with sarcasm. "You'll see in a moment." He put a hand at the small of her back and urged her forward. "Father's inordinately proud of the place, so pretend your horror is awe."

The door opened, and the butler's face practically shimmered as he restrained his smile. "Master Gareth, were we expecting you?"

"No, Bradfield, my wife and I are on our way to visit her parents in Scotland, and I wanted to show her the old place. Mrs. Sandison, this is Bradfield. Best butler in all of Britain. I'd steal him from the earl if Morton Hall wasn't entirely beneath his dignity."

Beau nodded, and Bradfield finally gave in and smiled as he bowed. The entry hall that he ushered them into was large and square, with an open colonnade circling it on the second story. The walls and pillars were of the same yellow stone as the façade of the house. The entire thing looked as though it were based on ruins. Her father, classical scholar that he was, would have loved it.

Beau glanced around with interest. She could just make out that there were paintings lining the upstairs walkway, interspersed with doors and the occasional commode.

"Is Souttar about?" Gareth said causally, as though it didn't matter in the slightest.

Beau licked her lips and tried not to appear as nervous as she felt. They needed his brother to be here and to corner him away from the earl.

"He is," Bradfield said. "As is Lady Souttar. Your parents are away though. Gone to Bath for the countess's health."

"She still thinking of going to Spa?" Gareth wandered familiarly about the hall as Beau divested herself of her coat, hat, and gloves.

Bradfield nodded, and Gareth laughed. "Stout as an ox, my mother, but she loves to pretend her health is delicate and to quack herself every chance she gets."

The butler's eyes widened reproachfully, but he said nothing, leading Beau to believe that her husband's assessment was generally correct. Bradfield draped her redingote carefully over his arm and extended a hand for the rest of her things. Beau dropped her gloves into her hat and relinquished it to him.

"Will you be staying for supper, sir? Shall I have your room made ready?"

"No, Bradfield. We have to be on our way, but could you send tea to the Tapestry Room in an hour or so? Thank you," Gareth said. "Well, love?" He held out his arm and Beau took it, letting him lead her across the open hall and up the stairs.

"Is the entire house carved of stone?" Beau trailed her fingers along the ornate handrail.

"Most of it, yes. Cold as a mausoleum," he added as they reached the colonnade. Carpets that had obviously been woven for the space ran along the floor, cushioning their steps. "My brother's most likely in his study. He has a whole suite of rooms, as far from the earl's as possible. Let's go flush him out."

A large double door, finished to match the stone walls, led to a drawing room furnished entirely in cream and gold. Gareth ran his fingers lightly over the keys of the pianoforte, trilling out part of a piece that Beau couldn't quite remember. She tipped her head. He glanced over, a hint of color splashed across the sharp jut of his cheekbones.

"I didn't know you played," she said.

"Only very indifferently," he replied, moving away from the instrument and leading her onward.

One room flowed into the next, without benefit of corridors. Beyond the drawing room was a snug library with a desk and window that overlooked the expanse of lawn behind the house.

Souttar spun around as they entered. "Gareth? What the hell are you doing in Yorkshire?"

"Looking to give you a hint, brother," Gareth said, a note of menace in his voice.

Souttar stared back at them both, eyes slightly wild. Beau knew that expression. She'd seen it on many a cornered fox just before it threw itself at the lead dog. "About what?"

"About the world of trouble that's about to come down on your head. Someone's been poking around. Sending out letters claiming Jamie's mother is still alive. At the moment, whoever he is, he thinks that I'm the father, but if he finds Jamie's mother, assuming he's correct about her miraculous resurrection, the jig will be up."

Souttar's face drained of color. Beau felt a pang of sympathy. He looked so much like Gareth that it was impossible not to do so. The same shock of white hair, same sculpted nose and high cheekbones. The only real difference between them was Gareth's superior height and his sad brows. Souttar's didn't dip downward. They were straight, dark slashes that nearly met over the bridge of his nose.

"So tell me," Gareth went on, stepping closer to his brother, crowding him, "*is* Jamie's mother alive? Because if she is, you'd best get to her first and get this settled as swiftly as possible."

Gareth's brother shook his head. "I told you. She died," he said a little too quickly and far too emphatically. "She died, and her brat got dumped on my doorstep."

"You mean your son," Beau said with a flash of anger. "Because we've all seen him, and there's no denying he's a Sandison. He's a butter pattern of you both."

Souttar stared at her dumbly, clearly not used to being spoken to in such a manner. Poor Olivia. Living in this mausoleum—for Gareth had quite correctly named it such—and married to such a dolt. Perhaps discovering that she was his bigamous second wife, and thus free to leave, wouldn't be the worst thing that had ever happened to her. Beau looked Souttar up and down in disgust.

"You've no right to look at me like that. No right to judge me." He twitched his coat down by the pocket flaps, staring back at her defiantly.

"She has every right, considering all the trouble that you've caused," Gareth said, cutting off her own reply. "You're a poor liar, Souttar. Always were. You should know the man behind the accusations has Jamie. He has him, and it's entirely likely that he'll use him to force a public declaration out of his mother. And if that happens, if it's even remotely possible that it could happen, the pretense of Jamie being mine won't stand."

"No?" Souttar lifted his chin, trying to brazen his way through the conversation.

"No," Gareth replied, a hard edge to his voice. "I was on the continent when this folly took place. People—father—won't be fooled, and Beau's family won't stand for it."

"I tell you she's dead." Souttar's voice rose an octave as he shouted, "She's dead, and there's nothing and no one to find."

Gareth shook his head and swept one arm toward the door, motioning her to precede him out. Beau took one last look at her husband's brother and did as she was bid. Gareth caught up with her before she was halfway across the drawing room.

"Hook baited?" she said.

"Baited and set, I'd say," he replied. "I suppose it was

too much to hope for that he'd simply confess the truth and help. Now all we have to do is wait and follow."

"And hope Granby is close enough to uncovering the truth that we can catch him."

"That too," Gareth said, taking her by the hand and leading her clockwise around the upper open corridor. He pushed open a door and motioned her in. "The Tapestry Room," he said, allowing her to precede him.

The room was small, really more of a closet than a drawing room. Just big enough for a fireplace and a writing desk. It had a window seat and was devoid of any ornamentation other than the magnificent tapestries that covered every wall.

"They were specially woven," Gareth said, crossing to sit by the window. "The countess wanted one comfortable room in the stone palace her husband built after the restoration of the monarchy. For the last several generations, it's been the domain of one of the younger children. Most recently, me."

Beau wandered from wall to wall, studying the tapestry. The main scene was a medieval hunt, hounds and men in livery pursuing a stag. But over the fireplace, a life-sized hedgehog roamed, and there were other small creatures and birds peeking out of bushes and through the leaves of the trees.

"Do you think your family would notice if we stripped the room bare and carried it all away with us?" Beau said, running her fingers over the hedgehog.

"The family? Probably not. But Bradfield most certainly would."

"Are they Gobelin?"

"Good eye."

"We've several at Lochmaben. One is original to the house, and the others Mother collected over the years. I'd love to show her this, though."

"There's no reason why you shouldn't. Unless the house burns to the ground—which is highly unlikely given that it's entirely made of stone—the room will be here any time you should choose to bring her."

"Assuming either of us is welcome here once this affair is concluded," Beau said, crossing to join him on the window seat.

"Well, there is that." He took one hand in his own, circling his thumb in her palm. "But I'm sure Bradfield could always be trusted to smuggle us in."

Beau watched his thumb, let the sensation of his skin on hers wash over her. "Do you love me?"

Gareth's thumb stopped and his hand gripped hers. "I could ask the same thing, Beau. Was I simply an expedient method of self-preservation?"

"That's not an answer." And she wanted an answer, wanted the actual words, not just veiled implications.

He sighed and lowered his head so they were eye to eye. The blue of his irises blazed in the sunlight. "I've loved you since the hunt ball, where I refused to come to heel like your devoted spaniel, brat. Maybe even before that, but that's the night I remember realizing it."

Beau nodded. "And so you avoided me," she said softly.

"I couldn't have you, so why torture myself?"

"And I ran after you like a child chasing a butterfly through the garden. How ridiculous I must have seemed."

Gareth chuckled softly. "You were adorable."

Beau bit her lip and then let it go. "You weren't merely expedient," she said. "If it had been Devere or Thane or any of Leo's other friends who'd found me, I'd have gone chastely home."

Gareth yanked her onto his lap and his mouth descended on hers. He kissed her fiercely, tongue tangling with hers, teeth clashing. "You're never again to say marrying me was a mistake," he said.

Beau grinned and caught her lips between her teeth. "If we've frightened Souttar sufficiently," she said, dragging herself back to the most pressing of their problems, "when do you think your brother will leave?"

"Not till after we've gone," Gareth replied with a lopsided smile. "We'll have tea and then be on our way. We can join your brother and Devere at The Bell and watch for Souttar. He'll have to pass through the village on his way north."

∼ CHAPTER 43 ∼

W ell, the hunt is on," Devere said, as he and Vaughn vaulted into their saddles. The dust from Souttar's coach was still visible, though it had been traveling at a rattling pace. Gareth nodded and sent them off with a slap to the hindquarters of Devere's mare.

One of them would circle back to report on Souttar's path, the other sticking close behind. They'd agreed on a specific series of inns, in case something went wrong and they had to send a message rather than meet up themselves. Once they reached Scotland though, they'd have to wait and see what direction Souttar chose.

He and Beau set off a short while later, Beau fidgeting and anxious. "I could take one of Souttar's horses and send you home," Gareth offered. "Or I could drop you at Lochmaben and you could try your luck explaining recent events to the duke."

Beau narrowed her eyes at him. "Feeling brave enough to face down my father? If Leo got a letter accusing you of being a bigamist, you can be assured that my father did as well."

Gareth smiled and shook his head. "Hence my concern," he said lightly. "Or are you out for my blood now too?"

"Just Souttar's," Beau said with a hard frown. "There's no way he comes out of this clean."

"Not if Jamie's mother really is alive, and I'm fairly certain that she must be. My brother looks fagged to death. A dead woman wouldn't cause that much worry." Gareth put his feet up on the rear-facing seat, one ankle crossed over the other.

"No, but a live wife with a suit before the commissaries would," Beau said.

"The what?"

"Commissaries," she repeated, turning in the seat to face him. "The court in Edinburgh that oversees petitions for divorce. We Scots aren't like the English. Women have the same rights as men when it comes to divorce, and the means of obtaining one are far simpler than in England. If Souttar's first wife really is alive, and she can prove that they were married, she could cause a great deal of trouble by suing him for either abandonment or adultery."

Gareth winced, sucking a breath past his teeth. "Given that the announcement of his marriage to Lady Olivia was widely published, the adultery part would be easy enough to substantiate." All the possible outcomes of such a suit swirled through his brain like a murder of crows, but his brain kept shying away from accepting the full horror.

Beau's eyes softened for a moment. She clearly understood exactly what was at stake. "And I'd wager that the man who brought Jamie to Ashburn is either the first wife's lawyer, or someone hired by her lawyer. She'll need a great deal of information to support her libel for divorce."

"So, Souttar put his own neck into the noose when he accepted Jamie," Gareth said, all hope of rectifying the situation quietly withering away like a plant uprooted and left lying in the sun.

Beau nodded grimly. "Though claiming paternity isn't the same as admitting to the marriage. She'll have to prove that first. If theirs was a typical irregular marriage, it will come down to testimony from their servants, neighbors, and clergy."

"Is there any chance at all of keeping it quiet?"

"Do you mean is there any chance of your father, Souttar's new wife, and the *ton* not finding out?" She shook her head, lower lip caught between her teeth. "No. She'll be entitled to a third of his property, just as though he'd died, and I imagine she'll have to sue in an English court to get it, which will cause additional problems and possibly drag the case out for years. Even if Souttar just wanted to give it to her, your father would have to be told in order for him to do so."

"So Souttar's best hope is that the marriage can't be proven, but even so, the scandal will be enormous. Once the suit is brought, and his name is attached, it will be in every paper in the British Isles."

"Do you think he even knows?" Beau said. Pity his brother didn't deserve was writ plainly on her face. Or maybe it was pity for Lady Olivia. Lord knew someone ought to be thinking of her in all of this.

"He must have an inkling by now," Gareth said. "The

sword of Damocles is dangling over his head and has been for months. Can you imagine his panic?"

"I'd rather not," Beau said with a shiver, lifting his arm and pulling it around her. "It's a disaster for everyone involved. All I want is to get Jamie back. Whatever else happens is secondary and beyond our control."

✈ CHAPTER 44 ✈

.

G ranby cursed as the street twisted again, winding
through the sooty streets of Edinburgh. Somewhere
in the muddle of stone buildings was his goal. At first, it
had been hard to pick up the trail in Yorkshire, but once he
had—thanks to a coachman with no love for their north-
ern neighbors—the man who'd delivered the child hadn't
been that hard to trace. A Scottish man traveling with a
child and no woman with them—well, that was unusual
enough to be memorable to many. Add in the fact that the
man's accent was so thick as to be unintelligible and you
had a very memorable man indeed.

Granby had gleaned enough of a description to trace
his way back along the route of the mail coaches that he'd
taken all the way to Edinburgh. Along the way, he'd discovered the man was a lawyer. One Mr. Budel. Further
inquires had uncovered offices in Bell's Wynd.

All that was left to do was find the child's mother, or
at the very least obtain proof of her marriage to Gareth
Sandison. If she was preparing a libel for divorce, all

the better. The news would be catastrophic, and it would travel the length of the country on mercurial wings. If she wasn't, she'd have to be pressured into doing so, and his possession of her son ought to be more than persuasive.

A trio of dogs ran yapping through the street, a boy in ragged breeches and coat chasing after them, a brace of rats hanging over one shoulder. A heavy dray shuddered to a stop, the driver cursing and waving his fist at the boy. Granby shrank back against the wall to avoid the mud-caked wheels. The door to Budel, Dunlop, and Piget opened, and a silver-haired gentleman stepped out.

Granby looked more closely as the man walked quickly past him. Not Gareth Sandison. His brother, Lord Souttar. A sick feeling crawled up his spine. He crossed the street and went quickly through the door that Sandison's brother had just exited.

"Can I help you, sir?"

"I'm looking for Mr. Budel," Granby said.

A squat man, well past his prime, stuck his head into the room. "Yes?"

"Mr. Giles," Granby said, extending his hand, the false name coming easily. "I'm working on behalf of Lord Souttar. I was delayed, and I think I missed our appointment. I need to see the file for his case."

"I can assure you it's all in order, sir. The marriage is thoroughly documented and attested to, and in light of his second marriage, my client will have no trouble obtaining her divorce. You may see it all when we go before the commissionaires."

"So the lady will be seeking to prove her marriage to Lord Souttar?"

"She will."

Granby ground his teeth as rage flushed through him. All this for nothing. Nothing. Without another word, he spun on his heel and marched out.

When returned to the inn where he'd left Nowlin, it was to find the man hurriedly packing. "Going somewhere?"

"There are men looking for you, sir."

"What men?"

"I don't know. I just know I heard a man asking after you by name. He gave a description as well: a one-eyed Englishman, possibly traveling with a child. It was the child they were most interested in. Offered a reward for any information leading to the boy's discovery."

"And what were they told?"

"Nothing. Only the innkeeper's wife was present in the taproom, and she hasn't seen you."

"Well, she has now. I wondered about the startled look she gave me."

"Then let's get out of here, sir." His voice had taken on a high-pitched whine. "Before she brings them down on us."

"A wise suggestion." Granby tossed his things willy-nilly into his trunk. "Take this down and have the carriage put to. I'll slip out the back and meet you in the yard."

The Irishman set his own bag atop the trunk and hefted them both. Granby spun about, mulling over the information. They wanted the boy back, did they? He might not be able to ruin Beau's marriage, but he could still take away something she wanted and leave her supremely unhappy. He just had to make sure that she could never find the boy.

He sauntered down the back staircase, slipping past a

harassed-looking maid in a checkered gown and mobcap, and emerged into the busy yard feeling better than he had in days. His postchaise had already been brought out, and the last of the four horses necessary to pull it was being hitched.

Granby climbed in and waited for Nowlin to join him. The Irishman swung the door shut behind him and threw himself into the rear-facing seat.

"Another thought occurs to me, Nowlin. Just what did you do with the boy?"

"Dumped him, sir. Just like you said to."

"And if we wanted to find him again?"

"Then you'd be searching all over England. I dropped him off near a gypsy encampment. Gypsy traders are always willing to take a stout boy on, or so I've been told. They could be anywhere by now."

❦ CHAPTER 45 ❧

G ot word from The Three Crowns," Leo said with a
martial gleam in his eyes. "A one-eyed Englishman
was seen leaving there in the company of an Irishman. No
sign of a child though."

Beau leapt out of her chair and ran to hug him, her
skirts nearly tripping her in her haste. "They could have
stashed him away. Do we know which direction they
went? Is the carriage being readied? Where is Devere?"

"Slow down," her brother said, hands gripping her
shoulders. "Devere is already on the road. As soon as
Sandison pays your shot, we'll follow."

Gareth burst into the room in a whirlwind, hair untidy,
a feral smile lighting up his face. Beau felt her heart turn
over. This was the man she'd fallen in love with.

"Let's go, love," he said, taking her by the hand and
hurrying her along. "He's on the move, and we've got him
in our sights. We just have to be patient a little longer."

"I'm not feeling patient at this point," Beau said as
they pelted down the stairs.

Her brother gave a bark of laughter, causing the inn's cat to bolt from her place at the bottom of the stairs. "If we have to resort to torture, we'll give you first rights."

Beau took Gareth and Leo both by the lapels of their coats, holding them tightly, bound together. "Promise me. Promise me we'll do whatever it takes."

Gareth covered her hand with his own and squeezed. "You know we will, brat. We're none of us good at losing. Your beastly brother least of all. Now up with you."

Beau let her husband boost her into the carriage. He and Leo stood with their heads together, one pale, the other dark, conferring in low, urgent tones. Just as though no estrangement had ever taken place. That was as it should be. If nothing else came out of this, at least one good thing had occurred.

"What?" Gareth said upon entering the coach.

"It's nothing." Beau swiped a hand over a misty eye and smiled back at him. How could she put it into words? Horror and pain on one side of the scale, friendship and happiness on the other. They didn't balance out, and one didn't make up for the other, but the warm glow inside her when she saw them together again was undeniable.

"Liar."

"I never lie."

Gareth raised an eyebrow in mocking disbelief. Beau reached out to cup his cheek, smoothing her thumb over the wayward brow.

"Ask Leo if you don't believe me."

Gareth caught her hand and kissed the palm, lips warm even through the leather of her glove. He tugged the glove off, using his teeth to loosen each finger. "The last thing I want to do is talk to your brother at the moment."

Desire mingled with guilt. Guilt over Jamie warred with the guilt of disappointing Gareth. She'd sworn to make him happy, and all she'd really managed was to cause him strife and trouble.

"Refusing the small pleasures in life won't bring Jamie back a moment sooner," Gareth said, hands already fumbling with the fall of his breeches. He took her mouth, hard, tongue dueling with hers. "Touch me." His hand guided hers to his cock.

Her hand closed around his shaft, and his breath hissed out of him. "I've been a bad wife," she said softly. A bad wife who hadn't lived up to her pledge, if only in her own eyes.

"No, you've been an understandably distracted one."

Beau held back a smile. He was, perhaps, being more generous than she deserved. She loosened her grip slightly and swirled her palm over the still-swelling head. With a slither of linen and silk, she slid to the floor of the coach.

Gareth held his breath as Beau swung herself out of his lap and onto the floor. Her mouth, hot and wet, slicked over the head of his cock. Gareth gripped the seat, wanting to thrust his hands into the head of curls spilling over his lap. Heat engulfed him, spread through his veins, and sapped his will. Her lips followed the tight circle of her hand, the stroke now slick. She sucked, and his vision fluttered.

Gareth grabbed a handful of Beau's hair and attempted to dislodge her. Her free hand shoved hard against his chest, the heel pushing up against his diaphragm, holding him in place.

"Beau—" His breath hissed out of him as his balls tightened and drew up, his release only moments away.

She sucked harder, squeezed harder. Her tongue swirled over the ultrasensitive rim, and Gareth spilled himself into her mouth.

Beau sucked lightly, and he shuddered in response. She released him slowly, trailing her tongue the length of his shaft, her hand still cradling the base. She smiled up at him, tongue darting out to lick the corner of her mouth. Gareth pulled his handkerchief from his pocket and held it out.

"You're indecently good at that for a newly married woman."

Beau shrugged and lifted her arms to re-pin her hair. "I always was a quick study when something was important."

She was still smiling like a naughty child when a horrible snapping noise broke the silence and the entire coach shivered around them. Gareth grabbed hold of her as the world tilted and lurched, landing them both in a haphazard pile of knees and elbows inside a suddenly dark coach.

The shouts and curses from the men outside were muffled by the wood. The coach shivered again as it was dragged forward, roughly. Gareth kept ahold of Beau and waited. A pounding knock reverberated through the coach.

"Sandison? Beau?" Vaughn's shout was easy to distinguish from the general din.

"Fine," Gareth shouted back. "Wheels off?"

"Smashed to flinders."

"Damnation," Beau grumbled, catching him in the ribs with her elbow as she attempted to climb up off him.

Gareth bit back an oath of his own and yanked her back down. "Stop squirming about, brat. Door's underneath us. Nothing we can do until they right the coach."

Vaughn said something to the same effect, followed by a shout to mind the horses. Gareth strained to catch the rest of what was happening but gave up when it became evident that it was impossible to eavesdrop from their current position.

Beau gave a gusty, annoyed sigh and dropped her head back onto his shoulder. "Leo should go on. We'll lose Granby if he doesn't."

"I wouldn't waste your breath suggesting it. Your brother's not going to just leave you here, trapped. I imagine once they've settled the horses, he'll ride on for help and try to pick up Granby's trail."

A disgusted snort was her only reply. Gareth pushed them both up a bit, and Beau yanked at her skirts and shifted about. "What are you doing?"

"Trying to get the pad that holds out my skirts to stop bowing out my back in the most uncomfortable manner possible. It's not meant to be laid upon."

After a few more minutes of struggling, she gave a growl of pure frustration and demanded that he help her. Gareth obligingly pushed her up, hands steadying her as she attempted to find footing in the dark amongst the jumble of dislodged cushions, hats, and traveling gear.

The rustle of fabric and the sound of her breath filled the coach. The hem of her skirts flicked across his cheek as she yanked them up. "Ha!" Her exuberance echoed inside the coach and something fell heavily beside him.

"What now?" Gareth said, hands sliding up her legs.

Beau made a tsking sound, like she was rebuking a horse. Gareth grabbed hold of her skirts and pushed himself up so he was kneeling. She pushed at him blindly, attempting to fend him off.

Gareth chuckled into the dark. "You have a better idea of how to pass the time?" he whispered, head already under her skirts.

"They'll hear us," she hissed back.

"Not if you're quiet," he said, hands on the naked flesh above her stockings. "You *can* be quiet, can't you, love?"

Beau sucked in a harsh breath. She moved slightly, bracing herself as he pushed her thighs apart, tongue delving into the sweet, hidden folds.

He found the tight peak at the apex and sucked hard. Beau whimpered and widened her stance. Her struggle to remain quiet only served to spur him on. Each little choked-back sound was like a gift or a prize.

Gareth huffed a breath across her and placed an open-mouthed kiss on the sensitive skin at the top of her thigh, and then he fastened his mouth back over her clitoris and drank her down until she collapsed, gasping and shaking, his arms the only thing keeping her upright.

He rolled back, taking Beau with him. She landed atop him, limp. Gareth kissed the top of her head and wrapped an arm about her. They lay curled up together until the coach heaved. It bounced and rose. Light leaked in, illuminating the scene of their debauch.

Gareth burst into laughter, and Beau rolled her eyes.

"Whatever my hair looks like, yours is just as bad, I assure you," she said.

The coach creaked upward and finally righted itself enough that the door could be opened. "Hurry," Vaughn said, shoulder braced on the side of the coach. "Not sure how long we can hold it."

Gareth thrust Beau out ahead of him and scrambled out after her. Beau stood beside the ruins of the coach, finger-combing her hair back from her face. She twisted the curls up and jammed them back in upon themselves. When she was done, she shook out her skirts and surveyed the scene like a newly arrived monarch disembarking from a ship.

"I suppose we shall have to wait here while someone fetches another carriage," she said, nose scrunched up with displeasure. Gareth repressed the urge to laugh again. His wife was adorable when playing the haughty queen.

"That you will," her brother said, swinging up into the saddle. "As monstrously unfair as I know you find it." His horse minced, knees lifted high, obviously eager to be off. Vaughn brought it quickly under control. "Either the postilion or I will be back as quickly as we can."

Without another word, he loosened the reins and his horse shot off down the road. The postilion raced after him, leaving them alone with the coachman and the three remaining carriage horses.

Gareth took Beau's small trunk from the boot and set it down under one of the blossoming fruit trees at the side of the road. Beau sat down and leaned back against the tree, lacing her fingers together over her stomach. She looked like a disheveled Fragonard. Beautiful, elegant, but with an underlying promise of wickedness.

She caught him staring and fiddled with her hair again. "What?" she said with a hint of a laugh.

"Nothing. Or rather, nothing of import. Just admiring the view. You should be painted just like this."

"Disheveled and blowsy?"

Gareth shook his head and sat down beside her on the damp ground. "Radiant."

❧ CHAPTER 46 ❧

Padrig Nowlin's gut churned uneasily. Granby hadn't said why he wanted to find the child, but it couldn't possibly bode well for the boy. As far as Padrig had seen, Granby had only the worst of intentions toward everyone and everything.

They'd stopped in London on their way south, and at the moment, Granby and Padrig's sister were screaming at one another, their shouts and recriminations barely muffled by the thin walls of the rooms that Granby had installed her in.

Padrig pulled the pillow over his head as the shouting turned to moans. He'd acted the lackey for months now in a bid to save Maeve, but it was impossible to believe it worth it in moments like this.

When the sounds of their coupling grew louder, he rolled out of bed and yanked on his clothes. He didn't have enough money to pay for a room elsewhere, but he had enough for a drink. He didn't have to be here, listening to that.

The walkway outside tilted toward the street, leaving Padrig with the sensation of drunkenness as he stumbled away. He chuffed his hands over his arms in an attempt to warm up. He should have grabbed his coat, but it was draped over a chair in the main room, which doubled as Granby's bedchamber.

To make up for his lack of coat, he walked faster. He passed one dram shop after another. Raggedy whores watched him from dark alleyways. Even more wretched-looking children huddled in doorways, piled together like puppies for warmth. It was no different from the slums of Dublin, but the sheer size of it was startling and depressing.

Padrig eagerly fell into the first decent-looking tavern that he could find. He fished in his pocket and came out with five shillings and a few-odd pence. More than enough to get good and drunk on.

He found a place near the hearth and paid for a mug of ale. He drank slowly enough that he could keep his seat until morning, and with each passing mug, the sound of his sister fucking Granby got a little bit dimmer...Dawn brought him up short and his last penny went for a bun, hot from the oven.

He pulled out his pocketbook and stared blearily at the notes jotted within. Number Twelve Chapel Street. That was where he'd delivered Granby's note. Where Lady Boudicea's brother lived. He washed the last bite of the bun down with the bitter dregs of ale in his mug and set off for Mayfair.

Viola was drinking tea and reading the morning paper when an unholy pounding on the front door startled her nearly out of her seat. Her butler's raised voice breached the walls, and she hurried out into the entry hall. Sampson never raised his voice. He never had to. His resemblance to a champion pugilist discouraged any type of violent interaction.

Sampson was in the process of physically restraining a man so drunk that he was babbling. "Sher'ladyship!" the man yelled, struggling mightily against the much larger butler. "Need to tell someone. Can't be trusted."

"I concur," her butler said, dragging the man toward the still-open door.

"Sampson," Viola said. "Bring the gentleman inside."

Her butler's eyes widened with disbelief and reproof, but he ceased attempting to eject the man and instead half carried him to the breakfast parlor. Once inside, Sampson thrust him into a chair and stood menacingly between Viola and her guest.

Pen growled, raising her hackles, and Viola shushed her. "I apologize, Mister … ?"

"Sh-Nowlin."

"Penthesilea doesn't like drunks, and I don't much care for men who abduct women and small children." Viola poured a second cup of tea and nodded for Sampson to pass it to Mr. Nowlin.

"Me either," Nowlin said, reaching for the cup. "S'why you need to find the boy before, before—" He hiccupped and held his breath for a moment, hand clamped over his mouth. "Before Granby."

"Granby doesn't have Jamie?" A flutter of panic and hope made Viola suddenly nauseous.

The man shook his head and downed the cup of tea.

"Gypsies have him. Least I think they do. S'where I left him. Tell Lady Boudicea. Got to get to him first. Oh, God." Nowlin put his head in his hands. "Ruined everything. Again and again. Please?" He looked up. "Promise you'll tell her?"

"I will." Viola nodded.

He blundered to his feet, causing Pen to growl again. Sampson caught him before he fell. "Have to go," Nowlin said. "They'll wonder where I am. Had to tell someone though. Too drunk to write a note."

Sampson looked at her, expression clearly indicating that he was by no means willing to let the man simply leave.

Viola shook her head. He might be right, but holding Nowlin would do them no good. He'd told them everything he could, and willingly. Keeping him would simply alert Granby to his betrayal and spur him to quicker action.

"Put him in a hack," she said. "And pay the driver to take him wherever he needs to go."

When she was alone again, she tossed the slice of toast she'd been eating to the dog and sat back in her chair to stew. Leo knew all the horse traders, and more important, they knew him, but there was no possible way of contacting her husband, which was infuriating.

If the boy was with the gypsies, Leo was the man they needed in order to find him quickly.

Leo could find them at this time of year, and word would spread...and the gypsies would keep Jamie safe until he could be returned.

With a growl of frustration, Viola tossed Pen another slice of toast and went upstairs to change into her habit. At a time like this, nothing but a good gallop would serve.

⊰ CHAPTER 47 ⊱

The interior of the mail coach stank of unwashed bodies and garlic. Beau was crushed into a corner by an enormous curate who took up far more of the seat than he had paid for. Her knees were fighting for space with those of a dour clerk. All in all, she'd have preferred to be back on the roof.

When it had become evident that it was going to take weeks to fix their own coach, Gareth and Leo had put her on the first mail coach to London with an available seat. Sadly, it had taken three days before there had been room for her. Three long, frustrating days.

There had been no sign of Granby or Devere when they'd reached Hawick, and she didn't expect to see or hear anything more until after she reached London. If she made it that far without killing the curate...Every time he coughed—and he seemed to do so incessantly—his bulk crushed her into the wall.

She fingered the tiny head of one of the pins holding her gown shut. She pulled it loose and crossed her arms, the sharp tip pointed at her seatmate. It might not solve the problem, but it might make him at least a slight bit aware of his encroachment. And if not, at least it would make her feel better.

He coughed again and then yelped and pulled back into his own corner as much as he could. Beau smiled to herself and lazed back into the seat, relaxing her shoulders for the first time in hours.

At the next stop, the curate didn't rejoin them, and Beau settled in with a sigh of relief. She had at least two more days to go before she reached London, and if she'd had to share the coach with that man the entire way, she'd have been hanged for murder long before she reached her destination.

It had been easy enough for Gareth to rent a hack and ride ahead with Leo in hopes of rejoining Devere, but there had, of course, been no horse broken to sidesaddle. Renting a lady's hack in London was one thing, but it simply wasn't done in the hinterlands.

Beau squirmed about, trying to get comfortable on the hard seat. If Devere had managed to stick with Granby, he might already know where Jamie was. He and Leo might even have reclaimed him by the time she reached London.

Beau tamped down the swelling of hope. The odds were against them ever finding Jamie, whatever Gareth might say. She knew it, and she knew that Gareth knew it. She could see it in his eyes. He wanted to find the boy, badly, if only because she wanted to do so. But he didn't truly believe they would and he was already preparing himself for her reaction to failure.

And even if they did find Jamie, there were still so

many issues to resolve. How did you make up for the loss of an earldom? Even if Jamie never knew what had been taken away from him, the guilt was going to haunt her. And if she wasn't careful, it was going to eat away at her marriage like a cancer.

Beau reached London in the middle of the night. The clatter of the wheels across the cobbles woke her. Gareth, as grim as an executioner, was waiting for her when she disembarked. What little hope she'd been clinging to dwindled and died.

He gave her a fierce hug. "Missed you, brat."

"Devere lost him?"

Gareth shook his head as Boaz materialized with her trunk slung over one shoulder. Together they followed him to the waiting coach.

"No, Devere stuck to him like a tick all the way back to London. Granby doesn't have Jamie. Not anymore."

"What do you mean *not anymore*?" Panic pushed everything out to the margins.

"According to your Mr. Nowlin, who paid Lady Leonidas a very drunken call, they haven't had him since the day they took him. Granby didn't want him in the first place. He wanted you, so they abandoned him."

"Where?" She was going to be sick. Her stomach churned and knotted. How could they do such a thing? Jamie was practically a baby still.

"Therein lies the conundrum," Gareth said, his irritation with the situation evident. "Nowlin claims to have abandoned him near a gypsy encampment. So, if we're very lucky—"

"Jamie was taken in, and it might be possible to find him."

"Might be," Gareth emphasized. "Your brother's ridden off to see if he can find any of the horse traders he knows and put the word out, but at this time of year, there's not a lot of movement. We might even have to wait until summer, when they all turn up at the horse fair in Appleby."

"But that's months away, Gareth. *Months*." They couldn't wait months. *She* couldn't wait months, not knowing if Jamie was safe.

He put an arm around her and pulled her close. Beau took a deep breath, letting the familiar scent of sandalwood and amber drive away everything else, if only for a moment.

"I know, love," he said, jerking her back into the moment. "I don't like it either, but at least we have some notion of where to begin looking."

❧ CHAPTER 48 ❧

Gareth awoke to his wife shaking him. There was shouting and the sound of someone pounding on a door.

"Gareth, open this door this instant!"

His father. Gareth grimaced and threw off the bed-clothes. "Best get dressed, love," he said. "I'm afraid we're about to endure a very trying morning."

He climbed out of bed and pulled on his banyan, and then strode out of the room, leaving the door ajar behind him. "Coming," he shouted back as the earl continued his assault upon the door. He turned the lock and yanked the door open, nearly catching a fist to the face as his father readied himself to knock again.

"Everyone in the building must have heard you by now," Gareth said, taking in his father's florid face and beetled brow with a sigh. This was going to go nowhere good.

His father glared at him and shouldered him aside. "What do I care? If you had a proper home in town, it wouldn't be a concern in the first place."

Gareth prayed for patience. Arguing with the old man wasn't going to help. Pointing out that he didn't have a *proper home* because the expense was out of the question wouldn't help either. The earl was as angry as Gareth had ever seen him, and he'd seen him livid and ranting on many an occasion.

"It's madness," his father said, his face betraying a hint of confusion. "Utter madness."

"What is, sir?" Gareth asked, though he already knew the answer. It has to be Souttar. Nothing else would compel their father to seek him out in such a way. Nothing else mattered so much to the earl.

"Some Scottish woman has sued Souttar for divorce," the earl said. "Word of it reached your mother and me in Bath yesterday. I'm sure Lady Olivia is having fits. When her father hears of this, there will be hell to pay. Your mother is prostrate and is refusing to leave her bed. I had to leave her behind while I came to town to see what can be done. And Souttar, damn him, has been playing least in sight like a damn whipped cur."

Gareth nodded sympathetically. Hysterical women couldn't be easy to deal with, especially when their hysteria was well justified. And with no one else to badger, of course his father had turned up here.

"You knew, didn't you, boy? Knew we were ruined. That your brother was going to drag our name through the mud and make us the laughingstock of England."

"Not precisely, Father. I'd hoped that I was mistaken in my conclusions, and that it might all be resolved without ever coming to Lady Olivia's notice."

The earl's normally devious gaze was shadowed, as

though he couldn't quite grasp what was happening, or accept that he had no control over it. "Something's got to be done," he said, as though simply saying it would make it so.

"Something is being done," Gareth replied. "It's just not a *something* you like."

His father's expression hardened, and Gareth knew that he'd gone too far. "Souttar's got to be saved. This nonsense can't stand."

"And I'm to be the one sacrificed in his place? Lady Boudicea to be ruined in Lady Olivia's stead? I think not."

"I think so, my boy," the earl said, the threat implicit in his tone. "Souttar's the heir. We can't have this. The two of you are like enough. You'll go to Edinburgh, you'll present yourself to the court and clear up this woman's *mistake*."

"I won't, sir." Gareth stared his father down. "I've helped as much as I can. I agreed to house Souttar's son. I even agreed to claim him as my own bastard, all to preserve Souttar's marriage and prevent Lady Olivia's ruin. But that was when I believed Souttar's first wife to be dead."

"Souttar's son?" The earl's face mottled, turning an ugly shade of puce.

Gareth pinched the bridge of his nose. Damn his brother for not making a clean breast of it. "He's still holding out on you, sir. If that Scottish woman proves her claim, the boy will be Souttar's heir."

"Heir? Have you run mad as well? A child in the mix makes it all the more imperative that Souttar be relieved of responsibility. A cutler's grandson to be the eighth Earl of Roxwell? It's preposterous."

"No, my lord," Beau said from the doorway between the two rooms. She'd pulled on just enough clothing to be decent. A frilled wrapper tied securely over several layers of petticoat. "It's a simple fact of law."

"You stay out of this—"

"Because it has nothing to do with me?" She crossed the room until she was standing directly in front of the earl. Gareth held his breath. His father had no idea what he was about to deal with. It was all that he could do to keep from grinning. With her hair in a braid down her back and her feet bare, she looked much younger than she was, and thus more innocent and more easily intimidated.

The earl made a dismissive, blustering sound, and Beau inhaled sharply. "It's my marriage and reputation you're proposing to sacrifice on the altar of Souttar's stupidity, and I won't allow it."

"You have no reputation, *my lady*," the earl said with a vicious smile.

Beau smiled back, every bit as cold a predator as his father. His father's smile faltered, and he glanced at Gareth, as though he expected help.

Beau's tongue darted out, wetting her lips. "You think the *duke* will take such an action lightly? It will be open war. And I swear to you, I'll drag every dirty bit of the proceedings through the gossip rags. Lady Worsley's divorce will be nothing next to what I'll give them. And I'll enjoy doing it. Remember," she said, leaning in so that her voice was barely a whisper, "I'll have nothing left to lose."

"You could remarry once the divorce was granted," the earl said, desperation leaking out.

"So could Lady Olivia," Beau parried.

"Lady Olivia isn't the hussy you are," the earl snapped, yanking off his wig and crumpling it in his hand. "And why would an heiress want to marry a man who already has an heir? She'd be throwing her fortune away. Her father would never allow it. It has to be you." He punctuated the *you* by shaking his wig at her.

"I don't think you've thought it through, Father," Gareth said before the two of them could come to blows. "The switch wouldn't stand up to even the most cursory inspection."

"Why not?" the earl said, clearly not ready to give up on his pet solution.

"The dates, sir. The dates." Gareth almost felt bad about having to point out something so basic to his father. It was a clear sign of how upset the earl was that he hadn't already worked it out for himself. "They must have already been clearly established in the libel, and while Souttar was in Scotland committing his folly, I was abroad committing my own."

Beau smiled triumphantly, and his father let loose with a blistering string of invective. "Look at her smile," the earl said when he was done turning the air blue. "A *lady* ought to be stunned. Offended."

"A *gentleman* wouldn't have put a lady to the blush in the first place, so I would propose we're even on that score, my lord."

"Saucy bitch," the earl growled.

Beau curtsied to him as she would have to the king. An elegant maneuver, even in her dressing gown and bare feet. Saucy bitch indeed. She was practically daring his father to strike her. Of all things Gareth was sure of in life, he was dead sure that he didn't want to contend with that.

"Father, I suggest you prepare for the worst. When the scandal breaks—and it will break; it's inevitable now—it's probably best that mother not be in town."

The earl flicked an angry glance over both of them, as though they were somehow to blame, as though he were still trying to concoct some logic by which they could be blamed.

"I suppose I shall take your mother to Spa after all." The earl turned on his heel to leave, clapping his mauled wig back atop his head as he walked. He stopped at the door. "The boy," he said. "I shall want to see him before we go."

"I'm afraid that's not possible, sir." Gareth said.

"Why pray tell?"

"He's missing," Beau said. "He's missing, and we've yet to recover him."

The earl blanched. "He can't be missing. You can't just lose the heir to a title. Do you know what that would mean?"

"It would mean the title would go into abeyance after Souttar's death," Gareth replied. The same horror that gripped his father rushed through him, making his pulse lurch unevenly. He hadn't thought it through until just now. Damnation.

"We can't have that, Gareth. You find that child. Find him and bring him to Ashburn. Whatever you have to do, do it."

"Everything that can be done *is* being done, my lord,"

Beau said. "When we find Jamie, we'll certainly bring him to meet you."

"Jamie?" The earl looked decidedly displeased with the name.

"James Gareth Sandison," Gareth said.

"Named him after the damn pretender, did she?" The earl shook his head in obvious disgust.

"You named *us* after the knights of King Arthur's court, sir. Being named after the first Scottish king to sit upon the English throne or his displaced descendant hardly seems more outrageous in comparison," Gareth said. "What would you have done if one of us had been a girl?" he added, the thought simply spilling from his lips before he could stop it.

"Named her Vivienne," the earl snapped and stormed out.

"The Lady of the Lake." Beau stretched her neck, rubbing the back of it with one hand. "I'd have thought him more inclined to choose Elaine, who died pining. It seems he likes women of power after all." Beau blinked up at him, doing her best impression of girlish innocence.

"Only in theory," Gareth replied dryly. "And certainly not when they stand up to him."

⫷ CHAPTER 49 ⫸

Gareth was ensconced at The Red Lion with Vaughn and Devere when his brother ran him to ground. His friends took one look at Souttar and melted away with only the sound of chair legs scraping across the floor to mark their departure.

From across the room, young Kettleston glared at them. Vaughn's forgiveness had been enough for most of the League to welcome him back into its ranks, but there were a few holdouts, especially among the youngest members, who seemed to share Kettleston's rather rigid view of right and wrong.

Ignoring the open hostility radiating off the boys gathered near the door, Souttar strode right past them and sat down heavily at Gareth's table. The viscount rested his head in his hands, the long cuffs of his shirt obscuring his eyes. "What did you have to go and tell him for?" Souttar said, hands balling up into fists in his hair.

"He had to know, Souttar. It would have come out sooner or later."

"He came home in a rage this morning. Yanked me out of bed and told me to leave. I'm cut off. Not welcome. Father said to come back with my son or not at all." He looked up, hair wild, falling all about his face. "I gave him to you to take care of. How could you lose him?"

"So this is my fault, is it?" Gareth picked up his glass and drank. It was just like his brother to want to shift responsibility onto his shoulders. He'd been Souttar's whipping boy any number of times over the years.

Souttar glared at him.

"Neither you nor his mother wanted Jamie," Gareth said. "You both made that much perfectly clear."

Souttar blanched. "I could hardly—"

"You," Gareth said with disdain, "could hardly be trusted with a puppy, let alone a child. What woman in her right mind would think her son would be better off with you?"

His brother flinched as though Gareth had struck him. "Her letter said she wants to marry again, and her prospective husband doesn't want Jamie underfoot."

Gareth fought down the urge to leap across the table and throttle Souttar. What a pair they were, he and his illicit wife. Neither of them gave a damn about Jamie.

"He was taken when Beau was attacked," Gareth said after he'd got his temper back under control. "There wasn't anything I could have done about it. And if you don't think that makes me sick, then you don't know me at all, brother. They were mine to protect, both of them, and I failed."

Souttar dragged a hand over his face, rubbing at the shadow of beard on his chin. "What's being done to recover him?"

"We've got men searching all over England. Searching and reporting back." Gareth pulled out his pocketbook and opened up the notebook inside. "These are all the gypsy encampments we've found and alerted."

Souttar leaned closer and Gareth pushed the list at him.

"Gypsies?"

Gareth nodded. "One of the men who took him said he abandoned him near a gypsy encampment. It's all we have to go on."

"Tell me what to do," Souttar said as though the words were being wrenched out of him with something sharp. "Tell me where to look."

Gareth studied his brother. The offer was utterly surprising, but he looked and sounded sincere. Being cut off must have shaken his world off its axis. Perhaps Jamie had one decent parent—or the makings thereof—after all.

"Well," Gareth said, "we have reports of an encampment near Burgess Hill. I was going to go, but if you like, you can go instead and I'll take the next one. If he's not there, don't forget to ask them where we might find other camps. Get names. Introductions. That's vital."

"Burgess Hill." Souttar nodded and stood, a little color flowing back into his face. "I'll leave at once."

When his brother had left, Vaughn wandered back over and reclaimed his former seat. "Will wonders never cease?" Beau's brother said, watching as Souttar pulled on his coat near the door.

Gareth took a deep breath and let it out in a long sigh. "I'd never thought to see the day Souttar put himself out for anything or anyone."

"Let's not be too generous," Vaughn said, his green eye unforgiving and his blue one flinty. "We both know he's not doing it for the boy."

Padrig stared down at the crushed and trampled underbrush and the ashes of what had clearly been a large fire. Gone. Gone for days already at the very least, and no sign that the boy had been left behind to starve. Thank heavens on all accounts.

If he and Granby found the boy before his family did, he didn't know what he was going to do. But he couldn't let Granby hurt the child.

Hell. He closed his eyes for a moment, hand splayed out across the grass. He couldn't live with any of the things he'd done, but this was one he still might have a chance to fix. That was all he had left at this point.

Granby stood holding their horses, mouth curled into a disdainful frown. Padrig swallowed hard, feeling sick. He'd felt that way every day since abandoning the boy. He'd become a monster in the service of this man. An irredeemable monster. And he was no closer to retrieving his vowels and rescuing his family than he had been when he'd first agreed to Granby's terms.

He claimed the reins of his horse and fit his foot to the stirrup. A rustle from across the little clearing stopped him swinging up. He kicked his foot loose, eyes locked on Granby. The Englishman had yanked his pistol from its holster on his saddle and was standing his ground, rage and hatred screwing his face into a mask.

"Damn you," Granby said, as a man leading a bay by the reins stepped into the clearing. Tall, lean, silver-haired with dark, slashing brows drawn into a frown. His identity was unmistakable.

Sandison raised one hand as if to hail them, as if he hadn't yet recognized them. Granby brought the gun up and fired. The concussion of the shot was deafening. Birds burst from the trees in frightened, chittering flocks, and then there was silence. Sandison crumpled to the ground without a word.

"What have you done, sir?" Padrig dropped the reins of his horse and raced across the clearing. He knelt down beside Sandison and put his hand to his chest. Nothing. He rolled him over and put his ear to his mouth. There was no stirring of breath, and a great red patch was spreading across his chest. He looked back at Granby. "I think he's dead."

Granby shoved the gun back into its holster and swung into the saddle. He flicked the skirts of his coat out and adjusted the set of his hat. "It's time we were leaving."

"We can't just leave him here."

One side of Granby's nose curled up. "That's exactly what we *have* to do, fool. I've no intention of hanging."

When Padrig didn't move, Granby sawed at the reins and swung his horse about. "Fine. Stay here and take the blame yourself, if you're so inclined."

He spurred his horse and galloped off, great clods of dirt flying up from the animal's hooves. Padrig stared at the body. The man was dead. Granby had shot him, and now he was dead. He staggered over to the nearest tree and vomited up his lunch.

What the hell was he supposed to do now?

~ CHAPTER 50 ~

Padrig forced himself to fish through Sandison's pockets. The man must have a purse or pocketbook. He himself had a grand total of three shillings in his own pockets, and though robbing the dead was yet another sin, it was the only way he could present a credible front when he turned up with a body.

And a credible front and story were going to be key to keeping his neck out of the noose. He found it at last in the tail pocket of Sandison's coat. Twenty pounds in bills, an odd collection of coins in the other pockets, calling cards...

Oh, God. *Viscount Souttar*, in fashionable copperplate. Nothing else. Just his title. Not Gareth Sandison, who'd robbed Granby of his first bid for revenge, but Sandison's elder brother, who'd robbed Granby of his second grand scheme.

Padrig stood as a sharp stab of panic hit him. He should leave. He should leave now and never come back. He vaulted into the saddle and then looked back at the crumpled body.

Knowing he was making a mistake, but unable to stop himself, Padrig climbed back down out of the saddle and tossed his mount's reins over the limb of a nearby tree. Souttar's horse had bolted, but he could see him now, cropping grass some distance away. With a resigned sigh, Padrig wove his way through the trees. It took him several minutes to capture Souttar's bay, and he was muddy and smeared in blood by the time he got the viscount draped over the saddle.

He was never going to stay there once they were moving. Damnation. Padrig dug through his saddlebags and pulled out his two spare cravats. He found three more in the viscount's bags. He knotted them all together, along with the one he removed from around his own throat, and managed to fasten the body to the saddle somewhat securely.

Once that gruesome chore was done, he remounted and led the dead man's horse out of the woods. He was going to regret this. It was foolish beyond belief. Granby was right about that. It was likely he'd hang.

He deserved nothing more.

"Souttar's dead," Leo said as Gareth entered the room.

Gareth looked green as he took the letter that Beau held out. Her eyes stung with the hot rush of tears. She blinked them away, swiping her hand across her face when one dared to run down her check.

Selfish beast that Souttar had been, they'd been brothers. And Gareth had loved him. Even when they'd fought, that much had been clear.

Gareth shook his head, as though trying to force his

brain to make sense of the words coming out of Leo's mouth. "The messenger said what?"

"He said Lord Souttar is dead. It's from Sir Tobias Montagu. His seat is in Kent, near Hawkenbury."

Gareth turned the sealed missive over in his hands several times. Beau put her hand on his shoulder and squeezed. After a moment, he cracked the wax and spread the letter open.

"Not just dead," he said when he'd finished reading. "Murdered. His body was brought to Hawkenbury by Padrig Nowlin, who claimed Souttar had been shot by George Granby in a fit of rage. He says they've posted a man to Dover to be on the lookout for a one-eyed man."

Beau sank down to the floor beside him, hands on his knee. There was nothing that she could say. It all kept coming back to Granby. She was going to be sick.

"Souttar was a fool, but he didn't deserve this. It's going to destroy the earl."

"Someone needs to go and claim the body," Leo said softly, the floor creaking beneath him as he shifted his weight. "And whoever it is, they should speak to Nowlin. He might know more about the whereabouts of the boy than he told Viola in his drunken confession."

Gareth nodded, but Beau wasn't sure that he'd actually heard or understood anything that had been said. She looked up at her brother. "Can you order the carriage put to?"

Leo flicked a finger against her cheek before turning on his heel and marching out. Beau forced herself to rise and went to direct Gareth's valet to pack for a short journey.

When she returned, Gareth was still sitting where she'd left him. He gripped her hand and squeezed back. What was there to say? They sat in silence until Leo came to fetch him.

Beau kissed Gareth as Leo frowned at them from beside the coach. Just a swift, hard meeting of the lips. "I'll take care of everything here, and I'll meet you at Ashburn."

Gareth and Leo piled into the coach. Beau turned back into the house as the door shut behind them. She had letters to write, arrangements to make, and, at most, two days to procure mourning clothes for both of them and get on the road. It wasn't impossible, but it was daunting.

Now was not the best time for them to leave London. They'd have to leave the hunt in the hands of her brother and Devere until Souttar was laid to rest.

Oh, Lord. The title. Beau sank down into a chair in the drawing room, heart pounding double time while her head swam. Jamie was Lord Souttar now. Or he would be if his mother proved her marriage was valid. And if she didn't, Gareth would become the heir.

≈ CHAPTER 51 ≈

Gareth stared at Padrig Nowlin. He was clean and well-groomed, but he looked hagridden. He'd aged a decade since Gareth had stolen Beau from his coach.

Sir Tobias had kept him under lock and key, not entirely sure what to do with him. Gareth wasn't sure what to do with him either. The man was villain enough that hanging didn't seem entirely unjust, but still...

"What have you told Sir Tobias?" Gareth said. If he'd told him too much, there'd be no saving him, even if he were to decide to try.

The Irishman swallowed hard, hands clenched together, knuckles white. "As little as possible, and almost none of it true."

"Cast yourself as Souttar's companion rather than Granby's?"

Nowlin nodded shamefacedly. "Said Granby kidnapped his child, and we were out looking for them both. Don't think the baronet believed a word of it though."

"But he's not certain, which is why you're still here,

locked up in a spare bedroom, rather than on your way to London to stand trial for murder."

Nowlin shuddered, seeming to shrink at the very thought.

"My brother's body should be loaded by now and ready for the journey home. I suggest you get your things."

"Going to deliver me to gaol yourself?"

Gareth sucked in one cheek and studied the Irishman. Truth be told, he felt vaguely indebted to the man. If not for Nowlin, he wouldn't have Beau.

"What happens next is up to you," Gareth said, suddenly sure that saving Nowlin was the right course of action. "You're our best hope of finding Granby, and our only witness to the crime, and I *do* want *him* to hang. What I propose to do is corroborate your version of events to Sir Tobias and take you with me. But if you'd rather, Lord Leonidas and I could tell the baronet the truth and leave you here."

"Why, sir?" He looked as though he were afraid to believe his luck. Afraid to hope.

"Because you told us how to find the child, and you risked your neck by bringing my brother's body back." Gareth stood, impatient to be gone.

"That hardly makes up for having participated in the crimes that led to both events. For abducting your lady."

"Which begs the question, why *were* you assisting George Granby? You don't seem to care much for the man—a perfectly natural sentiment as far as I can tell—so why help him?"

"Debts," Nowlin said simply, expression pained and full of self-loathing. "I lost hugely at table. Ruined myself and my family. Granby said he'd tear my markers up if I helped him abduct an heiress. It was her or my sisters…" He let his voice trail away.

Gareth exhaled in a rush. Feeling indebted was far better than feeling sympathy. "And you chose your sisters. I would have done the same, which makes neither one of us as good a man as we should be. Grab your things and let's go lie to Sir Tobias."

"You won't regret this, sir," Nowlin said as they strode toward the stables. The deep grooves of worry were still carved into his face, but his eyes had grown lively.

"The boy alive and Granby captured or dead, that's the only thing that matters. I'll expect word from you upon my return to London. If you need to reach me, see Lord Leonidas."

Nowlin nodded and disappeared into the stable block. Vaughn quizzed him with his eyes as the Irishman rushed past him. "Don't ask," Gareth said.

"You honestly trust him?"

Gareth shrugged. "I trust that he wants to be a better man than he has been. I'd rather be wrong than hang a man for a good deed. And right now, he's free to look for Jamie, and I'm not."

Vaughn nodded. "As am I. I'm sure Sir Tobias will loan me a horse, and I can keep an eye on Nowlin. You take Souttar home, and I'll hope to see you in a week with happier news."

~ CHAPTER 52 ~

The sound of pottery shattering greeted Gareth as he walked into the grand entry hall of Ashburn Park. A brief silence was followed by a storm of voices, all cursing and screaming at the same time. With his greatcoat still on, Gareth took the stairs two at a time, following the cacophony to his mother's drawing room.

"Why shouldn't I say it?" the countess said as he entered the room. "She's a widow. She should be in mourning."

"Lady Olivia—"

"Lady Souttar. Lady Souttar!" his mother screamed, cutting Beau off.

"We got word yesterday that Souttar's Scottish marriage was ruled valid. That Scottish woman is *Lady Souttar*, not me." Lady Olivia stood rigid by the fireplace, dressed in scarlet and pink, surrounded by a sea of shattered figurines. "I am *not* a widow," she said with a brittle laugh. "I was never truly married, so there is not the slightest *reason* for me to wear mourning."

His mother's Limoges snuffbox shattered against the fireplace, raining tiny bits of painted porcelain all over Lady Olivia's skirts.

"Throw all the figurines and snuffboxes and candlesticks you like. Doing so is hardly going to change my mind."

"Ungrateful girl!" His mother turned, clearly hunting for something else to smash. When she saw Gareth, she flung herself upon his chest, sobbing.

Beau, a slightly frazzled expression on her face, was standing across the room, her back to the long windows. Her gown was black, the sheen dull even in sunlight. Her face was pale, trapped between the dark fabric and her equally dark hair.

"Oh, thank God," she said as she saw him.

Gareth smiled at her over his mother's lacy cap. He'd missed her, though it had been only a few short days since he'd left her in London. He'd got rather used to having a termagant underfoot.

"And you." His mother pulled herself out of his arms and rounded on Beau. "None of this would have happened without you. I hate you. I hate you all, and I wish you'd leave me in peace."

"Gladly," Lady Olivia said. "I've been asking for the same courtesy for weeks now. And now that the decision has come down, I'm finally free to leave this horrible place."

"You'd be dancing on his grave if you could," the countess said as Lady Olivia stormed out.

"I just might," she shouted before slamming the door behind her hard enough to rattle the hinges.

Gareth surveyed the scene. Shattered figurines littered the floor. There were dents in the plaster walls, and a chair had been overturned. He glanced at Beau, and she rushed across the room, took him by the hand, and pulled him out behind her, completely ignoring his mother's protesting wail.

"You have no idea what we've been putting up with here," she said as she led him unerringly to the Tapestry Room and closed the door behind them. She leaned back against it, bracing herself as though she expected an assault.

"My apologies, brat. I should have thought before sending you here alone. I see you found my family on their very best behavior."

"It's bedlam. Your father is inconsolable. Your mother alternates between blaming me and berating Lady Olivia for not playing the dutiful widow. And one can hardly blame poor Livy. She's in the most unenviable position, neither fish nor fowl in this whole unfortunate mess, and now that the Commissaries has declared your brother's first marriage valid, well, her situation has gone from bad to worse."

"Why is she still here?"

"I asked the same thing when I arrived. It seems her father and your father agreed that it was best for her to remain, to stake her position as Souttar's legitimate wife—widow now. They want to fight on. To challenge the ruling here in England. The earl's solicitor found some sort of precedent they're hanging their hopes on."

"I take it Lady Olivia doesn't agree."

Beau shook her head and moved away from the door.

"Poor Livy. Scandal and humiliation are not her usual fare."

"Unlike you."

"Unlike me. I'd brazen my way through it. Livy can't."

"She seemed to be doing pretty well standing up to Mother just now," Gareth said, taking a seat and pulling Beau down with him. She settled into his lap and dropped her head to his shoulder.

"Livy's taking a stand now that Souttar's dead." She pushed herself up and turned her head so that she was looking him dead in the eye. "You never told me what a bully your mother is."

"I never knew she was," Gareth replied. And he hadn't. He'd never seen his mother behave as she had today, and he hadn't been around much during Souttar's brief marriage to Lady Olivia. He had no idea if the two of them had been fighting like cats and dogs since day one, or if this was something brought on by grief and disappointment.

"Well she is, and I'm telling you right now that I won't put up with it as Livy has."

"Good thing we don't have to live here with her then," Gareth said.

"She seems to expect that Jamie will though," Beau said, worry marring her brow. "She vacillates between railing about '*that Scottish woman's bastard*' and crying to be united with '*all that's left of her beloved son.*'"

Gareth let his breath out in a long sigh. He'd been worried about this for days. "My mother's right to want him at Ashburn," he said.

"No." Beau shook her head, dark curls tumbling across her eyes, her tone accepting no disagreement.

"I can fight my parents, but I won't win. I suggest we encourage '*the Scottish woman's bastard*' line of thinking then. If mother refuses to accept him, it will be easier to justify leaving him with us, at least until he's old enough to go to school."

"It could take that long before this is all concluded if your father fights to have the marriage declared invalid under English law."

"And if he doesn't?" Gareth smoothed his thumb over the soft skin on the inside of her forearm, stopping when he reached the pulse point in her wrist. Her pulse leapt.

"Then as Souttar's widow, she'll be entitled to a dower, and your father can send her on her way with a pittance and a curse, which is about all she deserves after abandoning Jamie because his existence was inconvenient. And in the eyes of the law, she's got no right to Jamie, so even that need not concern him."

Gareth's thumb moved in tiny circles across the thin skin at her wrist. "You're right," he said. "And even if the laws were different, they'd have a hard time forcing an English earl to give up his heir to the mother who abandoned him."

Gareth's lips brushed across her cheek. Beau nodded, unable to muster a verbal response, and Gareth captured her mouth for a long, devouring kiss. Beau moaned softly, going pliant in his arms. Still kissing her, he half carried, half dragged her to the adjoining bedchamber. He let her legs fall, but kept one arm securely about her waist as he shut the door behind them.

"That room doesn't have a lock, but this one does," he said as he turned it.

Beau shoved his coat off his shoulders with rabid

haste. He let it fall to the floor. He fought with the hook and eyes holding her gown closed, but gave up as they hit the bed and tumbled into it.

She kicked off her shoes, and they clattered noisily across the floor. Her nimble fingers attacked the buttons of his waistcoat and those that held his braces in place. Lord, she'd have him spilling himself in her hand if he wasn't careful. He'd missed her far too much for this to end so quickly, so ignominiously.

Gareth slid off the bed, Beau's mewl of protest almost drowning out the rustle of fabric and the creak of the floor as he settled on his knees. He ran his fingers up her legs, the transition from silk to even softer flesh tantalizing and full of promise.

Beau propped herself up on her elbows, barely able to see over the rise of her petticoats. She raised a brow and placed her stockinged foot on his shoulder, pushing him back slightly, staving him off.

Without dropping her gaze, Gareth pushed her foot back over his shoulder, and he pushed her legs apart with both hands, palms flat against the tender skin of her inner thighs. He leaned forward to lave his tongue along soft, secret flesh. Sweet, like a plum plucked from a tree on a hot summer day.

He opened the fall of his breeches as he traced every hill and valley with his mouth. He dipped his tongue inside her, licked up the length of her, locked his mouth over the engorged bud, and sucked until she thrashed.

"Now." Her hands locked in his hair. "Now." Beau dragged him up, impossible to resist. No *please*. No begging. Just a command that she expected to be obeyed.

Gareth entered her swiftly enough to catch the last pulsing contractions of her release. Beau smiled, lazy, self-satisfied, replete. She threw her head back, offering him the tender expanse of her neck.

Gareth placed an open-mouthed kiss below her ear, added a hint of teeth, and sucked harder. Beau gasped and arched, legs locking about his ribs with a now-familiar strength.

She bent upward, head tucked hard against his shoulder, hair falling about her in waves, its pins scattered all over the bed. Her hands slid up his back, beneath his waistcoat but over his shirt. Beau clung to the fine linen, wrenching it in two directions, using it to draw him to her, to hold him, trapped, entangled.

The fabric gave way, the sound loud and sharp against their mingled breaths. Beau's nails slid across his back, dug in, spurring him on. His heartbeat thundered in his ears, Beau's gasps and cries almost too soft to hear beneath it. With an exultant shout, he spilled himself inside her.

~⊱ CHAPTER 53 ⊰~

Beau pushed her fingers through her hair and massaged her scalp, trying to stave off the headache that was steadily building behind her left eye. Dinner had been blissfully quiet, since both Lady Olivia and the countess had chosen to eat in their rooms. Breakfast, however, was rapidly turning into something of a nightmare.

"Father," Gareth said with a flare of temper. "Lord Leonidas is, at this very moment, along with Sir Tobias Montagu and the entire constabulary of Kent, hunting for Jamie and for George Granby. Would you prefer I be there? Because I assure you, I would much rather be doing something other than kicking my heels here."

The earl grumbled something under his breath about being cursed with disrespectful children, and Gareth sliced into his steak as though he were picturing his father on his plate. Beau refilled her teacup and piled her muffin high with marmalade, ignoring them both.

"The burial is scheduled for eleven, is it not?" Beau said into the strained silence.

The earl blinked as though he'd forgot that she was there. "Yes, the vicar will meet us in the churchyard."

"Then I propose to have our things packed and the horses harnessed and ready to leave by one," she said before taking a bite. The marmalade was bitter and sweet on her tongue, much like everything else in her life at the moment. "There's no reason to tarry."

Gareth nodded his agreement and stabbed a piece of meat with his fork hard enough that the metal squealed sharply against the plate. His face was flushed with anger, his brows drawn down over narrowed eyes.

This was not a salubrious household, and she would not be sad to leave it behind. How Lady Olivia had survived in such an atmosphere was beyond her. She'd have come to blows with one of Gareth's parents if she were forced to share a home with them.

She finished her toast and excused herself to pack. Upstairs, she found Lady Olivia lying in wait in the Tapestry Room.

"You have to take me with you, Beau," she said. "I can't stay here another day. I simply can't. And I've no other means of escape."

Beau claimed the chair beside her, smoothing her skirts as she sat. She'd known Lady Olivia for years. They'd shared their first Season together. Pinned up each other's trains at balls, fought over flirts. It could so easily be her trapped here. "Livy, I'm sure your father—"

"Doesn't want to accept the truth," she said, voice shaking with anger. "He thinks if I just hang on everything will come about. His last letter advised me to remain here, stand my ground, and not give up my claim. I could strangle him."

Beau curled her hand over her mouth, thinking. The earl might object, but Gareth certainly wouldn't. "Do you know where you'll go?"

Livy gave her a mocking smile. "I shall go to grand-mamma, of course. I don't think my arrival will come as a surprise to her, and she's the only person I can think of whom my father will hesitate to cross. He'll have to leave me in peace—they all will."

Beau found herself nodding. If anyone could knock heads together and force a resolution, it was the Dowager Duchess of Cherbury. "Pack what you can," Beau said, squeezing Livy's hand reassuringly. "But don't let them see you. Let us be well on the road before they discover you've flown."

The first shovel of dirt hit Souttar's coffin like a cannon going off, the sound loud enough to make his father wince. Gareth took a deep breath. His brother was gone. The grave didn't make that fact any more real than it had been an hour previous, but somehow the feeling of finality, of futility and waste, was heightened by the sight of that scar in the earth being carefully refilled.

Gareth took the earl by the arm and led him slowly back to their waiting coach. His father didn't say a word as they rolled slowly back to Ashburn Park. He just stared, unseeingly, at his own hands.

When they reached the stables, his father nodded silently and staggered toward the house. Beau was standing in the yard, black gown harsh against the pale stone, directing the footmen in the stowage of their baggage.

"Did you really bring that much luggage with you?" he

said, eyeing the numerous trunks and portmanteaus that were being strapped down.

"I have my mourning clothes, your mourning clothes, as well as everything we were traveling with previously." She put her foot on the step, jet sparkling on the buckle of her shoe, poised to enter and depart. "I wasn't sure what I would need and I didn't want to take the time to sort it."

She ducked her head, climbing inside. Gareth followed her, and the coach pitched slightly under his weight before righting itself as he took the seat beside her. Lady Olivia smiled nervously back at him from the far corner, eyes wide, begging him not to object.

Gareth smiled. "Making good your escape, my lady?"

~ CHAPTER 54 ~

Gareth's head snapped up as Padrig Nowlin came racing into The Red Lion. The man's face was alight with excitement. "We found him!" Nowlin said loud enough that the entire room stopped to stare. He blushed and swallowed nervously.

"Jamie?" A surge of excitement flushed through Gareth's veins. He set his cup down before he dropped it and spilled coffee all over himself and the table.

Nowlin's face fell. "Granby. When he wasn't at Dover, it occurred to me that he might try Ireland first. He has money there. And a house. From there, he might escape with his fortune to America, or the Continent. Sir Tobias wrote to the local magistrates of all the cities where a man could get a packet to Ireland. A one-eyed man boarded a packet in Bristol two days ago. Sir Tobias has sent a man to Dublin, and I've come to report to you."

The rush of excitement built inside him. Catching Granby wouldn't bring Souttar back, but it was a start. Watching him hang would bring some small amount of satisfaction, and it would mean knowing that Beau was finally safe.

Gareth stood and dusted off his hands. "Race you to Bristol?" he said to a grinning Devere.

Mud spattered across Gareth's face as Devere cut him off and shot round the mail coach. Beside him, Nowlin cursed and clung to the seat as they did the same. The light sporting phaeton bounced as it hit a rut, shimmying in a disturbing manner for several seconds as they flew after Devere.

Gareth snapped the whip and sent it curling back on itself as it recoiled. His team surged, edging up on the other vehicle. Devere laughed as they passed him, making a rude gesture with one hand.

They'd been running half the night. They were changing horses every eight or ten miles. Money flowing through their fingers like water.

Nowlin adjusted his muffler, pulling it up to cover his mouth and nose. Gareth flexed his hands on the reins, working to keep some feeling in them. It was cold. Freezing. And they couldn't afford to stop.

"Hot bricks at the next change if they have them," Gareth said, and Nowlin nodded back.

When they reached the outskirts of Bristol, Devere was in the lead, but it was Gareth who rolled into the quiet yard at The Stag first, setting off a squabble as to who had won the race.

"You're a cheat," Devere said, jumping down and handing over the reins to his tiger so his team could be walked.

"I was carrying a full-size passenger." Gareth braced his foot and held the team in place as the ostlers ran to their heads. "You had only Wilkins, who's barely bigger than a child."

"We need an outsider's opinion, Mr. Nowlin." Devere turned to the startled Irishman. "Was the bet first to Bristol, or first to reach the port?"

Nowlin's gaze flew to Gareth, eyes wide with trepidation. "First to Bristol, sir. But I think first to reach the port, that being our destination, was implied."

Devere rolled his eyes and shook his head. "I need a drink."

"Next boat for Dublin doesn't leave for a couple of hours," Nowlin offered.

"Plenty of time for a drink or two, and a meal besides then." Gareth pulled his portmanteau from underneath his seat and pushed past Devere and entered the inn.

Every inch of him ached. His bones felt as though they'd been rattled from their sockets. The others must feel the same. He should be exhausted, but anger seemed to be serving as a very good substitute for sleep.

⊱ CHAPTER 55 ⊰

Dust motes filtered through the shafts of sunlight that cut across the darkness of the barn. Beau put her forehead against Gunpowder's neck and let the scent of horse and hay wash over her, through her, until that and the warmth of the sun on her back were the only things that existed.

The gelding stamped his foot, knocking his hoof against the door of his stall, an impatient demand for one of the lumps of sugar that he knew she kept on her person. She reached into her pocket, hand pushing carefully down past her gown and petticoats. Her fingers slid over the toy monkey she'd carried there since Jamie's disappearance. She paused, then dug deeper, finding the lumps of sugar beneath the toy. She pulled several out and offered one to her horse.

"Greedy beast," she said as Gunpowder took it, lips brushing across her palm, ears swiveling at the sound of her voice.

"Beau?"

Gunpowder tossed his head at the sound of Leo's voice. Beau put a hand across his nose and brought his head back down, offering him another lump of sugar.

Leo was flushed, eyes bright with excitement. Beau's pulse fluttered, and she braced herself against the stall door.

Leo smiled as he strode toward her. "We have an emissary," he said, gesturing toward a man behind him. The man was swarthy, with dark curls spilling out below his red woolen cap, and he wore a sash instead of a waistcoat. He barely reached Leo's shoulder.

"They have Jamie?" The lump in her throat pushed into her chest, burning as it went.

Leo glanced down at the man before speaking, "Tobar, the *rom baro* of one of the large clans of horse traders, has invited us to visit him. He sent Yoska here to bring us to them."

The gypsy smiled, teeth flashing against his dark skin.

"That's all he said? That we've been invited to visit?" She couldn't keep the disappointment from her voice.

"Yoska doesn't *seem* to speak much English," her brother replied, stressing the one word. "So he didn't even say that much. What he did say was *Tobar* and *come*. I spoke to Tobar myself not a week ago. He wouldn't send for us for no reason. If he doesn't have Jamie, he knows who does. If we leave now, we can be there by nightfall."

When they reached the Romani camp, the moon had already risen, a tiny sliver of silver filtering through the trees. Beau was shaking with anticipation. She flexed her hands and then balled them into fists, skirts clutched tight within them. There was music in the camp. And a fire. And horses. Lots and lots of horses. Beau recognized Tobar immediately. She'd gone with Leo on more than one occasion to the various horse fairs, and Tobar was always there. A big, bluff man with a quick smile and two missing front teeth.

A hush fell over the camp as they were spotted, and their guide disappeared into the crowd. Tobar stood up and came to greet them. "Lord Leonidas, I think we have your lost colt."

"We certainly hope so," Leo responded. "And we're very grateful."

Tobar motioned with his hand, and a woman broke away from the fire. "Plenty of *Romanipen* in this one," Tobar said. "Like you, my lord. I almost hate to give him up."

"Where did you find him?" Beau said, knowing she should stay quiet, but unable to do so.

Tobar turned to look at her. "With my cousin's people, lady. But they were too afraid to return him. After all," he said bitterly, "everyone knows gypsies steal children."

Before Beau could respond, the woman whom Tobar had sent to fetch Jamie returned, leading a sleepy boy by the hand. Jamie yawned and blinked before flinging himself at Beau.

Beau crouched down and smoothed her hand over his curls. "Hello, puss."

"Want to go home. Want Mokee."

"Yes, little man," Beau said. "I've got Mokee right here." She pulled the battered toy out of her pocket and handed it over. Jamie held up his arms, and Beau scooped him up, staggering slightly under his weight. "What have you been feeding him? He feels like he's gained a stone."

Tobar smiled and winked. "That one eats anything."

❧ CHAPTER 56 ❧

The house Nowlin led them to in Dublin appeared unoccupied. The knocker was off the door, and there was no sign of servants or Granby. Gareth tried the door, but it remained stubbornly locked. He retreated to the walk and stood studying the house. It was narrow, made of soot-darkened stone, and identical to twenty others running in a solid row down the street.

Devere shook the handle.

"We could break it down," Nowlin said. "Or slip in a window and have a look around."

"You're sure this is the right house?" Gareth asked, glancing up the street.

"Yes, sir. Number six."

"Well, then, I suppose one of us should wait here while the others return to confer with the Lord Magistrate."

"I say we have a look around and wait in comfort," Devere said, pushing the door open.

Gareth raised a brow, and Devere held up a pen knife before folding it shut and shoving it into his pocket.

"So now you've added housebreaking to your list of crimes?"

Devere shrugged and walked into the house. "I suggest we have a quick look around for signs of habitation."

Gareth drew his pistol from his pocket as Devere did the same. Nowlin hurriedly shut the door behind them. Devere walked off to explore the ground floor, and Gareth moved toward the stairs. At the top of them was a small hall with doors on three sides. The stairs twisted up another floor behind him.

There were footprints in the fine layer of dust that covered the dark wooden floor. Gareth followed them to the middle door and pushed it open. The chair was still swaddled in a linen drape, but there was a coat tossed carelessly across its back.

A trunk, open and belching forth its contents, sat under the room's only window. One drawer of the clothespress lolled open, overflowing with scraps of paper. Granby's belongings were strewn all across the bed, as though he'd been sorting them.

Gareth picked up a stack of paper and sorted through it. Debts of honor. Markers and IOUs in at least a dozen hands. He swiftly leafed through them. Nowlin's appeared to be mixed in with the rest. With a smile of grim satisfaction, he collected them all and went to inform Devere and Nowlin of what he'd found. They had him, and after they burnt his cache of markers, he'd have no hold over Nowlin.

Devere checked the frizzen of his gun for the hundredth time. Gareth uncrossed his ankles and flexed his calves. The Irish constable that the Lord Magistrate had sent to arrest Granby motioned for them to stay still.

They'd been lurking in one of the spare rooms beside Granby's bedchamber for several hours, while Nowlin and another constable hid on the ground floor in case Granby managed to get past them. Two more constables, including the man that Sir Tobias had sent, were waiting outside.

A whistle, like the cry of a starling, was followed by the sound of the front door opening and brought Devere's head up. It shut with a solid *thump*, and then someone could be heard ascending the stairs. The bedroom door likewise announced its use, and Devere cocked his pistol.

Gareth climbed carefully to his feet. The others did the same. The wood of the gun butt had grown warm in his hand. The deadly little instrument had only one purpose, and Gareth very much wanted to use it.

The constable gave them a stern look and eased the door open. He'd oiled the hinges when they first arrived, and the door swung as silently as they could ever have hoped.

"Mr. George Granby," the Irishman said, voice deafeningly loud. "I've an order here for your arrest on the charge of murder."

When no response was forthcoming, the constable lifted one foot and smashed open the door. By the time Gareth reached the room, Granby was halfway out the window, backlit by the moon like a silhouette. The constable had him fast by the skirts of his coat.

"Come back inside, sir. Nothing out there but my men and a hard drop to the cobbles. And that's if you miss the spikes."

A shout from below caused Granby to lose his grip and lurch outward. The constable hauled him back inside, the sound of tearing stitches loud as he did so. Granby landed with a thump and came up swinging.

He took the larger man down and lunged for the door. Gareth sent him sprawling with a kick. Devere's gun went off, wood splintered, and the stench of saltpeter filled the room.

Granby skittered across the floor and scrambled up, armed with a poker. Devere and the constable closed in on him, hemming him in on both sides.

Granby ignored them, eyes trained on Gareth. His breathing was heavy, labored, like a dog at the end of a fight.

Gareth raised his gun as the constable took hold of Granby's wrist. A grimace passed over Granby's face, and he took a deep, audible breath.

"I'd love to shoot you," Gareth said. "Watching you hang won't give me nearly the same satisfaction. Swing. Swing, damn you."

Granby's hand opened, and the poker clattered to the floor.

The constable took a firmer grip on Granby and shoved him toward the door. Granby's boot heels dragged heavily across the floor.

"Coward," Gareth said as Granby passed by him.

❦ CHAPTER 57 ❧

Gulliver yawned, showing a great, pink gullet like the inside of a whale, and flopped back down onto the grass beside Beau. They made a sight, the group of them all in black and white, as though matching their color scheme to the house.

Gareth repressed the urge to laugh. Jamie was safe. Beau loved him. And he was home. Jamie and Beau hadn't spotted him yet. He was free to simply watch them, a happy protectiveness sweeping through him. This was his. All of it.

Jamie glanced over at Beau, indignation writ large on his face. "Not down, Gully," he said. "Sit."

The dog continued to ignore him, but its tail swished. Gulliver had clearly been washed and groomed since Gareth had last seen him. His white fur was actually white, and the mass of matts and tangles had been trimmed and combed out.

Jamie bent close and patted its face. "Gully, up."

The dog rolled over, exposing its belly. Beau rubbed the expanse of pale skin.

"I don't think you're going to win that one, Jamie," Gareth said loudly enough that all three of them jumped.

Jamie screwed up his face, nose scrunched like a rabbit. But he didn't fling himself at Beau and hide as he'd been wont to do. Beau grinned up at him, the purity of the welcome utterly humbling. She held out a hand. Gareth strode across the lawn and tugged her up.

"Granby?" she said, eyes searching his.

"On his way to Newgate." When Jamie squatted down next to the dog, back facing them, Gareth swooped in for a kiss. Her lips were soft beneath his, soft and warm and welcoming.

"And Mr. Nowlin?" she said.

"He'll have to testify, but he'll be a free man after that. He can take his sister and go home. Granby certainly won't be in any position to press his claim, even if he wasn't going to hang."

Beau's mouth curled into a smile. "Found his markers, did you?"

"And burnt them, every last one," he said with deep satisfaction.

Laugher overwhelmed her, leaving her breathless and clinging to him. "I missed you," she said simply.

"I missed you too."

"Good. You're supposed to." She glanced over her shoulder. Gareth followed her gaze. Jamie was sitting next to the dog, getting a very thorough tongue bath.

"Kiss me again and tell me that you love me."

"Do I?"

She pinched him hard, scrunching her nose at him much as Jamie had at the dog. Gareth kissed the tip of her glorious nose, dropped another kiss upon her cheek, and then found her lips. He swept his tongue across the seam of her lips, dipped inside her mouth, and broke away.

"I love you, brat. Never doubt it."

Look for the sexy conclusion of
the League of Second Sons trilogy!

Ripe for Seduction

Available April 2012

Please turn this page for a preview.

❧ CHAPTER 1 ❧

B ird chatter split the morning air, the sharp cries entering Roland Devere's ear and cracking his head apart. He turned his face away from the sunlight streaming from the window and draped his arm over his eyes.

Never try to outdrink Anthony Thane. Never bet against Leonidas Vaughn, and never fence with Dominic de Moulines. Three rules to live by.

And he'd broken all of them last night, though thankfully not in that order. The evening had begun with a bout of fencing at Angelo's Salle and ended in an utter debauch at Lord Leonidas Vaughn's house on Chapel Street. Vaughn's wife had abandoned them to it, not even bothering to scold.

The soft tread of someone in another room finally forced his eyes open. It sounded as though whoever it was were tiptoeing about in their stocking feet, but the soft creaks of the floorboards was almost more irritating than the birds.

Roland pushed himself upright, head pounding

uncomfortably as he did so. His coat was bound up at the shoulders, and he yanked it about. He was still fully dressed save for his shoes, which lolled beneath a chair across from the settee he'd spent the night on. His unbound hair swung into his face, and he shoved it back, hooking it behind his ears.

The last time he'd downed that much port he'd woken upstairs in one of the finer houses of the impure with a troupe of disgusting little *puttee* staring down at him from the bed's canopy, their sly smiles and tiny pricks lurid in the morning light. Vaughn's drawing room was an infinitely more welcoming sight.

The League of Second Sons had caroused their way through London, their band growing larger and more raucous as they went. They'd stormed Lady Hallam's ball and invaded the Duke of Devonshire's rout, and had been ejected from The Red Lion—the coffee house the League had made their own—by the elder members. Ultimately, they had finished their night here in Vaughn's drawing room, or at least he had.

Roland had a vague memory of Thane flirting with Lady Ligonier just before his memory went black. Perhaps he'd been lucky enough to accompany the lady home. For the life of him, he couldn't remember anyone taking their leave, but he must have been in quite a state if they couldn't even get him up the stairs and into one of the guest chambers.

Roland ran his hands down his chest as he took a deep breath, yanking them away as a pin dug painfully into his flesh. He glanced down. A thin, brass dress pin held a slip of paper secured to his coat. Roland tore it free.

His own drunken handwriting crawled across the paper:

> *I, Roland Devere, bet Anthony Thane one guinea*
> *I can beat him into the bed of Lady Olivia Carlow.*

His signature and Thane's were scrawled below the statement. Roland crumpled the note in his fist. How many witnesses had there been? Who'd been left by the time they'd degenerated into boasts and bets? Good Lord, if Lord Leonidas knew—and how could he not—he was sunk. What the hell had they been thinking?

Lady Olivia shimmered insubstantially before his eyes: A heart-shaped face, brilliant blue eyes, a jumble of blonde curls. She had been hotly pursued during her time on the marriage mart. An heiress and a beauty. She'd married well. Or so it had seemed.

She'd been through a lot in the last year. He ought to know, having borne witness to all the most humiliating details of the scandal that had ended her marriage. She didn't need the gentlemen of the *ton* making sport of her, but it was inevitable that she would be pursued like a vixen by a pack of hounds now that she'd returned to town.

Lady Olivia wasn't quite a widow, nor was she ruined in the traditional sense of the word. Her situation was unique.

Numbness spread through Livy's hands as she finished the letter that had arrived on the silver salver with the morning post. The tingling spread up her arms and coalesced into a blinding ball of fury inside her chest. She stared dumbly at the words, raking her eyes over the sentences that sloped haphazardly across the page.

She'd known returning to town was a mistake. Had known it bone deep. But just when she'd convinced her father that it was a terrible idea for her to accompany him back after the Easter recess, her grandmother had started in, siding with the earl—against her—for the first time since her marriage had ended.

Her marriage. Livy's stomach churned, and she tasted bile at the back of her throat. Her not-quite-marriage had been the great scandal of the *ton* the previous year, eclipsing even the runaway marriage of her former not-quite-brother-in-law.

Bigamy. It was still nearly impossible to grasp that the man she'd married, the man her father had chosen so carefully from her legions of suitors, had already had a wife. Some low, Scottish cutler's daughter, who was, even now, happily remarried and living in Canada.

The crinkle of paper brought her head up from the insulting letter. Her father was staring at her over the sagging upper edge of *The Morning Post*. Livy forced herself to pick up her teacup and take a drink. The tea was stone cold, and the sugar had congealed in the bottom, but it served to settle her roiling stomach all the same.

"Bad news?" the earl asked, brows rising to touch his gaudy silk banyan cap.

Livy shook her head and refilled her cup. "No, just country gossip from Grandmamma," she said, the lie coming easily to her lips. Lying was a new skill, but it had become a necessary one. She couldn't possibly have been truthful about how she'd felt since her marriage had been invalidated. Not even with her father.

The earl smiled, his attention already slipping back to the news of the day. There were ink stains on his fingers. A sure sign that he'd torn himself away from his desk to join her in the breakfast parlor.

He was a man of intellect. A man who waged war with verbs and won battles with synonyms. But it wasn't magic. He wasn't like the bards of old, who could raise blisters with a word or lay waste to an army with a song. And today, she rather wished he was. Surely Devere deserved some sort of reprimand?

Livy smoothed the letter on the table and read it over again, sucking the marrow out of every word. Devere's penmanship was atrocious, and there was a dark ring where a glass of wine had been set down on the sheet of foolscap, making the ink of several words blur, but his offer—and the insult therein—was unmistakable.

Devere was offering himself as the sacrificial lamb for the pyre of her marriage. Every widow must start somewhere, and he thought, perhaps, she would like to start with him. Arrogant bastard.

Livy toyed with a muffin, breaking off a piece and slathering it with ginger preserves. She chewed thoughtfully. This was just the beginning. Just a warning shot across her bow. She was damaged goods, and men who'd once vied for her smiles would be expecting something more—and offering a great deal less—this time around.

She swallowed and took another bite, letting the heat of the ginger linger on her tongue. Roland Devere was a pompous ass, and he deserved to be punished. No, not just punished. He deserved to be tortured over an extended period of time for his presumption, and he should serve a higher purpose as penance.

Livy smiled and slipped the letter into her pocket. Not only should Devere do penance, he should serve as a warning to others, and she knew exactly how to go about making him of use.

THE DISH

Where authors give you the inside scoop!

♥ ♥ ♥ ♥ ♥ ♥ ♥ ♥ ♥ ♥ ♥ ♥ ♥ ♥ ♥

From the desk of Christie Craig

Dear Reader,

As an author of seven humorous suspense romance novels, I'm often asked how I come up with my characters. Since the truth isn't all that fun to describe—that I find these people in the cobwebs of my mind—I usually just tell folks that I post a want ad on Craigslist.

One of those folks replied that she'd be checking out my ad and applying for the position of romance heroine. Right then I wondered if she'd ever read a Christie Craig book. Well, it's not just my books—every good story is really a triumph over tragedy. (Of course, I have my own lighter spin of tragedy.) And by the ending of my books, my heroines have found a man who's smoking hot and deserving of their affection, and they've experienced a triumph that's sweeter than warm fudge. Friendships have been forged, and even the craziest of families have grown a whole lot closer. And I do love crazy families. Probably because I have one of my own. Hmm, maybe I get some of my characters from there, too.

Point is, my heroines had to earn their Happily Ever After. The job requires a lot of spunk.

Take poor Nikki Hunt in DON'T MESS WITH TEXAS, the first book in my Hotter in Texas series, for example. Her cheating ex ditches her at dinner and sticks her with the bill. She then finds his dead body stuffed in the trunk of her car, which makes her lose her two-hundred-dollar meal all over his three-thousand-dollar suit. Now, not only is Nikki nearly broke, she's been poisoned, she's barfing in public (now, *that's* a tragedy), and, worse still, she's a murder suspect. And that's only the first chapter. Nikki's fun is just beginning. You've hardly met Nikki's grandma, who epitomizes those family members who drive you bonkers, even though you know your life would be empty without them.

As we say in the south, Nikki's got a hard row to hoe. For certain, it takes a kick-ass woman to be a Christie Craig heroine. She's gotta be able to laugh, because sometimes that's all you can do. She's gotta be able to fight, because life is about battles. (I don't care if it's with an ex-husband, a plumber, or a new puppy unwilling to house-train.) And she's gotta be able to love, because honestly, love is really what my novels are about. Well, that and overcoming flaws, jumping over hurdles, and finding the occasional dead body.

So while in real life you may never want to undergo the misadventures of a Christie Craig heroine, I'm counting on the fact that you'll laugh with her, root for her, and fall in love alongside her. And here's hoping that when you close my book, you are happy you've met the characters who live in the cobwebs of my mind.

And remember my motto for life: Laugh, love, read.

Christie Craig

www.christie-craig.com

♥ ♥ ♥ ♥ ♥ ♥ ♥ ♥ ♥ ♥ ♥ ♥ ♥ ♥

From the desk of Isobel Carr

Dear Reader,

I've always loved the "Oh no, I'm in love with my best friend's sister!" trope. It doesn't matter what the genre or setting is, we all know sisters are forbidden fruit. This scenario is just so full of pitfalls and angst and opportunities for brothers to be protective and for men to have to really, really prove (and not just to the girl) that they love the girl. How can you not adore it?

Add in the complications of a younger son's lot in life—lack of social standing, lack of fortune, lack of prospects—and you've got quite the series of hurdles to overcome before the couple can attain their Happily Ever After (especially if the girl he loves is the daughter of a duke).

If you read the first book in the League of Second Sons series, you've already met the sister in question, Lady Boudicea "Beau" Vaughn. She's a bit of a tomboy and always seems to be on the verge of causing a scandal, but she means well, and she's got a fierce heart.

You will have also met the best friend, Gareth Sandison. He's a committed bachelor, unquestionably a rake, and he's about to have everything he's ever wanted—but knew he could never have—dangled in front of him… but he's going to have to risk friendship and honor to get it. And even then, things may not work out quite as he expected.

I hope you'll enjoy letting Gareth show you what it means to be RIPE FOR SCANDAL.

Isobel Carr

www.isobelcarr.com

♥ ♥ ♥ ♥ ♥ ♥ ♥ ♥ ♥ ♥ ♥ ♥ ♥ ♥ ♥ ♥ ♥

From the desk of Hope Ramsay

Dear Reader,

In late 2010, while I was writing HOME AT LAST CHANCE, something magical happened that changed the direction of the story.

A friend sent me an e-mail with a missing pet poster attached. This particular poster had a banner headline that read "Missing Unicorn," over a black-and-white photograph of the most beautiful unicorn I have ever seen. The flyer said that the lost unicorn had last been seen entering Central Park and provided a 1-800 number for tips that would lead to the lost unicorn's safe return.

The unicorn poster made me smile.

A few days later, my friend sent me a news story about how hundreds of people in New York had seen this poster and had started calling in reports of unicorn sightings. Eventually, the unicorn sightings spread from Manhattan all the way to places in Australia and Europe.

At that point, the missing unicorn captured my imagination.

The worldwide unicorn sightings proved that if people take a moment to look hard, with an innocent heart, they can see unicorns and angels and a million miracles all around them. As we grow up, we forget how to look. We get caught up in the hustle and bustle of daily living, and unicorns become myths. But for a small time, in New York City, a bunch of "Missing Unicorn" posters made people stop, smile, and see miracles.

The missing unicorn and his message wormed its way right into my story and substantially changed the way I wrote the character of Hettie Marshall, LAST CHANCE's Queen Bee. Sarah Murray, my heroine, tells Hettie to look at Golfing for God through the eyes of a child. When Hettie heeds this advice, she realizes that she's lost something important in her life. Her sudden desire to recapture a simple faith becomes a powerful agent of change for her and, ultimately, for LAST CHANCE itself. And of course, little Haley Rhodes helps to seal the deal. Haley is a master at seeing what the adult world misses altogether.

I hope you keep your ability to wonder at the world around you—to see it like a child does. You might find a missing unicorn—or maybe a Sorrowful Angel.

Hope Ramsay

♥   ♥ ♥ ♥   ♥ ♥ ♥

From the desk of Dee Davis

Dear Reader,

Settings are a critical part of every book. They help estab-
lish the tone, give insight into characters, and act as the
backdrop for the narrative that drives the story forward.
Who can forget the first line of *Rebecca*—"Last night I
dreamt I went to Manderley again." The brooding house
in the middle of the English moors sets us up from the
very beginning for the psychological drama that is the
center of the book.

When I first conceptualize a novel, I often start with
the settings. Where exactly will my characters feel most
at home? What places evoke the rhythm and pacing
of the book? Because my books tend to involve a lot of
adventure, the settings often change with the flow of
the story. And when it came time to find the settings for
DEEP DISCLOSURE, I knew without a doubt that Alexis
would be living in New Orleans.

One of my favorite cities, I love the quirky eccentrici-
ties of the Big Easy, and I wanted to share some of my
favorites with readers, including the Garden District and
the French Quarter. Of course, Alexis and Tucker don't
stay in New Orleans long, and it isn't surprising that they
wind up in Colorado.

We moved a lot when I was a kid, and one of the few
stable things in my life was spending summers in Creede.
But because I've used Creede already in so many books, I

Find out more about Forever Romance!

Visit us at
www.hachettebookgroup.com/publishing_forever.aspx

Find us on Facebook
http://www.facebook.com/ForeverRomance

Follow us on Twitter
http://twitter.com/ForeverRomance

NEW AND UPCOMING TITLES

Each month we feature our new titles
and reader favorites.

CONTESTS AND GIVEAWAYS

We give away galleys, autographed copies,
and all kinds of exclusive items.

AUTHOR INFO

You'll find bios, articles, and links to personal websites
for all your favorite authors—and so much more.

GET SOCIAL

Connect with your favorite authors, editors, and
other Forever fans, and share what's important to you.

THE BUZZ

Sign up for our monthly romance newsletter,
and be the first to read all about it.